A PRETTY
IMPLAUSIBLE
PREMISE

ALSO BY KAREN RIVERS

You Are the Everything

A PRETTY IMPLAUSIBLE PREMISE

KAREN RIVERS

ALGONQUIN   2023

Published by Algonquin Young Readers
an imprint of Workman Publishing Co., Inc.
a subsidiary of Hachette Book Group, Inc.
1290 Avenue of the Americas
New York, New York 10104

Printed in the United States of America
Design by Carla Weise

LIBRARY OF CONGRESS CATALOGING-IN-PUBLICATION DATA
Names: Rivers, Karen, 1970– author.
Title: A pretty implausible premise / Karen Rivers.
Description: New York, New York : Algonquin, 2023. | Audience: Ages 12
and up. | Audience: Grades 7–9. | Summary: Connected by experiences only
they understand, teens Hattie and Presley fall into a whirlwind romance, but
when the unrelenting trauma that haunts them jeopardizes their relationship,
they must find a way to overcome their losses without losing each other.
Identifiers: LCCN 2023006317 | ISBN 9781616208165 (hardcover) |
ISBN 9781523526239 (ebook)
Subjects: CYAC: Psychic trauma—Fiction. | Grief—Fiction. | Dating—Fiction. |
Athletes—Fiction. | LCGFT: Romance fiction. | Novels.
Classification: LCC PZ7.R5224 Pr 2023 | DDC [Fic]—dc23
LC record available at https://lccn.loc.gov/2023006317

10 9 8 7 6 5 4 3 2 1
First Edition

To Linden and Lola,
who teach me every day
how to love;

and to my parents,
who have been teaching
me how to be loved
for my entire life.

And to you:
I hope you're loved.
I hope you love.

All fiction is true.

—BIANCA STARK, *THE SHARK CLUB*

**Triggered Tastes: Lexical-Gustatory Synaesthesia
and Childhood Trauma—Interview #1
Subject: Hatfield, Isabella G. Interview by Brady R. Finch
(UNEDITED TRANSCRIPT)**

BRADY: Hey, thanks for agreeing to do this. I'm turning the recorder on.

HATTIE: That's very official. I'm impressed. It's like you're a real . . . grown-up. Incredible. Next up: A real shirt and tie, an office with your name on the door, a creased look of constant sweaty exhaustion as you run on life's treadmill to pay bills for things you don't want. Your future is rosy, my friend.

BRADY: Ha ha. Okay, so are you ready?

HATTIE: I'm as ready as I ever will be. But you owe me, big-time. I'm only doing this because you're like a brother to me, which would be weird because you're literally only seven years younger than my dad. But maybe like a sibling from a different dad. And mom. A cousin or—

BRADY: You're being avoidant. Let's start with your earliest recollection of tasting a word. Do you remember how old you were and what the word was?

HATTIE: Ugh, I don't. I don't think I do. I'll tell you what I think, but there's a caveat: I might be making it up. It might be one of those stories I've told so often that it's become true.

BRADY: Try.

HATTIE: Fine. I think I was six. The word was guitar.

BRADY: *Guitar?*

HATTIE: It tasted like steamed spinach, all green and metallic and . . . slippery.

BRADY: What was your reaction?

HATTIE: I threw up, just like I threw up that one time my mom made me eat steamed spinach. She went through a health thing. It was terrible, truly the worst, all vegetables, all the time, but it didn't last. Nothing she did ever lasted. After *guitar*, I threw up for a week. I felt stuck in it. I'd fall asleep and wake up and remember the word *guitar*. Dad thought I had the flu. I had to go to the hospital. I lost six pounds, which was a lot, because I was, you know, little. I don't know how much six-year-olds weigh but not much.

BRADY: No, not very much.

HATTIE: At the end I weighed less than not very much.

BRADY: Do you still taste it when you say *guitar?*

HATTIE: I taste it when you say *guitar*. I taste it when I hear *guitar* or think *guitar* but especially when I say *guitar*.

BRADY: After *guitar*, what was next?

HATTIE: There were a bunch all at once, words I didn't say very often, like *orangutan*, which tasted like caramel apple—I love those so much—and *encyclopedia*, which was a burnt marshmallow, which were my favorite. I used to always try to set them on fire when we were making s'mores and Mom would get so mad, she was a perfect-golden-marshmallow person and my dad and I were blackened-on-the-outside-runny-on-the-inside people. I remember that she got mad because she said we were lying, that we were just trying to leave her out, which was . . . I don't know. I was six.

Anyway, sorry, I got sidetracked. What was I saying? Oh, I'd try to work the words into conversation because I liked the taste, but I didn't want my dad to know, because he'd maybe pack me up and send me to a place for broken kids. I totally thought I was broken. I thought that's why mom left: because she could see through to my broken self. I remember asking my best friend Bug at some point if she thought it was funny that *grapefruit* didn't taste like grapefruit and realizing that words didn't taste like things to anyone else and it was like the bottom fell out of my entire life. I was hopelessly, fatally weird. My dad eventually noticed because what six-year-old says *sequoia* in every conversation?

BRADY: What did it taste like?

HATTIE: Root beer.

BRADY: Do the tastes of words ever change or go away?

HATTIE: No. They can just start out of nowhere though. Like last week I said *Rottweiler*, which I must have said before more than once, but this time it tasted like steak sauce. My mom used to put it on everything and when I used to beg for it, she'd say it wasn't for kids, that I wouldn't like it, but I was sure I would. So one day, I snuck the bottle and took a sip. It was so shocking how awful it was, like vinegar and something that burned. She laughed and laughed. Anyway, it felt new, but maybe I just didn't notice it when it happened before. Saying that out loud makes me feel like I'm doing it wrong, like you're going to say, "Oh, that's not how lexical-gustatory synaesthesia works, you don't have that, you are broken," even though I know that *broken* isn't part of the *DSM-5* or anything. But I don't know how it's supposed to be. I read about other people's experiences on Reddit and when they aren't like mine, I feel like . . . broken. Sorry, there's no other word for it, just broken broken *broken*. Like I can't even get my own weird thing right, I have to have it even more weirdly. I don't know. I don't think all people with synaesthesia are freaks, just that I'm one because I don't even get my own weird wiring right.

BRADY: There's no right and wrong here, Hattie. I'm studying you and your unique experience. Can we go back a bit? What emotion do you feel when you say the word *guitar*?

HATTIE: I don't feel an emotion, I feel nauseated. Do you have a piece of gum?

BRADY: I appreciate you, Hattie. Thanks for doing this.

HATTIE: I have regrets. I'm never getting this taste out of my mouth.

HATTIE: I'm kidding! Don't look like that. I'm fine. This is fine. Everything is fine.

ZING

HATTIE

Hattie's leaning on the kitchen island eating Cheerios, except she isn't really eating Cheerios so much as she's sinking them to the bottom of the bowl and watching them bob back up to the surface.

"So resilient," she says after a beat, savouring the too-sweet doctor's-office-yellow-lollipop taste of that word. "We could all learn a serious life lesson from this cereal."

"What's that, hon?" Her dad glances over at her from where he's stirring eggs in a huge cast-iron pan. "Are you sure you don't want eggs? These are going to be muy delicioso!" He kisses his fingers and flings them wide, then salts the eggs with a flourish.

"Absolutely not." Hattie's dad loves eggs. He loves lifting weights and Taylor Swift. He loves mornings and hyperbole and El Amado and his job as a child psych professor at El Amado Community College.

In the Venn diagram of Hattie and her dad, the overlap is Taylor Swift, but sometimes she wonders if she even *does* love Taylor Swift or if she just loves loving Taylor Swift with her dad . . . and now she's overthinking Taylor Swift and overthinking *overthinking*, which is another area where they overlap.

They've both been overthinking her mom's departure for eleven years—her old toothbrush is still by his sink, her hiking boots by the front door, her surfboard in the shed out back—even though there is not *that* much information to overthink:

She went to Switzerland. She didn't come back.

"So . . . eggs for you then?"

"*No*, Dad. God. Those eggs smell like wet dog."

"They'll taste like heaven itself has stirred itself into a pan to be fuel for *these* babies." He flexes his massive bicep.

"Only if you have no sense of smell. Please put that arm away before someone gets hurt." Hattie spins her phone on the counter. The glittery case reflects the lights like a tiny disco ball. Inside it, lurking behind a notification, there's an email from her mom that she hasn't opened and can't open and won't open. The subject line says: Fwd: Fwd: Save the Date.

"Any big plans today?" asks her dad.

"It's the first day of school, Dad, so you could say that school has made plans for me. Then I'm going to work, because someone has to pay for . . ." Her voice halts, slamming on the brakes before it gets to *college*. She's not even going to college now that she's quit swimming. How can she? Swimming scholarships make swimming necessary. Her dad looks at her expectantly. "Stuff," she finishes, quietly.

"Let's make it Taco Tuesday then!" he says. "We'll celebrate!"

"I'm always down for tacos . . . but it's Monday."

"Rules were made to be broken."

"So you say until I break them." Hattie can tell from his good mood that her dad did not get the Fwd: Fwd: Save the Date email. She's equally sure that what's in this email will break his big stupid heart. Again. And he'll overcompensate by doing something ridiculous like taking up the lute and becoming a Renaissance musician or signing up for a macrame art class and opening an Etsy shop. It's not normal. *He's* not normal. His reactions all veer toward alarming positivity. *Normal* people get angry and sad when bad things happen, not enthusiastic.

Not that she *wants* him to get angry or sad. She wants to keep the email locked in her phone forever so he doesn't have to get angry or sad or angrier or sadder than he's already over-correcting for.

She also wants to know what the email says so *she* can be angry and sad, which would validate how angry and sad she always feels when she thinks about her mom.

Or she could just delete it.

She could never think about it again.

That, she decides, would definitely be the power move.

But then she wouldn't know. She has to know.

Her dad tosses the spatula in the air, spins on one foot, and catches the utensil behind his back. "Ta-da!"

"OMG. Stop." She holds up her hand. "I'm googling how to get you an application for Cirque du Soleil. Those skills can't go unshared with the world."

"Do you look miserable because you'll miss me when I'm touring the world with French Canadian acrobats and my spatula or is there some other reason?"

Hattie takes a sip from his coffee cup and makes a face. "Ew. That's terrible."

"That's why I didn't pour you a cup. But excellent avoidance." He bobs, ducks, and weaves. "Bob! Duck! Weave!"

"Dodgeball rules don't apply to conversations. And I get to be angsty on my last first day of school. It's a legitimate developmental stage. It's senioritis. Definitely in the *DSM-5*. Check it out."

"Noted." He inhales deeply over the pan. "Mmmmmm. Gordon Ramsay is probably turning over in his grave."

"I'm pretty sure Gordon Ramsay isn't dead."

He gives her his signature look, one eyebrow raised so high, it practically disappears into his hairline. Scooping his mountain of eggs onto a bright yellow plate, he slides it onto the counter, sits down next to her, and starts eating. His fork scrape-scrape-scraping catapults her through the atmosphere and into deep space where, even then, she can still hear it, and she shatters into a million pieces, all her molecules dissipating into the eternal darkness of the multiverse . . .

He taps his fork on his plate, jerking her back. "So . . . is this really just first-day blues or should I worry?"

"It's nothing. It's . . . whatever. It's *scraping*."

"Scraping?"

"Forget it. Never mind."

On the fridge behind her dad, there's a photo of her mom wearing a faded pastel orange plaid sundress—it's one of Hattie's favorite things to wear now—holding Hattie's hand in front of her lime-green VW bus, which is also now officially Hattie's and dubbed Applejack after her favorite My Little Pony. Hattie's mom looks impossibly young in the photo. She looks like a kid. She *was* a kid. She was less than a year older than Hattie is now. In the picture, toddler Hattie is crying with her mouth wide open. Her mom is staring at something in the distance, above Hattie's head, outside the frame.

Hattie took the picture down once. It had been there so long that it left a ghost of itself on the fridge, a perfect square. She'd tucked it into the back of the cutlery drawer, under the tiny forks they never used. The next morning it was back, perfectly lined up with its own shadow.

It's the only photo of her mom they have. Before she left, she deleted all the photos from the hard drive of the family computer. She factory-reset Hattie's dad's phone and deleted the cloud. She took every photo out of every frame. She deleted her entire existence from their lives, like someone purging an ex from social media, but a million times worse because in doing so, she also erased Hattie's early childhood.

This photo only survived because it was in her dad's office.

They don't talk about how all the photos are gone yet the things they'd thought mattered to her mom had stayed, the things they'd thought she loved: her surfboard, the VW, her favorite Nikes, a rack of sundresses, her bright blue guitar, her collection of vintage mix tapes . . . and her daughter and her husband.

"You sure you don't want to talk about it?"

Hattie startles. "No. Talk about *what*?" She shuts her eyes so she can't see the photo or the eggs, picks up her bowl, and walks with her eyes still closed to where she thinks the sink is, gropes around, and puts the bowl down with a clatter. "There's nothing to talk about. I'm fine."

Fine tastes like fresh milk. She can't remember when she stopped drinking milk, but Mr. Kim, her favorite teacher, taught them that human cells regenerate completely every seven years, so maybe it's just that the cells of her that liked gulping down a glass of milk have been extinguished by the passage of time.

Seven years.

Elijah Johnston was only seven years old when he died on Hattie's watch, so he never had a chance to become someone else. Thinking about Elijah makes his face appear over the kitchen island, with his wide smile and missing top teeth and huge dark eyes . . .

"Shit." She presses the heels of her hands into her eyes, darkening everything.

"You're fine but also . . . shit?" Her dad pushes his empty plate away. *Scraaaaaaape.*

She flinches. "I contain multitudes." She is not going to tell her dad about Elijah's presence. Her dad is a psychologist. He'll *diagnose* her. She wants to change the subject. She wants to run away from Elijah's face. She wants . . . another life. A different life! In a parallel universe, Elijah did not drown at his seventh birthday party. She, the lifeguard on duty, *saw* him slip under the floating island and jumped in and saved him in time. There was no CPR needed because she stopped it from getting that far. He didn't freaking *die*, her hands uselessly pressing his chest, her breath uselessly puffing into his mouth. And if none of that happened, then she also wouldn't have started having panic attacks in the pool. In *that* world, she'd be at practice right now with the rest of the team, hauling herself up and down the lanes until every muscle in her body was spent, waiting for the whistle that meant it was time to shower and go to school.

Elijah's death is why Hattie believes in the multiverse.

She has to.

Somewhere, somehow, there's a world where Elijah isn't dead, and one where her mom didn't leave, and even one where she still likes drinking *milk*.

She takes a deep breath. "Your obsession with me is comforting but unhealthy, Dad. Consider your own needs. How are *you*?"

"I'm more than fine. Thanks for asking." He does a drum roll on the island. "I'm tied together with a smile, baby." He starts to sing the song with the same name.

"It's *way* too early for the kind of energy T-Swift brings to the table."

"Hang on, kiddo." He leaves the room, coming back with a folded black T-shirt that he tosses to her. "I can tell you need this today. Wear the power."

She pulls the giant *Fearless* T-shirt from their first Taylor Swift concert over her cropped tank top and jean shorts. It's been washed so often that it's almost transparent in places. It's soft and perfect and smells like her dad: some inexplicable yet fitting combination of a specific type of cookies—the kind you give to teething babies—and ancient rainforests. "Thanks, Dad. I think you're right. This is exactly what I need." She holds up her fist for a fist bump.

"Untouchable!" they say, at the same time, bumping fists, then waving their fingers.

She doesn't necessarily feel better, but she does feel *slightly* closer to fine now, and that's something.

PRESLEY

Presley wakes up with the vibration of his phone alarm, his heart already in his throat, half-remembering something he doesn't want to know. He blinks up through the skylight, which is only inches from his face, his brain scrambling like someone trying to regain their footing on a collapsing slope. He squints in the dazzling sunlight. A bird flies by, small and frantic, as though it's trying not to crash.

He's never related to something so hard.

Pinching the skin between his thumb and fingers, he reminds himself that it's like this every morning. He's fine. Everything's fine! Or it will eventually be fine! Probably. Maybe. Possibly not. Sweat beads on his forehead.

Mac is dead, he reads on a Post-it note, taped to the ceiling six inches from his nose, illustrated with a stick figure with x's for eyes.

Dad is in prison. (Stick figure behind bars.)

Mum and Ellie got married. (Two stick figures in dresses.)

We live in California now. (Stick figure standing under a palm tree.)

This tiny house is temporary (watch your head!). (Stick figure bending over in a too-short room.)

Last night, he added a new one:

It's the first day of school (don't be late!). (Stick figure with a backpack.)

He reads them every morning so he's not taken by surprise. It helps to remember everything all at once instead of letting it creep in gradually, like a really terrible rising tide. Or maybe it makes it worse. He isn't totally convinced either way.

He peels the First Day of School note down and shreds it into confetti, sprinkling it with other one-time-only reminders on the shelf next to his mattress, a colorful flurry of paper snow. The others stay.

He can hear his mum and Ellie not snoring exactly, but sleep-breathing in unison from the bedroom below his loft. It's sweet, if a little too intimate for comfort. But their new, big house overlooking the cliff is going to take months to build and is currently only a skeleton, bones stark and pale in the sun like the ribs of the Santa Barbara Museum of Natural History's blue whale. So, for now, they're embracing the tiny house lifestyle. He wears headphones a lot.

Keep it together, trash-hole, he tells himself. (This, he guesses, is probably *not* the kind of motivational up-talk Ellie suggested he give himself, but it's as close as he can get right now.)

Trying not to make too much noise, he reaches over to his pile of clothes and grabs some layers: Mac's old dark gray Nirvana T-shirt ("Smells Like Teen Spirit"), the soft flannel plaid button-down he used to wear for luck when he traveled for skating competitions, his favorite cargo pants, a too-big vintage Levi's jean jacket. He'll be way too hot, but he needs something between himself and the sharp reality of today: the stares of the other kids; the sympathy of the teachers who probably know the bare bones, at least, of his past; the way his head after a few hours will feel like it's full of nails, scraping his skull from the inside.

Once he's dressed and brushed his teeth in the tiny bathroom, he gulps down a glass of water with his pills, throws his water bottle and a sandwich Ellie made into his backpack with a binder, an iPad, and a bunch of pens. Then he slips his silent phone into his pocket, steps outside, giving his eyes a few seconds to adjust to the dazzlingly painful Southern California sun . . . and immediately seizes up.

It's a thing that happens to him now, in his own personal After: Tonic seizures that disconnect his body from his brain for tiny spasms of time, locking him rigidly, although fleetingly, in place. After one numbly clenched minute, he manages to take a deep, slow breath and his muscles release like elastic bands, all popping at once. His nose fills with the cloying scent of the bougainvillea that grows over the trellis-covered patio behind the tiny house and the acrid smoke from the distant wildfires that stain the eastern sky.

"You all right, Pres?" His mum's voice from behind makes him jump. He turns, and there she is, wild curly hair in disarray, looking half-asleep. Her British accent is stronger in the mornings.

"I'm fine, Mum. Go back to bed."

"I thought maybe you were . . ." She shakes her head, then yawns. "Never mind. Love you to the moon, sweetheart."

"Yeah, sure, Mum." He waits for her to close the door, then presses play on Catfish and the Bottlemen—turns it up so loud his ears hurt, then louder still, so loud he can feel it reverberating in his joints, vibrating his skin.

I'm fine, he thinks. *This is fine. Everything is fine.*

Fine is the goal.

His goals once had words in them like *exceeding, exceptional, excellent.* Those days are long gone. Now he shoots for *fine* and misses more often than not.

He hasn't walked more than fifty yards before he trips over . . . a goat. An actual real, live goat. His knees hit the ground first and explode in a firework of pain. The place where his left leg is pinned together shoots a lightning bolt of tingling agony to both his hip and his foot. "What the actual fuuuuuuuck." The goat, who's exactly the same shade of dusty brown as the dirt, blinks at him slowly, unmoved.

Presley flips over onto his back, his heart racing, and stares up at the hazy sky, trying to regroup. *Just because one thing has gone wrong doesn't mean the whole day is a write-off!* Ellie would say. She's the human equivalent of a motivational podcast playing constantly in his brain, but he can't even hate her for it because sometimes it helps. Without her, he's pretty sure he would've fallen into the abyss that's permanently yawning around his feet, waiting to pull him in. *Keep it in perspective!*

"Yeah. Right. Sure." He closes his eyes. There was probably a time in his life when he would have turned this situation into a funny story. But now, he just feels . . . defeated. "You win, goat." His headphones have bounced off and the noises of this new place are an unfamiliar assault on his ears: distant freeway traffic, the surf smashing against the base of the cliffs, the wind pushing through the long grasses, low shrubs and scattered wildflowers, a cacophony of strange birds, the dull roar of a jet overhead.

Then, out of nowhere, a voice. Mac's voice.

"What?"

I asked if you had a good trip, drawls Mac. *Yodiot.*

Presley takes a breath, his voice cracking slightly. "Takes one to know one."

Yodiot was one of their favorite made-up words, an insult they invented when they were little kids, one that wouldn't be (couldn't be) on their mum's list of forbidden bad words.

The spinning world accelerates like a broken fair ride trying to buck him off. It's an existential dizziness that's made both worse and better by Mac, who is real, even though he can't possibly be real. Presley stopped questioning his presence after a quick Google floated the possibility of *post-TBI psychosis*, which he . . . doesn't want to have. The traumatic brain injury is more than enough already, and the seizures and anxiety in his After are about all he can handle. So Mac's a real ghost as far as he's concerned—why the hell not? He's fine with it.

Fine!

Fine.

"So, bromigo, where have you been?" He hasn't heard from Mac since they moved, so while talking to a ghost is not a sign of good mental health—his mental health is a dumpster fire, there's no point pretending it's not—he's honestly just happy Mac's here. "I thought maybe you got stuck at the border."

No idea, man, but I'm pretty sure I don't need a passport. SoCal, eh? Why didn't this happen when I was alive?

"Do you really want me to answer that?"

Nah. You gonna lie there hitting up that hot goat all day? She's obviously just not that into you. Mac's voice seems to be coming from Presley's headphones. He picks them up, puts them on, only to find Catfish still playing. He pauses the song. His hands are shaking, but they're often shaking now. ("Essential tremor," said his last doctor, shrugging, as though that were the least of Presley's problems. "Totally benign.")

"She said she's saving herself for you, so I'm out of luck."

There's no reply from the ether, the goat, Presley's headphones, or anywhere else, just the uncomfortably dry sound of the goat's lips smacking as he nuzzles the back of Presley's head. When it becomes apparent Mac's ghost has nothing more to say, Presley gets up slowly, blood roaring in his ears, and starts limping in the direction of El Amado High, the day already feeling impossible in every way. He hopes the goat didn't actually eat a chunk of his hair.

"The nice thing about being new is that you can be whoever you want to be, Pres," his mum had said. "You can start over, reinvent yourself. Be anyone! Like, if I could reinvent myself, I'd be a bloody Swedish supermodel with a PhD in astrophysics. Or at least a Kardashian."

Obviously, if Presley could reinvent himself, he'd start out with an intact body and brain. Beyond that, he can't even imagine who he'd *want* to be except the person he was before everything happened: a nationally top-ranked figure-skater with a twin, a still-married mom and dad, two delightfully weird best friends, a yellow house in Canada, and a three-legged cat named Buck.

But it's not that simple, or even possible.

The house is sold. His brain is fucked. He hasn't talked to Henry or Big Tee since . . . Before. Buck ran away. His mum married Ellie. His dad is in jail. And the cherry on the top of the shit sundae that's his life now? *Mac is dead.*

So his mum's wrong. You don't get to pick who you want to be. He *was* who he wanted to be. And now he can't ever be that person again.

HATTIE

Jada leans impossibly close to Topher. Her shiny black hair slips out of its loose bun, and he feels it brush his cheek. "Come on. Love is bullshit. You know it, I know it, everyone knows it."

He steps back, fast, as though she's hit him, his unruly hair flopping down over his forehead. She's torn between fixing it or slicing it off.

Slicing would be so satisfying. So satisfying and so wrong.

But she has no scissors, lucky for him. She reaches over and fixes it. "Better."

"I just . . . But . . . I love you," *he says pitifully.* "What am I supposed to do with that?"

She shrugs. "Let it keep you warm at night? Sell it to Hallmark for a few extra bucks? Cross-stitch it on a pillow?"

He looks pained for a second and then he realizes she's (probably) joking and a smile opens his face, wide and bright,

and he's laughing

and she's laughing, too,

and then they're kissing

because that's how it is with them,

it always leads to kissing, or at least it does now.

It's taken them a while to get here, but the wait was

worth it, even if she doesn't believe in love, at least not the eternal magical pixie dust dream kind, sold to kids from birth as forever.

She can say whatever she wants about it, he thinks, but no one kisses like that—long, slow, tender, a whole goddamn orchestra of sensations—and thinks it's anything less than love.

"I still think love is bullshit," she murmurs into his mouth, just so he doesn't get the wrong idea.

Lunchtime. Hattie is outside the school, cross-legged on the ground, reading. She loves this part of the book.

She is officially *gotten*. By a novel.

"Hey, Cal?"

Calliope doesn't react, doesn't even open her eyes. Hattie flicks a tiny sugar ant off her shin where it's been weaving between her fine blond stubble like it's navigating the Amazon rainforest.

They aren't supposed to be outside—the wildfires sweeping toward them from the east have made the air quality in El Amado "unsafe"—but everyone else is inside so they're not. The kids from the swim team, who Hattie has easily avoided all summer, are impossible to avoid at school, but they'd never come out here, not into this smoke-cloaked hellscape.

She stares at the open book on her lap. She tries to not think about her former teammates or swimming, or Elijah. She pretends to read, pretends his face isn't looming, pretends to not feel the tightness in her lungs, the pink flesh of them absorbing the gray air and turning into something else, something poisoned and sick.

She runs her hand over the page, squints at the words that have turned into black ants crawling across the page, blinking hard until they swim back into focus.

"What if everyone just accepted that love is bullshit?" Her voice is loud in the stillness and the word *bullshit* is surprisingly sweet and minty, like the spearmint fluoride her old dentist used to use, the one who had clowns painted on the ceiling and gave out balloons you had to pop to retrieve plastic rings or tiny bouncy balls, like some kind of trauma trifecta: Clowns! Popping balloons! Dentists! "It would change everything. Think about it. Songs. Movies. Books. If love wasn't, like, the *only* goal, wouldn't everything just be more . . . interesting?"

Calliope's eyes stay closed, not even a flicker. Only she could nap so hard out here, sprawled like a chalk outline on the ground. Hattie takes in the precise cat-eye of her friend's perfect eyeliner, her fanned-out blue box braids, her twitching lips. She nudges her with her foot. "You're faking it, Cal. Come on. Wake up and talk to me."

Calliope sits up abruptly, simultaneously flinging one AirPod out of her ear. "I never fake it, but, girl, if you're reading *The Bullshit Club* again, I'm staging an intervention."

Hattie laughs. "I'm *not*. Well, I *am*. But that's not the point. Anyway, it's called *The Shark Club*. It's a future classic. A hundred years from now, people will be heralding it as the most important book of the millennium."

Calliope looks at the book, raises her eyebrows slowly. "Uh-huh."

"Why do you doubt me? This book has literally everything, including a message that will save us all: Love is bullshit."

"I hate to burst your bubble, but (a) that's not true and (b) no one gives prizes to love stories and (c) that book literally says *A LOVE STORY* in all caps on the cover. It's a goddamn romance."

Calliope's not wrong. The book's title is *The Shark Club: A Love Story*. And below that, the quote says: *A slow-building, heartfelt, genuine Gen Z romance*. But she also *is* wrong.

"It's a *meta* love story that understands we're fundamentally wrong about love. And, technically, it's not a romance, so they should have used a different quote. Romances *always* end with happily ever after. It's a rule."

Calliope stares at her. "I don't think that word means what you think it means."

"*Romance?*"

"No, *meta*. And the fact that you seem invested in the definition of *romance* is kind of adorable, but mostly just deeply nerdy."

"Good. I like to consider myself a deep nerd."

Calliope rolls her eyes. "Didn't you tell me that she's literally mouthing 'I love you' at him as she dies or whatever at the end?"

Hattie turns the book over and lays it carefully on her leg so it doesn't get dirty. "Yes, but please stop trying to confuse me into thinking I think the opposite of what I think."

"LOL, well, that's what happens when you use a love story to defend your misguided anti-love stance. Love is what makes this shit world *fun*." Calliope coughs. "Jeez, we probably have lung cancer now. Remind me why we're out here?"

Hattie tucks wayward strands from her long, messy blond bob, which now smells like a campfire, behind her ears. She stares at Calliope without blinking until Calliope sighs.

"Oh yeah. Well, you can't avoid them forever. What are you worried about, anyway?"

Hattie ignores the question. "All famous love stories end with tragedy. *Romances* are fun, but they don't win prizes; *love stories*, which are serious and intense and depressing, do. See: *Romeo and Juliet*. We take them totally seriously, but we haven't learned anything of what they're trying to tell us, which is love equals tragedy. Straight truth. And I've had more than enough tragedy in my life. Ergo, I'm love-averse." She tucks her knees up under the *Fearless* T-shirt. "It's smart, if you think about it."

"*Ergo!* I can't. I'm dead. Tell the coroner *ergo* was my cause of death." Calliope clutches her chest. "Good-bye, cruel world!"

"Oh, stop. It's a *great* word." Hattie doesn't add that it tastes like the watermelon Kool-Aid powder her mom let her dip her finger into when she mixed it into her white wine-Sprite spritzer to make it "taste like summer," but she takes out her red Moleskine notebook and writes it down.

"Literally no one in the world needs to fall in love as badly as you do. You need to *understand* it. You need to feel it. You don't get what you can't get, you know? Love gives life it's . . . va-va-voom. And the only looming tragedy in your life is that you're going to be a virgin when you graduate. You're a senior now. It's time, girl! Find love. Be love! *Make* love. That's what that book is trying to tell you." She taps Hattie's notebook. "That was good, write that down."

"Jada and Topher don't even have sex, so you're wrong." Hattie closes the notebook and puts it back in her bag.

"*You're* wrong. It's a cautionary tale. That's the tragedy:

They died before they lived." Calliope widens her eyes, cocks her head. "What about Javi? He's already half in love with you. You could throw that poor boy a bone."

"What are you even *saying*? Do you hear yourself?" Hattie shudders and makes a face. "Hard pass. He's not *any* fraction in love with me; he's just pissed I'm impervious to his dubious charms. And what I feel for him is . . . Let me think of the right word . . . Oh, I've got it: *repulsed*." She leaves out the part where Bug made her promise that she'd never, ever like Javi Sanchez, who happens to be Bug's cousin, and Hattie is nothing if not true to her word, even if it was a promise she made when they were twelve.

"He's hot. You could do worse for your first."

"That's what you think, but when I googled *the worst for my first*, guess whose pic was there?"

"LOL. Well, I'd hit that. At least he's had lots of practice." Calliope laughs with her whole body, with her arms and legs, with her head and neck, with her braids and piercings that glitter. Her laugh is as bright as the sun, which is still blinding even behind the haze that's working so hard to snuff it out. Wiping away a tear, she makes a heart with her hands and looks through it.

"I love you, too." Hattie sticks out her tongue. "But I also hate you." She opens *The Shark Club* again at random. She's read it so many times that reading it in order doesn't matter. But before she can lose herself in it, the bell interrupts with its clanging old-fashioned chime. They stand up, brushing the dead grass off each other's clothes, and Hattie knots the huge T-shirt at her waist so her shorts show and it doesn't look like she forgot her pants.

"I love Leo and *I'm* happy. We have sex. We have fun! We laugh. Not everything has to be so . . . *intense*," Calliope says as they walk toward the side door of the school.

"Um, yeah. Okay. Well, you're . . . lucky, I guess." Leo's only notable quality, as far as Hattie can tell, is that he's been expelled four times for painting dicks on Mr. Stevens's car. "But if you think about it, the whole concept of True Love™ is a tool of the patriarchy." Hattie yanks open the heavy glass door, and they're hit by a wall of cold, fresh, filtered air. "It's an idea that's sold to us so that we—"

"OMG." Calliope stops so abruptly, Hattie walks into her. "Ouch! Watch it."

Calliope holds her arms up, as though she's embracing the air itself. "I must love *you* to have breathed that crap when I could have been breathing this sweet elixir instead."

Ever since Hattie has known Calliope, she's flung her heart at people and air conditioning and girls with wild hair and lost puppies and boys with tragic pasts and spiders and the old guy who plays a ukulele outside the 7-Eleven. Hattie's own heart thuds hard and then painfully in her chest, cramping like a charley horse. She bends over slightly, letting out a small "oof," fingers automatically reaching for her pulse.

"Are you feeling the pain of an existential love-related crisis? Come here. I'll save you with a hug, like your favorite goddamn My Little Pony movie."

"Oooooh, *Friendship Is Magic?*"

"Exactly." Calliope pulls Hattie up and drapes her arm around her and starts steering her toward the classroom wing.

"You're my hero, Princess Sparkle Butt." Hattie drops her head on Calliope's shoulder, then straightens. "You know they always die at the end of all capital-L Love stories because they have to stop the story abruptly before the *real* part, where they have a kid and get married and live normal lives, until one of them walks out the door and moves to Switzerland."

"Hat, you know not everyone is like your—"

"See also: *Romeo and Juliet*." Hattie doesn't need Calliope to say *your parents*. "If they didn't die before they got to know each other, the whole idea that it was some magical forever *love*, not temporary lust, would've fallen apart and they would've hooked up and then started hating each other's annoying mouth sounds or terrible taste in pizza toppings." *Lust* and *love* both have very sharp and conflicting flavors, making Hattie's mouth contort, flooding her tongue with something that lands somewhere between hot dogs with sauerkraut and stale popcorn, the classic swimming-pool-concession-stand food of her childhood, of her *life*.

"I kind of like *Romeo and Juliet*, tbh. It's hella old, but it's a whole mood. Big love! Big feelings! Big twist ending! Big emotional catharsis! And you said they die at the end of *The Shark Club*, too, and you love that stupid book. You need to change your relationship status to 'in a relationship with hypocrisy.'"

The second bell rings and Mr. Stevens, stepping between them to open the door to the classroom, clears his throat. He smells like must and mothballs, as though all summer he's been stored in a closet in someone's attic and has just been dusted off and unfolded. "Ms. Hatfield, you're late. Not a good look for the first day, hmmm?"

Hattie ducks under his arm and into the room, glancing back in time to catch Calliope blowing her a kiss before turning around to make a run for the art room. She slides into her seat next to Bug and whispers, "Gum? I'm desperate." Her synaesthesia is sometimes no big deal, but at other times it feels like a life-destroying curse bestowed by a vengeful crone in a fairy-tale forest.

Bug hands her a cinnamon Altoid, and Hattie lets the candy burn her tongue, sizzling away the lingering flavors.

"You okay?"

"Love." She makes a face. "The worst tasting of all the words."

Bug shakes her head mock sadly, her long dark bangs swinging across her eyes. "Cinnamon will save you. Hey, it would've been ironic if that was a cinnamon heart, right? Because *love*? But you can only get those around Valentine's Day, which sucks donkey balls, because they're the best."

Mr. Stevens tugs morosely on his bushy gray mustache, then raises his hand to get their attention. "You all have fifteen minutes while I'm preparing. I trust you to manage yourselves. You're seniors now. Act like it, please."

"Love should taste like doughnuts," Bug continues. "But good ones, not those crappy Dunkin' Donuts ones. Like those mini-doughnuts from the carnival! God, I love those."

"Even love knows itself better than to be delicious."

"I know, I know. Love's a lie, blah, blah, blah." Bug makes angry eyebrows with her fingers. "Frowning emoji."

"It's not that it's a lie, it's—"

"If you say *bullshit*, I'm going to throw that goddamn book into the sea. Feed it to the sharks, for real. Then I'm going to buy up every other copy and do the same until all the sharks are full and none of those books exist anymore."

"I know you're kidding, but this book means a lot to me. The author gave it to me when I—"

"I know! I was literally *there*, Hatfield. She saw you crying in the airport, and you told her everything and the book changed your life, et cetera. But it's not like it's a secret coded message just for you that means you should reject love. It's. A. Love. Story."

"This book just says that love is . . . a pretty implausible premise. It's not exactly news, it's just . . . validating. And true."

Bug sighs and starts sketching a girl on her notebook, her pen moving in short confident strokes. "I happen to believe in True Love™ so stop shitting on my implausible dreams." Bug holds up her notebook. "Future wifey. Isn't she gorge?"

"Nice. Wife, though? Did you time travel here from an Up with Marriage conference in 1962?"

"Call me old-fashioned, but I want what I want. Anyway, *lesbian* marriage is hardly archaic and my future is whatever *I* want it to be."

"Did you get that from Instagram? True inspo. Really." Hattie bends her fingers into a heart shape and presses them on Bug's forehead. "Like."

Bug ducks away. "Eff you, Sarcasmo."

Hattie tries to laugh like a normal person, make it a joke, but it comes out strained. She knows she's being a jerk but the word *future* contains too many things she can't think about, like . . .

"Oh no." For the millionth time, Hattie reminds herself that Elijah Johnston is not a *ghost*. He's a hallucination, his face just some nightmarish new extension of her synesthetic curse. According to the *DSM-5, the* reference guide to psychiatric disorders that Hattie's dad keeps a copy of in the bathroom, there are a multitude of mental illnesses that can explain why she keeps seeing him. It's chemicals. It's neurotransmitters. It's a short-circuit in her system. But she's not going to swallow a bunch of medication and erase him either. This is what she deserves in *this* world where it was her fault that he died. She makes herself stare directly at him, meeting his eyes.

Somewhere else in the multiverse, he didn't die. She holds on to that thought, her heart clenching around it like a fist. She wants to tell him, to explain how it works.

"What?" says Bug. "Did you say '*oh no*'?"

"No. Nothing." Hattie doesn't tell Bug this latest wrinkle. She hasn't told anyone. How could she? *Hey, guys, guess who I just saw? Guess who I can't stop seeing?* It's like a bad knock-knock joke: *Knock-knock! Who's there? The ghost of Elijah Johnston!* "It's just . . . I hate talking about the future." *Future* tastes like the egg-and-mayonnaise sandwiches on Wonder Bread that her mom was obsessed with, would eat for three meals a day sometimes. *Tastes like a picnic!* she said, every time. *What's not to like?* "Where did Mr. Stevens go? Surely abandoning a class like this is a fireable offense." She presses her fingers against her eyelids until she can see nothing but Rorschach-like blobs of light and dark, dancing poodles of pink and gray and red.

"He's getting more chalk from the supply closet so he can write your name on his naughty list."

"LOL, for real."

"You know, Hattie, you can still future it up with the rest of us. It's not too late. It's literally the first day of senior year. There are lots of colleges, and swimming isn't your only—"

"Don't." It comes out more sharply than she intends.

Bug has her life all mapped out, like Hattie did once. Bug's vision board looks like a life-insurance ad: a series of perfectly filtered snapshots of smiling people aging happily with college educations and nice cars and big houses and family dinners and *true love* and obviously a solid insurance plan, as if you can insure against people abruptly leaving the picture. Bug's naivety is annoying and also kind of sad. Two people can never permanently stay on the same page. Hattie knows this. People die. People leave. People get pregnant in high school. People have regrets. People run away to Switzerland, lured there by political neutrality, mountains, chocolate . . . and yodeling.

Hattie snorts. The only map she has now is her meticulously collaged map of Jada and Topher's road trip from *The Shark Club*. She made it using a huge vintage driving map from AAA, carefully marking the roads they drove in the book with a thin purple ribbon. She pasted over the whole thing with precisely cut-out scenes of stops they made—the Santa Monica Pier, the giant Paul Bunyan and the redwoods, the Oregon coast, Mount Neahkahnie, the Pike Place Market—which she found on the internet and had printed at Walgreens. She made a hand-drawn version of their Seven Days of Us and marked the locations where each activity took place. It's . . . a lot. The map covers the entire wall above her bed. It has colorful pins marking times and dates and chapters, labeled with newsprint words snipped from the *El Amado Weekly News*, making up quotes from the book. The whole project is *maybe* the tiniest bit obsessive . . . but that makes sense because she's the tiniest bit obsessed.

"What?" Hattie says. "Sorry, I drifted. What did you say?"

"I was just saying that . . . like, I *get* it, okay? But you can't punish yourself forever. It's time to move on. You have to live your *life*." Bug's expression is all sympathy, which makes Hattie cringe. She can't stand it—can't stand that her friends feel sorry for her, but equally can't stand if they don't, or if they ask her about her future, or if they don't, or if they let her act like a bitch and get away with it or if they shut her down or if they tell her to *let it go*, which she can't do, which she'll never be able to do.

"I'm not *punishing* myself." Hattie swallows it all down, all the feelings, the burgeoning scream, the rest of the mint, everything. She chokes, coughs, swallows again, then moves the book from her backpack to her lap. She'll stop reading it soon. Maybe. Probably.

"Don't you, like, get sick of reading the same book over and over again?"

"Nope. You should read it. You might even like it."

"Hard pass. Hetero couples are so predictably depressing. And that story sounds like it is already depressing. It's a double bill of *nope*."

"Your loss. But it's more sad than depressing. Sad is kind of beautiful. Ask the poets and the songwriters."

"Okay, Taylor Swift, but so is *happy*. Please don't make *sad* your brand unless you can turn it into a bajillion gold records." Bug reaches over and squeezes Hattie's hand, and Hattie lets her for about three seconds before she pulls away, forcing her gaze to land anywhere but on Elijah, who's shimmering in the corner like a silent rebuke.

His mom probably doesn't find sadness beautiful, Hattie thinks, and digs her fingernails so hard into her thigh that when she looks down, she sees four bright red crescents.

She forces her eyes back to Elijah, making herself take in his grin, his missing front teeth, the birthmark on his fore-head, the tiny scar on his chin.

PRESLEY

The school day is almost over, and Presley has done an impressively shitty job of reinventing himself so far, unless what he was aiming for is "creepy loner with serial killer vibes." He's knocked *that* out of the park. It's definitely too late to swap it out for "Swedish supermodel." He knows he's coming off all wrong, but he can't shake the feeling that he's just returned to Earth after being in an alternate galaxy for so long that he doesn't remember *how* to be, how to even exist in a body. His hands are too small or too big, or things are too far away or too close—it's hard to put his finger on the problem, but every proportion is distorted, wrong, off.

His brain hums with static, the thud of a brewing headache. He's *tired*, both physically tired and tired of the way the other kids are looking at him, sizing him up, wondering where he came from, then deciding things about him they can't possibly guess, unless they *know*, unless they've seen the memes or, worse, the humiliating viral TikTok, unless they've figured out who he is, unless they actually know everything about him, about Mac, about who his mother is, about what his dad did, about who he used to be.

There's no way, he thinks, but he can't really know for sure and not knowing makes his brain prickle. *They don't care. Don't think you're so important.*

In the back of the classroom, someone yells, "Yo, yo, yo!" Goose bumps rise on his arms. Mac would *yo* back, and like owls, they'd recognize each other's calls and become instant buddies and he'd have a whole group of yo-friends who would absorb him into their yo-parliament.

He could *yo*. But . . .

I'm not *Mac*, he reminds himself.

When Mac first died, it was easy for him to take on Mac-isms, to fake his way into being a *yo*-er. People who knew Mac and missed Mac wanted Presley to *be* Mac—they were identical twins, after all—and he kind of subconsciously obliged. But Mac is nothing to the people here. He's a *yo* no one else can hear: a voice, memories, a hazy outline, and a bunch of ashes kept in a hideously ugly, misshapen pottery urn their mum made that's temporarily being stored under the bathroom sink because it's the only spot where it fits in their tiny house.

"Oh my god! Dude! You're slaying me!"

Presley glances back. One of the boys is lying on his back on the floor, writhing. "I'm slayed," he keeps saying. "All hail Roberto, the slayer of slayed slayers." He's laughing so hard he's crying. Presley can't remember ever finding anything that funny, but he knew he did. Once. *He* used to be funny! Now he's . . . not.

There was a time when he would have stolen the scene for a comic, recreated it with stick figures, but that time is long gone. Mac was his Stwins audience (and inspiration) and now he doesn't exist, so the Stwins don't either, and Presley doesn't know what to do with his doodling hands. A wave of panic rises in his throat. He looks around the room, trying to find something, anything to distract him from the abyss that's gaping around his feet, threatening to absorb him like a dinosaur in the La Brea Tar Pits. His eyes land on a blond girl in the far row, a book open on her lap, heavy black-framed glasses obscuring the parts of her face her messy blond hair doesn't hide. He can't see what book it is, only that her posture makes it look as though she wants to climb into it and disappear. She looks up, straight at him. *What?* her expression says.

It's all he can do to not say *Sorry* out loud. He shrugs, but he doesn't look away.

He can't.

The thing is that her face is instantly the most familiar face in the world, even though he's never seen her before. It's not that she's pretty (although she's fucking beautiful), it's more like some part of him recognizes some part of her.

Oh, he thinks. *It's* you.

HATTIE

The New Kid is staring at her.

Hattie pushes her glasses up her nose so she can see him better. She's noticed him in passing, but what she's mostly noticed is that he looks like someone who doesn't want to be noticed. As someone who *also* doesn't want to be noticed, she respects that.

He was there in chemistry when Mr. Kim taught them that water is the only substance that expands when it freezes, each molecule pushing the next away, holding it at arm's length.

He was there in drama, sitting close to the door, staring at it as though he was only just barely stopping himself from running away while the new teacher joyfully expounded on the time she played Juliet in an off-off-off-Broadway musical version of *Romeo and Juliet* set in a 1970s disco.

He was there in math when Mr. Harris surprised them all with a first-day pop quiz.

And now here he is in English, waiting for Mr. Stevens to bore them all to death, releasing them only when they've been reduced to brain-eating zombies, a horde of the undead unleashed on the unsuspecting population of El Amado.

The only difference is that this time, the New Kid is staring directly at her.

He's *noticing* her.

She stares back. A jagged purple scar softens and interrupts his features, leading to his unusually full lips. His hair is long in the way that more suggests he doesn't have the energy to cut it than it being a style choice. He gives the impression of being somehow both broad shouldered *and* skinny but sinewy as opposed to bony. His eyes are so dark they appear to be black.

He looks . . . terrified.

She smiles at him like she would at a kitten hiding under a car.

He shrugs, a tiny movement of his shoulders.

"Who are you smiling at?" says Bug. "The New Kid?"

"What? No. No one. Nothing. I was looking at the sky," Hattie lies. "The smoke. The looming apocalypse."

"Nice," says Bug. "*The end is nigh.* Very upbeat."

"Laugh it up, but it's the truth, Shakespeare. El Amado has burned to the ground once before, remember? Have you packed your go-bag?"

"Um, yeah, of course. Duh. Have you?"

"I keep everything I care about in Applejack. My life is portable as long as her engine doesn't stall during my getaway drive. Where did you go at lunch, anyway?"

"Drama club. It was *so good.* OMG. The new teacher is . . ." Bug makes heart-eyes, tucking her bangs back behind her ears. "I don't know if I want to *be* her or be *with* her, tbh. I'm pretty sure it's B though. She's freakin' gorge."

"There's so much wrong with what you just said, I don't know where to start, but she's teaching *Romeo and Juliet* and . . . ugh. Have no new plays been written in the last four hundred years?"

"Maybe we can do *Juliet and Juliet* instead. Do you think she's queer?"

"No," says Hattie. Then she reconsiders. "Yes. Maybe? Does it matter?"

"Of course it matters. Hey, whether you were smiling at the New Kid or not, he's totally smiling at *you*."

Hattie squints as though she isn't already very aware of his gaze. "Oh."

"You're making him blush."

"Maybe he's shy. Don't stare. You'll scare him." She holds up her book so Bug's view is blocked.

Bug snorts, pushing it away. "He'll be okay, I promise. What is he *wearing*?"

"Maybe he's from . . . the north?"

"The *north*? That's very specific. I'm worried for him. He does not look like he'll fit in here. He's dressed like either a thru-hiker on the Appalachian Trail or a time-traveler who took a wrong turn on his way to *Mallrats*, circa 1990-something. Is that mean?"

"Um, yeah. He looks okay to me. He looks . . . fine."

"Fine-fine? Or *fine*?"

"Neither," says Hattie. "Just . . . regular fine." She blushes, giving herself away.

In the Venn diagram of the school population, the overlap for most kids in El Amado is partying. Surfers, burnouts, rich kids, artsy kids, mathletes, whoever: They all party like it's their full-time job. The New Kid doesn't look like software money. He doesn't look like a surfer. And he doesn't look like a partyer either. He looks, to Hattie, *different*.

He's a singular dot on the Venn.

"He reminds me of someone." Hattie frowns. Shrugs.

"Everyone reminds everyone of someone," says Bug. "Did

you know everyone has a doppelganger? Somewhere in the world, there's another person, just walking around with your face. They could be anyone, doing anything. Maybe right now, someone with your face is murdering their neighbour with a chainsaw or . . . I don't know, something you can't even imagine, something super-weird, like counting penguins in the Arctic."

"I think penguins live in the Antarctic. And of those things, was counting penguins really the *weird* option?"

"Whatever. Anyway, if you ever see your doppelganger and *touch* them, even accidentally, the multiverse collapses."

"No pressure."

"You know, I bet Ms. Singh isn't even *that* much older than us. She might have just graduated college. And you know, we're closer to being adults than not. A four-year gap isn't terrible in the big picture. Like when I'm twenty-one and she's twenty-five, no one will even raise an eyebrow. It's nothing."

"Seriously? People will raise both eyebrows. They'll draw on extra eyebrows so they can raise those as well. You'll live a life where everyone is looking at you like *this*, 24/7." Hattie raises her eyebrows to demonstrate, adding two more with her fingers. "So many eyebrows. Even if we're almost eighteen, that *almost* means a lot in court. See also: *teacher.*"

"LOL, for real. But soon I won't be her student anymore. We might bump into each other at Starbucks and . . . the rest will be history. Let me have my dream and I'll let you pretend *The Shark Club* is giving you personalized lessons tailored to your specific life experience."

"Deal." Hattie tries to pretend what Bug said didn't bother her, but the truth is, she doesn't even *feel* almost eighteen. She feels like a kindergartner playing pretend: pretending to be a senior, pretending to be mature, pretending to know what the hell she's doing. Bug and Calliope are practically halfway out the door to college already, and she can't picture herself leaving home, being on her own, being an *adult*. It was different when she was swimming. Swimming was its own path, a particular route that would also have led to adulthood, but it was still a version of who she's always been, with coaches guiding the way. There weren't many ways to go wrong. The path was clear and if you drifted off it, someone would blow a whistle and get you back in your lane. Being unguided sounds . . . deeply and intensely impossible.

So what if *The Shark Club* is her guide?

She glances over at the New Kid again.

He's smiling at her.

She looks away, her face burning for no good reason. She can't summon the energy to smile back, to engage, to connect. She flips to a new page in her book, trying to orient herself to Topher and Jada through time and space and reality, to where the characters are staring at each other across the classroom, smiling and blushing, and she can stop being here, stop being herself, stop avoiding eye contact with Elijah's near-constant presence.

PRESLEY

The blond girl is reading *The Shark Club*, holding it up almost as though she's showing it to him.

No fucking way.

But also, *of course.*

Lately Presley feels like his life is a punch line to a joke he doesn't get. Looking at the cover of *The Shark Club*—solid blue, a graphic shark centered under the messy font and as familiar to him as his own face—makes him want to throw himself out the window or, at a minimum, set himself on fire.

Ideally both. He pictures it in stick figures because he can't help it. He almost sketches it right onto the desk but stops himself.

But . . . why *that* book? Literally hundreds of thousands of novels are published every year. The odds are astronomically low.

It's just as easy to apply a positive filter as it is a negative one! Shine a golden light, don't be surprised by a warm glow! Ellie chirps in his brain, like the goddamn blue bird of happiness. He squints, trying to think of a way to spin this situation positively. On the plus side, he's read it and he could talk to her pretty knowledgably about the plot and the characters. But in the minus column, it's also pretty much the last thing he wants to talk about.

Then, suddenly, Mac: *Yo, chill out. You look sweaty.* Right in his ear.

The room lurches. He doesn't dare move in case he falls out of his seat into the tarry eternity of oblivion bubbling up around his shoe. If he lets go, he'll become just another fossilized skeleton in the abyss.

He presses both hands down on the flat surface, holding on.

"Whoa, New Kid." The laughing boy slides into the seat next to him. "You okay there?"

"Oh. Me? Yeah. Totally." Presley turns his head, tries to smile and simultaneously unclench his jaw, resulting in what can only be a grimace. *Be normal.* "Sure. I'm good. Sorry."

"I'm Javi." The boy is all Axe body spray and dimples and muscles. He's wearing a surf-branded T-shirt with a tear across the nipple and sunglasses on the back of his head. The kids here all look they're on a TV show where they've been cast to portray themselves, only better. "Why are you sorry, man?"

"I . . . Presley." He points to himself, then immediately regrets the weirdness of that. *I . . . Presley.* Javi grins even more widely, revealing his big white straight teeth, exactly like Presley's own. *American teeth*, Presley's British mum calls them. "I'm Canadian. We're, um, an apologetic people. Being sorry is kind of our thing."

Javi laughs and Presley looks away. There's a possibility Javi's laughing at *him*, not at what he said, that he's seen the video, that he's already been sussed. He pulls his sleeves down over his hands, tries to feel invisible in the cocoon of his clothing.

"So where ya from?" Javi leans back, puts his feet up on his desk, somehow managing to sprawl.

Presley clears his throat, tries to relax his shoulders. "Yeah, I'm from, um . . . Canada." His voice is creaky. Apart from the goat and Mac, he hasn't spoken more than a handful of words to anyone all day.

Javi nods, looks serious but his eyes are laughing. "You said that already. But Canada's a big country." He taps Presley's arm lightly with his fist.

"Oh, right. True. It's very . . . big. Huge. It's actually the second biggest country in the world. By land mass. Not, like, population." He rubs his arm. Next to the board-short-sporting, shaggy-haired, shell-necklace-wearing Javi, he feels skinny and tense, as if he's holding every muscle in his body taut like the rabbits that his dad hunted, stuck forever in that split second when they froze before—too late—trying to flee. "Hunting makes real men," Presley's dad would say, chortling. Or was it "Hunting separates the boys from the men"? Whichever. He's glad he's forgotten.

"USA is number one!"

"Um, but . . ." He stops. America is a lot smaller than Canada, smaller still than Russia, but he doesn't want to start something.

"You sure you're okay, man?"

"We lived near Victoria," Presley says, after a beat. "That's where I'm from. It's on the West Coast. Vancouver Island." Just saying *Victoria* nearly flattens him with a wave of longing for the place, for the smell of their old house—trees and petrichor and kelp-strewn beaches—things he'd totally taken for granted, hadn't even realized that he cared about. He blinks.

"Oh yeah?" says Javi. "Rad. Canada seems cool. Snowy, right? I want to try snowboarding so bad." He makes a swooping gesture with his hands. "Like snow-surfing, you know? What's it like there?"

Presley shrugs. *Green*, he almost says, but Javi wants to hear about snow, not foliage. "Snowboarding's okay. We used to drive to the mountain and . . . Anyway, yeah, there was lots of . . . um, good powder." He wants to literally punch himself in the face. Like he knows anything about *powder*. It hardly ever snowed at home, and they went to the mountain exactly once. He *did* snowboard on that trip, but cautiously because he didn't want to risk an injury on the slopes that would keep him off the ice. Mac, who instantly mastered a dozen tricks, said Presley boarded like an old man with a walker. (And then they'd fought, as usual, but that time, no one had gotten hurt.) Presley's tongue goes reflexively to his teeth.

"Well, you're going to love it here, Canada," says Javi. "El Amado's freakin' paradise. You can't ever be bored with waves like these, ya know?" He points toward the window, the ocean, the relentless hypnotic roll of surf that actually gives Presley vertigo.

"Wow, yeah. For sure," says Presley. "Lots of . . . So far, it . . ." He lets his voice fade, realizing suddenly how much he actually hates it here: the unbearable heat, the strip malls along the freeway exit into town, the straggly bent pines masquerading as trees, the unwelcoming ocean that churns and foams, never holding still, the wildfire smoke slowly suffocating the sky. There's not enough oxygen, period. He's suddenly light-headed. He takes a swig from his water bottle.

"I'll take you around. You want?" Javi does a drum roll on Presley's desk with his fingers. "This weekend, yeah? We can throw the boards in, catch some waves, then head to Phantom Fest with the boys. It's what El Amado's all about. I mean, seriously, raddest party of the year. Your timing is perfect."

"Oh, yeah, nice. But . . . you know, I don't surf. I'm . . . Yeah. No. I'm good." Presley searches for the teacher, willing the man to start teaching, something, anything to get him out of this.

"I'll teach ya," says Javi. "No worries, man."

"Okay, great, cool, awesome," says Presley, like he's listing the dorkiest words he knows. Maybe the abyss wouldn't be so terrible, after all. Better than *this*, whatever the hell this is. He imagines the thick permanent peacefulness of tar filling his ears. The relief he'd feel knowing there was no point bothering to try to claw his way out. *It's metaphorical tar*, he reminds himself. *It's not fucking real.* He yawns to hide the fact that he's possibly, probably, hyperventilating.

"What's your number? I'll drop a pin. Meet me there at eleven. Saturday." Javi makes a hand gesture that could mean anything. Hang loose. Or peace. Or some obscenity in a different country.

Presley automatically does it back. He tries not to think about how ironic it would be if he were bitten by a shark. Or if he drowned. Or hit his head. Or just . . . died, seized on the board and sank into the depths. "Okay, yeah. Thanks. Cool."

"You got a wet suit?"

"Wet suit? Sure. Totally." He's apparently only capable of speaking in single words and of course he doesn't have a wet suit. But hopefully Ellie will know how he can get one or borrow one. She seems to already know everyone and everything here. She's become instantly connected. It's just how she is. She had a job at the college lined up before she even got here. She'll be proud of him. He's doing what she wants him to do: *trying*, reinventing himself as a character who isn't afraid of surfing and who has buddies and who goes to community events.

It's fine.

He's fine!

He *will* be fine.

He'll be a surfing, partying American teen, someone who owns a wet suit and says *rad* with a straight face, a kid who might one day wear puka shells and board shorts to school.

HATTIE

Hattie watches the New Kid talking to Javi, a bead of sweat trickling from his temple, down the path of the scar, to the corner of his mouth. She hopes they don't become friends because then she'll be forced to rethink the New Kid and she doesn't even know him yet . . .

"Ugh," she says.

"What?" Bug turns to her, just as Mr. Stevens slams the door with a bang. The whole class knows what he's like, so they fall silent. Without preamble, he launches into a memorized-sounding lecture about term papers, research notes, rough drafts, and quizzes, and then he taps the chalkboard where he's written out the reading list from which they can choose two novels to study.

The Shark Club isn't on the list. All the books on the list are written by straight, cis white men who have been dead for so long that even their reincarnations have lived full lives and died of old age. None of them have a subtitle like *A Love Story*. They are serious, stodgy, unsubtitled books.

Under her desk, Hattie texts Bug: *This reading list is a tool of the patriarchy.* She adds a shaking fist emoji, a wrench emoji, and a white man's face.

Bug smiles and texts back. *See also: Heteronormative propaganda.*

HATTIE:
See also: Male, pale, and stale.

BUG:
See also: Racist AF

HATTIE:
See also: boring as &#$^&

BUG:
Poop emoji

HATTIE:
You don't type it out, u nerd.

BUG:
Or do I? heart emoji nerd emoji heart emoji

Hattie hides a giggle with a cough. Mr. Stevens goes on. He has *expectations* and *standards*. He has a *grading rubric*. She starts reading again, her book hidden from his view by her desk.

"Sharks," says Mr. Hanks, smiling widely. "That's a first for me. Not sure your parents will sign off on the permission slip for that one, but you can always try. If they say yes, I'm not going to say no. Even though I'm not-so-secretly terrified on your behalf."

"It's fine," says Jada. "Cage-diving is a legit business. We're not just going to jump into the middle of the Pacific Ocean at night in a known feeding location and take our chances on not being mistaken for a seal. My dad will sign, no problem." She leaves out the part

where her mom is dead and her dad will absolutely, defi-
nitely not sign, which is fine, because she's been signing
on his behalf for most of her life. She has to do this.
This is a very real chance to get up close with a great
white, and she's not going to let that opportunity pass
her by.

"Exactly," says Topher, nudging her. "We're smart.
And we'll stay far away from Amity Island."

"Amity Island is not a real place," says Jada. "Are
you even serious?"

"I know! I was joking."

His arm is so close to hers they're almost touching.
She can feel the warmth pulsing off his skin and she
steps away. "Topher, we aren't friends; we just hap-
pened to pick the same book. Don't get excited." Like
she's the popular one and he's the quiet nerd and she can
put him in his place.

He looks confused.

"I love this outlandish idea," says Mr. Hanks, look-
ing up from their proposal. "I'm in. I'll support your
project. But if it doesn't fly, think of how else you can
find a way into that book without the need to sign legal
documents saying that your family won't sue if you die."
He signs the paper, humming the theme song from Jaws
ominously. "You know, I don't think I could do it, even
in a cage. That movie scarred me for life."

"Wimp," they say at the same time, exactly, their
voices overlapping to the point that they make one note,
a singular sound. Then, also at the same time, "Hey,
don't copy me."

It's the first time they belly-laugh together, clutching at each other's arms, laughing until they cry, even though later, when Jada is regaling Eva with the story, Eva will say, "Huh, was it really *that funny? Or are you in love or something?" And Jada will stop talking about it, turn up the music, and pretend to herself that the answer is "Of course not" when she's not absolutely sure that's true.*

Something is happening, she thinks, and she kind of hopes it's a brain tumor and not that she's falling for this boy. She has more important things to do and they all involve a huge and terrifying shark who, in real life, is a wild animal with a prey drive and not just a movie-version caricature of a shark named Bruce. Sharks might not eat *people, but she knows from experience that they sometimes take an exploratory bite and spit you out again. And sometimes, that exploratory bite severs your femoral artery, and you bleed out, fifty feet from shore, on a snorkeling holiday in Hawaii while your kids obliviously eat shaved ice on the beach and bicker about whose turn it is with the boogie board.*

Absorbed in the story, Hattie lets out an involuntary "Oof."

Bug kicks her under the desk. "Carefulllll," she singsongs, under her breath.

"Ms. Rodriguez," barks Mr. Stevens. "You can consider yourself warned." He writes her name—*Estrella Rodriguez*—in cursive on the board under the ominous heading: *Warnings.*

"Okay, okay," says Bug.

"Sorry!" Hattie mouths at her.

She shrugs. "Eyeroll emoji!" she mouths, rolling her eyes.

Hattie drops her face onto her desk to stop herself from laughing, pressing her cheek against the solid cool wood. The book slides off her lap and smacks down onto the floor.

"Oh crap!"

"Ms. *Hat*field," says Mr. Stevens. "Now you are *both* on thin ice." He adds Hattie's name under Bug's, pressing so hard the chalk snaps in two: *Isabella Hatfield*. Her full name written out in his looping cursive looks like nothing to do with her. The only person who ever called her Isabella was her mom.

Hattie's eyes suddenly flood embarrassingly with tears, and she roughly wipes them away. "My bad," she manages to squeak out, her voice cracking.

Her dad would tell her to go to her happy place and she would say, "You're such a cheeseball, Dad. We should spread you on a cracker." But still, she closes her eyes and imagines the pool, which always *was* her happy place even though now it's her panic trigger—can it be both?—the aqua blue of the water, the cool gray tiles, the huge plants that Bethanne, the daytime receptionist and technically her boss now, insisted on putting along the wall of windows, which grew so tall they formed a jungle, the air heavy with their greenness. She pictures herself—the dawn light streaming through the greenery—the first one out of the changing rooms, standing on the block in her red suit layered over her black one for extra drag, the sandpapery roughness against her feet, the crouch, then the dive: Her hands punching through the surface cleanly, hardly any splash, her body a blade, following. She'd keep her head under, eyes open, the tiles on the bottom of the pool blurry and distorted, holding her breath halfway down the length of the lane before exploding out of the water and taking a lungful of pool-scented air.

She gasps out loud, coming back to English class with a start, her heart racing. She doesn't know how to not think about Elijah when she thinks about the pool. It's impossible. They're inextricably linked. Her lungs tighten down like fists.

Avoiding Bug's questioning stare, she looks out the window straight at the sun—still pinkly shining through the brownish haze of smoke—and Elijah's face fades into the dust motes in the too-bright light and the sunspots the sun leaves behind on her retinas.

PRESLEY

The class is blurring and fading around Presley, tiny pricks of light sparkling around the periphery of everything, his own private constellations. He takes out his pen and starts sketching on the back of his left hand. He used to do this all the time, stick figures obviously, always with stick figures, but this time . . . something different. The pen nib tugging sharply at his skin anchors him just enough to keep him from spinning out entirely. By the time the room swims back into focus, there's an orca on the back of his hand. A sketchy orca, but still an orca. He stares at it, tracing it with his finger, almost as surprised to see it as he was every time they spotted one in the wild. *Home.*

"Ms. *Hat*field," Mr. Stevens says. "Now you are *both* on thin ice."

Presley glances over and the blond girl's eyes meet his and there's that *feeling* again, then she says, quietly, "My bad." She looks upset, like she's crying or about to be, and Presley sees what he hadn't registered before: She's shimmering like heat on blacktop.

"Oh *fuck*," he says, and Mr. Stevens whips his head around, ready to scold him. He keeps his eyes down, stays invisible.

"Whoa, dude," murmurs Javi admiringly.

Presley's heart feels like it stops, starts again, stops, then explodes. Isabella Hatfield has a mesoglea. He keeps his eyes on Mr. Stevens, registering nothing he's saying, aware only of the girl and of the blurry moving layer of light around her. He blinks, hard, trying to focus. In front of her he sees a faint face he can *almost* discern, one he senses as much as sees. Every part of him is tingling.

"I see it, too!" he wants to tell her. He *needs* to tell her. He wants to shout, to grab her, hug her, high-five her, *something*. His heart skips erratically. Other than himself in the mirror, he's never seen anyone else with that particular, impossible to describe but as real as anything, haunted *shimmer*.

He's never seen someone else's ghost.

The thing is . . . if he can see hers, she can see his. Maybe. And maybe that means he's not completely insane.

Maybe it means that Mac is not just a hallucination brought about by PTSD or his head injury or both.

He swallows the hysteria that's threatening to bubble up, not unlike what happened when they drove through El Amado the first time, seeing the GHOST CAPITAL OF THE WORLD! banner, the WELCOME GHOST HUNTERS sign outside the Haunted Inn, the ghost mural on city hall painted above a sign about the people who died in the 1987 fire, the Ghost Emporium, and the painting of shadowy specters on the wall of a Dairy Queen. He'd started to laugh and couldn't stop. He'd laughed and laughed, tears rolling down his face, and Ellie and his mum had exchanged *that* look, the worried one, the one that said *What should we do?* and *I don't know!* then pulled into the Dairy Queen and bought him a milkshake. For the whole drive, they'd been stopping and buying him milkshakes, like instead of losing everything that mattered, he'd only lost his teeth.

But now . . .

He feels like his heart has slipped down and is beating where his spleen should be. Or maybe it's just that, after a long period of feeling like everything had been glued together wrong, it's finally falling back into place again.

HATTIE

"You don't *have* to be here." Bug leans against the window of Starbucks, waiting for the line to inch forward. "Especially if you're going to be all . . ." She makes a gesture with her hands.

"I'm not all . . ." Hattie moves her hands the same way. "Or maybe I'm *always* all . . ."

They're interrupted by the squeal of brakes, someone honking at the end of the block. A car revs its engine as it roars past, kicking up a cloud of dust.

"Jeez, what an asshole."

"Talking about me?" Javi materializes behind them, his buddies clustered around him like he's a magnet and they're nails and can't help themselves but stick to him.

"At least you recognize yourself, Eavesdropper."

"You're funny. I like that about you, Hattie Hatfield." He grins and leans closer, dropping his head on her shoulder. She smells shampoo and sunscreen and mint and Axe body spray and automatically steps back. Javi is always so . . . unsettling or maybe just really good at getting people to feel *liked*. Instinctively, Hattie glances at Bug to see if she's noticed, to see if she's annoyed, but she just laughs.

Hattie's irritated by him, irritated by Bug's nonchalance, irritated in general. She turns her back on all of them. Her phone buzzes.

DAD:
Rate your first day on a scale of 1 to Taylor Swift.

Hattie pauses before she types.

> **HATTIE:**
> Sad Beautiful Tragic, I guess.
> The usual. Yours?

DAD:
Breathless . . . (Just hit the gym with B-Finch)

> **HATTIE:**
> Gross. Go take a shower.
> (Don't forget to pick up tacos.)

DAD:
On it. Love you more than T-Swift's Red tour.

> **HATTIE:** As if.

She smiles and pockets the phone, but even as she slips it into her backpack, she remembers the Fwd: Fwd: Save the Date! email still lurking in her inbox and her smile falls away.

"Can Save the Date ever mean anything except . . . a wedding?" *Wedding* tastes like curdled milk, sour and strong, like the time her mom didn't check the date before pouring it on Hattie's Rice Krispies, thick and chunky. Hattie had cried, but her mom just laughed and said the date on the carton meant nothing, when it obviously did. She nearly gags, but Bug doesn't even notice. She's fully engrossed in looking at something on Roberto's phone—Roberto is never more than a few feet away from Javi, as far as Hattie can tell, stuck to him like a very tall shadow—while Javi drapes his arm over her shoulders and Hattie's left asking her own reflection in the coffee shop's front window.

She makes a face at herself. She already knows the answer: It can't be anything else. Her mom is getting married. Probably. Definitely. She just can't bring herself to click the email to find out because then she'll have to figure out how she feels about it and that's too hard to even contemplate.

PRESLEY

A few too-tall palm trees throw down too-small patches of shade as Presley walks down the main street where half the school is lining up at Starbucks. He crosses the road abruptly, without looking both ways, and there's a screeching of brakes, a honking, and a car narrowly misses him, a man yelling out the open window.

Presley freezes.

He watches the car peeling away, a big gray dog hanging out the window, tongue lolling. He literally *can't* move—all the muscles in his body have temporarily disconnected from his brain. There's nothing he can do but wait it out, glued to the ground, hoping he doesn't actually fall over, acting like he means to be here, standing in the middle of the road while everyone from school stares at him. He hopes Isabella Hatfield isn't there . . . But of course she is, or someone who looks like her, a flash of blond hair and black-framed glasses.

Look at me, he thinks.

Don't look at me.

Look.

Don't.

A girl with bright blue box braids steps in front of him, looking amused. "You okay there, New Kid?"

He manages to make eye contact with her and then, just like that, his muscles unlock and he manages to shift from one foot to another, then: "No, yeah," followed by "Yeah, no." It isn't exactly articulate, but close enough. "Sorry. I'm good. Thanks."

"Okaaaaay," she says, and he knows it really isn't, but what can he do?

He raises his hand, a salute or a wave, and starts to walk away, every step feeling steadier as his body remembers how to *be*. He puts his headphones on.

"Welcome to El Amado," she calls to his receding back.

"Yeah, thanks, you too." He cringes and hits play and cranks the volume until he drowns out everything: his mortification, his heartbeat, his thoughts, the sky, the entire world.

HATTIE

"The New Kid is super weird," announces Calliope, joining Hattie and Bug in the Starbucks line.

"Is he?" says Bug, ducking out from under Javi's arm. "Hattie thinks he's . . . What was it? *Fine.*" She makes a heart and peers at Hattie through it.

"Who is fine?" Roberto hangs over them, grinning.

"Probably talking about me," says Javi. "You know anyone else who is *all this?*" He frames his face with his hands, blinks at Hattie mock-flirtatiously.

"I have to go," says Hattie. Her face feels hot. There's still a terrible sour milk taste in her mouth that's so bad, she's worried people can smell it. Her pulse is picking up, too, but also skittering in an alarming way: *Beatbeat beat beeeaat beatbeatbeat.* She can't have a cardiac arrest *here*; there's no defibrillator in sight. Surreptitiously, she presses her fingers to her wrist and starts counting. Dana Vollmer, her swimming idol, has seven Olympic gold medals and long Q-T syndrome. She travels with her own defibrillator.

"He just about got run over. Did you not see it?" Calliope points at the road. "Just now. Then he just stood there, like he was waiting for the next car to come along and finish the job. And he was kind of staring blankly and smiling like this . . ." She demonstrates. "Maybe he's high."

"He's not. I'm leaving," Hattie says shakily. "I have to go." She wants to run. "Fight or flight," her dad would say. "That's normal."

Calliope looks at her, head cocked. "Don't you want a coffee? Why are you being weird?"

"Hattie doesn't drink coffee, remember?" Bug says, speaking for her. "She gets freaked out when her pulse speeds up. Caffeine is her enemy."

Hattie shakes her head and shrugs at the same time, raising one hand in a wave.

"Are you okay?" Calliope calls after her, half-laughing, but Hattie pretends not to hear, forcing herself to walk away slowly until she's out of sight, and then she starts to run. Running hurts but it also feels good. She's way too early to go to work, but the farther she gets from everyone, the easier it is to breathe. She runs fast and then faster. Her sneakers make clouds in the dust. Bug's wrong, she likes it when her pulse speeds up, but only when she's in control of when and how. It makes her feel strong. Alive. She runs and runs, faster and farther, farther and faster, until her lungs are wheezing for oxygen, burning from the smoke, her muscles screaming, her blood thundering powerfully in her veins, her eyes stinging in the terrible air, her T-shirt soaked with sweat.

PRESLEY

Presley had thought there were stairs along this part of the cliff, leading down to the beach, but he must have imagined them, because as far as the eye can see, there's just . . . cliff. It feels like a metaphor, but he can't think of what it might be for, exactly. His brain is only half-working, the other half numb and humming.

He scrambles down the steep rocky slope on what *might* be a trail, hoping he can get back up just as easily (or at all), then walks as far down the beach as he can, stopping only when he gets to the massive boulders that form a breakwater.

The tide is high. Tiny flecks of ash swirl in the air, disappearing into the water. The stench of rotting seaweed in the foam at the edge of the tideline smells like home. He crouches down, breathes it in. It makes him nostalgic for the gasoline-tinged air on his dad's boat, for all the days he and Mac spent on the deck, nauseated by the rolling swell, waiting for something to happen, for their dad to be done with work, for orcas to swim by and break the monotony.

"Shark!" Mac would yell at intervals, pointing at imaginary dorsal fins, pretending to shove Presley over the side.

"We're 'gonna need a bigger boat,'" Presley would say, quoting *Jaws*, Mac's favorite movie.

He misses Mac so much he wants to puke. His grief is all nausea and twisting gut-ache, which isn't how the poets or songwriters talk about it, but grief—at least his grief—is more like food poisoning or IBS than *poetry*. His stomach rolls in rhythm with the swell. He presses on it with his hands, willing himself to not throw up.

Then, in the heat shimmering over the black boulders, he sees Mac, faint but definitely present.

"Yo, bro!" He's nearly collapsing from relief, but Mac only answers when he wants to and this isn't one of those times.

Presley stares at the spot until the image vanishes into the stones. He drops his bag, along with his phone, jacket, and flannel into the sand and walks straight into the waves.

He's in up to his knees.

Then his thighs.

Stop, he tells himself. But there's another voice: *Keep going.*

The swell pushes up as high as his waist, then higher. The water is too cold and is hitting him too hard, seems to want to toss him back to shore. His feet have to fight to stay grounded on the slippery, uneven rocks.

Feel what you're feeling—that's what Ellie says to do when he gets like this, overwhelmed and desperate. *Be present, Pres.* (Staying in the moment is definitely his biggest problem, his brain is always pinballing into the past and bouncing around there before exploding into his blank future.) He puts his hands in the water, splashes some onto his face, steps deeper and deeper until he's practically swimming, the water nearly up to his armpits. It would be easy to just let his feet lift away, to reach for deeper water, to . . .

To *what*?

Then he hears Mac, clear as anything: *Get out of the water, trash-hole. You wanna drown in a rip? Were you raised by wolves, son?*

That's another thing their dad always said—"Were you raised by wolves, son?"—and they'd say, "More like a dogfish." And he'd say, "Lucky for you, that is. Least you can swim."

That was their dad's specialty: dogfish. Not even an *impressive* shark, one small enough you could easily hold it in your hands.

"Yeah, whatever, Macaroni. Maybe I just wanted to come see you." But he turns around and lets the waves push him toward the beach. He's limping slightly and his clothes stick to his skin. He grabs his things, swaps his T-shirt for his flannel, and finds a hot rock to lean against, the water pouring off him, puddling at his feet.

He looks around to make sure no one saw him, but the beach is empty, and he's struck by the sensation that he's not really here, that none of this is real. He takes a selfie to prove he exists and there he is, alone on his phone screen, soaking wet and squinting in the sunlight. Here, but not here.

Nowhere.

Keep it together.

He opens Instagram but instead of posting the pic on his currently blank grid, he scrolls until he finds Maeve, poking the bruise of his past. She's deleted him, purged her page of even the outline of his elbow, but she's still posting like the so-called influencer she is. There's something comforting in knowing she's unchanged: same natural hair, same leather jacket with embroidered roses, same dimples carved into her cheeks, same wide-mouthed smile. But there's a different boy hanging over her shoulder, an unfamiliar boy who's obviously not Presley, and may be the opposite of Presley in every visible way.

He expands the picture. He doesn't want to look, but he can't *not* look either. The guy looks like someone who does something with a ball on a muddy field, someone who breaks his ribs and sustains concussions without noticing, someone who can bench-press a piano or a live bull.

Fine. It's fine! He doesn't care.

He wants to not care.

What's the difference?

Sweat stings his eyes. Maeve is a shitty human being who happens to be pretty. He's over her. He didn't love her. She didn't love him. They both loved Mac, which was something altogether different than liking each other.

He starts scrolling again, stopping when he sees skating. Vertigo threatens to topple him, turns his stomach inside out—that grief-puke thing also applies to the rink—but he also can't *not* look. The surf smashes the shore noisily. His ears fill with the noise and for a second, he feels disoriented.

It's Sergei Gorgov's story. Serg looks the same but taller. No more acne. He looks good. Strong. *Coming for you, Russia,* says the caption over a clip of Serg cleanly landing a perfect quad toe, with a speed in the air Presley can feel on his skin. He knows without wanting to know that the Junior Grand Prix of Figure Skating is in Russia next week and he has to grab his wrist to keep from throwing his phone into the waves.

It could have been you, he tells himself. *It should have been you.*

But . . . would it? Maybe that's just another bullshit story athletes tell themselves—"I'm the best! I'd have won gold if I hadn't been injured!"—because there's no way for them to prove otherwise. Maybe the closest he ever came to the

Olympics was in his head. He might have flamed out, even if he hadn't had his chance stripped away by the accident.

Maybe he was never as good as he imagined.

But maybe he *was*.

His heart is beating too fast now, panic coming at him from all directions. His breath is shallow.

He tips back his head and opens his mouth. "FUCK!" he screams into the wind. "FUUUUUUUUUUCK!" Then, nearly toppled by that effort, he drops down hard on the sand and stares at the photo of himself.

He scrolls through his contacts. Then he types, *Wet my pants. No one can tell, right?* attaches the pic, starts a group chat with Henry and Big Tee. The last messages in their chat were from Camp Thunderbird. *Heading home, I guess, gotta go to the dentist* his message said, attached to a pic of him grinning with broken front teeth. *What happened?* was the reply and *Are you okay?* then more questions, spaced out, then: *I'm sorry about Mac, call us, we want to help,* then . . . nothing.

He ghosted them.

He hits send on the pic.

Then, because he can't stop himself, he clicks on TikTok and opens the video that spawned the meme. It's as bad as he remembers. Maybe worse. And it has 1.4 million likes. Almost *ten* million views. That's the equivalent of the entire population of Sweden.

He clicks off the video and rubs his eyes.

The wind sighs, like even *it* is rolling its eyes at him. He's unbearably uncomfortable. He peels off his wet, gritty pants—there's no one around except a handful of seagulls riding the wind—and squeezes them out, stuffs them in his pack with his uneaten lunch and pulls on his skating pants, his legs still sticky from the salt water. Then he picks up his pack and starts scaling the steep cliff path—the surreality of the scene making his head spin, the abyss threatening to pull him over the edge of the barely there path—the skates in his bag banging into his kidneys with every step he takes.

HATTIE

Hattie sits down at the front desk of the El Amado Activity Center and spins in her chair.

"Don't *break* it," says Bethanne, gathering her purse and fanning herself with it. "That's my favorite chair. You're early. Did you just work out or something? Why are you so sweaty?"

Hattie shrugs, wiping the sweat off her face with the hem of her *Fearless* shirt. "I ran here. You can leave. I've got it." She takes off the shirt, swipes it under her arms, and then stuffs it into her bag.

"Is that tank top work-appropriate?"

"Bethanne, please. It's the best I can do. Go home."

"Huh. I guess I *could*. Might be nice to leave early. It's too quiet here with the pool being closed. Talk about bad timing. Is it hot out there?"

"How can you even ask me that? There's a record-breaking heat wave fueling out-of-control wildfires. Pretty soon all of humanity will be dead and the insects will feast on our cooked-by-the-sun flesh. It's hot in *here* and we ostensibly have air conditioning." *Ostensibly* has a barely perceptible but definitely present fishy aftertaste, like the smell of the herring she used to throw to seals off the end of the pier when her mom took her, calling "Lunchtime!" and shrieking appreciatively when they stuck their little heads out of the water, looking for more.

Bethanne sighs. "Well, don't forget to do the filing. And please stop putting your feet on my desk."

"Sorry," says Hattie automatically, not meaning it. She takes a bottle of water and a bottle of Diet Coke out of her bag—her friends are wrong about caffeine, she loves her Diet Coke—and lines them up next to the phone. She puts her red Moleskine notebook and her black felt-tipped pen on the desk pad, then flips it open and writes *ostensibly* so she doesn't forget.

"Skating lessons start today," says Bethanne. "You're in charge of the soundtrack, remember? And the pool reopens next Tuesday. Got it? Do I need to write it down? You can only do homework if it's dead in here."

Hattie drops her head to her chest and groans. "Yes. I know, Bethanne. I've got it. Skating. Pool closure. Bye."

Bethanne starts to leave, then turns back, a wide smile plastered across her face. "Are you sure because—?"

"It's *two* things, Bethanne."

"Well, okay. Anyway, don't forget that today's a great day to have a great day!" She taps her bejewelled nails on the counter twice and then finally leaves Hattie alone with the humming of the ineffective air conditioner, the silent phone, and the empty waiting area. She has a love/hate relationship with being alone. If she's alone, no one can ask anything of her but also, if she goes into cardiac arrest, no one will be there to save her. She presses her fingers to her wrist and feels her heart beating steadily, reassuringly, strong. She's young and healthy. She's not going to die.

But Elijah was only seven and he was as healthy as a human can be.

Her eyes automatically dart around, searching, and there's his face in the corner, smiling.

"No, please, not now."

Each time she sees him, she thinks she'll know how to respond. She'll stay calm, she'll just *be*, but each time, her brain says, *Oh shit*, and starts spinning. Maybe it's her negative energy that's keeping him around, but how can she control it? It's out of her hands.

She gets up, unlocks the vending machine and retrieves a Snickers, puts her feet up on Bethanne's desk, and focuses on Rusty, driving the Zamboni down on the ice, sweeping it in perfect laps around the rink, not missing even the tiniest sliver.

PRESLEY

Presley takes off his shoes and puts on his skates, pulling the laces tight. The place is too quiet, the sound of the Zamboni muffled by the glass, every other noise magnified a million times: the zipper on his bag, the *thock-thock-thock* of his laces fitting into the hooks, his own breathing.

"Hey," he practices. He stands, leans forward like he's talking to imaginary kids and forces himself to smile so his voice sounds happier. "I'm Presley. Who wants to learn how to skate?"

"Hi, guys, listen up. I'm Presley and we're going to kick some ass today!"

The Zamboni drives off and the newly cleaned ice gleams behind the glass, smooth and blank and terrible and beautiful, the smell of the rink so utterly familiar, it nearly crushes him with a wave of longing and nostalgia for everything he was and can't ever be again. He breathes it in deeply, like he's breathing real air for the first time in months, breathing too much, hyperventilating. His hands are shaking. His legs are shaking. He's so fucking *scared*. What if he can't remember how to teach? How to skate? He blinks hard, pressing the heels of his hands into his eyes, a flurry of lights swirling around his periphery, and when he opens his eyes again, there's the glimmer of Mac, bulky with goalie pads, taking up so much more of the ice than Presley ever did.

He's waving. *Bromigo!* He flips Presley off and does a corny spiral and falls on his ass, whooping. He laughs, wavers, vanishes into the blank whiteness.

"Hey." Presley presses his hand against the glass. "Wait!"

But Mac is gone.

He turns away, his whole body trembling, then makes himself climb the stairs to the office, his skate guards rocking on the tile floor, rehearsing what he's going to say in his head:

Hi, I'm Presley. It's my first day.

Hey. Presley Jablowski, I'm the new skating teacher.

Any idea where I find Coach Kat?

But as he approaches the girl at the desk, whose back is to him, all his words vanish because his cells know who she is before he does.

"Hi" is what creaks froggily out of his mouth. He has to repeat it, loud enough for her to hear. "Hi?"

Isabella Hatfield turns around.

Their eyes meet and there's a practically audible *click*, which makes him think of how he and Mac once taught themselves to break into lockers by holding combination locks against their ears, listening for the metal components to fall into place.

Click,

click,

click.

"Hi," he repeats, stronger, his voice echoing in the space around them.

HATTIE

The New Kid's mouth is forming an already familiar smile, pulled crooked by the scar on his cheek. Hattie finds that she's leaning toward him, like her body is reaching for his over the counter before she has a chance to consider how weird that is. She straightens up abruptly.

In an alternate world in the multiverse, she'd do it. She'd just *kiss* him. But—

"I . . . Are you okay?"

"Yes! Sorry. Um . . . I just . . ." Hattie's heart skitters dangerously in her chest. "I mean, *hi*. Just hi." She stands up straighter, takes a deep breath, regroups. "It's you."

PRESLEY

Presley's fingertips are tingling.

"I'm good," he says.

Isabella Hatfield tucks a stray piece of hair behind her ear. She raises one eyebrow slowly. "I didn't actually ask how you were."

"Well, I'm good," he repeats. His tongue is taking up too much room in his mouth. "Now you know. Saves you having to ask, which is . . . You're welcome."

She smiles, a smile that crinkles the corners of her eyes into what will one day be laugh lines.

Feel what you're feeling.

He's feeling euphoric. And weird. Weirdly euphoric. Euphorically weird.

"I'm good, too," she says. "Now you're also off the hook."

There are a million things he wants to say, but what he says is: "Okay. Right. Yeah. I'm Presley? Presley Jablowski. I work here. I need to find Coach Kat because I'm teaching today. Coaching, that is. Skating."

"That explains the skates," she says gravely. "I work here, too, coincidentally." She gestures around her work area. "Work is my middle name."

Be funny, he tells himself, but he can't remember how. He closes his eyes, pictures only stick figures, and opens them again. "Um, your middle name is Work? That's . . . I like it. Isabella Work Hatfield. It has a nice ring."

She looks uncertain. "I was joking?"

"I know!" he says quickly. "So was I."

"Oh, right. But how do you know my name? Should I be scared?"

He backtracks. "English! I'm in your class. It was written on the board. Mr. Stevens." He mimes writing on a board. "God, I don't know why I did that. Pretend I didn't . . ." He does it again.

"Did what? Anyway, my middle name is Grace. I go by Hattie, because . . . Well, because." She pushes her glasses up her nose. "What's yours?"

He swallows. *Be funny. Be a Swedish supermodel. Be better.* "Are you asking for my middle name? Is it because you already know everything about me or because you want the answer to my LiveJournal security question?"

She laughs but she sounds nervous. He wants her to not be nervous, but he's also nervous and the nervousness of them both *has* to be something.

"For starters, are you famous? Why would I know anything about you? And second, I wasn't going to hack your LiveJournal before, but now . . ."

He smiles. All the trembling in his body has stopped. "No one has a LiveJournal anymore outside of YA novels, where it's a convenient plot device. But I'm an open book. Ask me anything."

"Okay . . . Well, I guess I still want to know because you're avoiding answering: What *is* your middle name?"

He looks at her pretty, serious face, at her slightly chapped lips, the gap between her teeth, the piece of wavy hair tangled behind the arm of her glasses. "You won't believe this, but it's also Grace."

She laughs, a real laugh. "Is it really? That's . . . beautiful."

"I kind of wish it was. Maybe I'll change it." He leans closer and whispers, "Full disclosure: It's Bearnard." He pronounces it with the full-on Scottish accent, heavy on the *bear*. He does not mention that it's his father's name and that he hates carrying his dad around with him, inside his own name like that.

He focuses on her nose piercing, a tiny gold heart.

"Bearnard?" She makes a face. "What kind of name is Bearnard? *That* is a truly terrible name." She looks at him as though she's inspecting his skin for flaws, of which he knows she'll find plenty. The scar, for one. He fights the urge to put his hand over it, to turn his face so she can't see it.

"It's Scottish, lass," he says, in a heavy version of his dad's burr, a glottal stop in the middle. *Sco-ish.*

"Bearnard." She rolls the *r*'s so hard she sounds like she's gargling. "Still awful. Truly." She takes a sip of Diet Coke, swishing it in her mouth as though she can wash the taste of his terrible middle name away. "Suits you though."

"Ouch. Because I look like a bear or because you can already tell I'm a terrible person?"

"Now that you mention it, you do look like a bear." She leans toward him, squinting, like maybe she's examining his ursine features. "A bear who's just woken up from hibernation: long winter, no food."

Which is funny, because that *is* how he feels, like he's been hibernating for eighteen months.

He smiles at her.

"What?" she says. "Is there something on my face?"

"No, it's just . . . This is good."

She reaches over and touches his hand. Once. Lightly. "Yep," she says.

"Did you know . . . I mean, this will sound weird, but I can see your . . . When he's here, you have a mesoglea," he says, before he can stop himself. He has to tell her. He wants her to know. He needs her to know that he *knows*. He needs to know that she knows, too. And if she does . . . if she can see Mac . . . The sentences he could say that would make it make sense get stuck in his mouth, tangling on his tongue. "I can . . ."

But at the exact same moment, she says, "Coach Kat's office is down the hall from the changing area, orange door, you can't miss it! Good luck!" and then, at the same time, they both say, "What?" and then the phone starts ringing, and she slides the papers across the counter, and he says, "Got it," and he walks away, still smiling, as she talks into the phone, his skates the only thing keeping him firmly on the ground.

THE MESOGLEA

HATTIE

Hattie doesn't tell him that *Bearnard* tastes of salt and hot mustard, but she opens her notebook and carefully writes it on the list she's keeping for Brady. *Bearnard stings my tongue but makes me want to keep saying it, a street pretzel dipped in spicy gold bought at Golden Gate Park on the day we went to play Frisbee and I skinned both my knees and Mom put her socks on me and pulled them up to my thighs, the blood seeping through them, because she had no Band-Aids.*

She can never ever, ever, ever give this notebook to Brady. It's *way* too cringe.

("This is good," Presley had said. And she had known exactly what he'd meant.)

She shivers and traces her pen over the name *Bearnard.* Over and over and over until it makes a dent in the paper.

Stop, she tells herself. *You are losing your shit.*

She puts her feet back up on the desk. Then off again. Then back. She wants to climb out of herself, maybe fly up to the ceiling or out through the skylights and into the smoke-choked sky. She goes over to the vending machine and gets another Diet Coke, this one ice-cold, and holds it against her neck, presses it to her chest, rests her cheek on it.

"Wait, what's a mesoglea?" she says suddenly to the space where he was standing. Whatever it is, it tastes like grape jelly, the kind she used to eat on crackers in Applejack after preschool, leaving purple stains all over the upholstery. The stains were why Hattie started renovating Applejack. Now the seats are reupholstered in the perfect shade of coral-pink vinyl. It wipes clean.

Mesoglea (sp?), she writes in her notebook. *A rushed snack before swimming, a grape-jelly stain left on the Cinderella pool towel Mom used to wipe my mouth.*

"Cringe-o-rama," she says out loud, and stuffs the notebook into the bottom of her backpack so she doesn't have to look at it and wonder if she'd literally die of embarrassment if anyone read it. She pulls out her phone.

> **HATTIE:**
> Is "mesoglea" a real word?

> **BUG:**
> It sounds like something you should cough up and spit out.

> **CALLIOPE:**
> "mesoglea: a gelatinous substance between the endoderm and ectoderm of sponges or cnidarians" See also: Why Google exists.

> **BUG:**
> Yeah, obvi cnidarians, Hat. Everyone knows that. Sarcasm emoji eyeroll emoji scorn emoji

> **HATTIE:**
> Middle finger emoji. Follow up question: Is "cnidarian" a real word?

PRESLEY

The mesoglea was the reason why Maeve broke up with Presley in the middle of her parents' twenty-fifth anniversary party.

They'd been together ever since Presley returned to school after the accident—he'd missed the last two months of tenth grade, but the teachers passed him in all his classes since he'd always been an A student. He'd returned at the start of junior year patched together and stunned in a way that reminded him of when they used to catch fish and his dad would smash them on the head with a rock until they stopped moving. Maeve had been one of Mac's best friends. Maeve was . . . impulsive. She was fun and a little unhinged and *really* pretty. She was definitely a *type*. Mac's type. She probably would have been Mac's first girlfriend, but Mac was dead, so she was Presley's, a fact he chose at the time to not examine too closely.

Maeve's parents' party shouldn't have surprised him, but it did. Unlike his dad's boat, which had been held together with duct tape and fiberglass patches, every surface of this boat was polished to a high sheen. Even the people seemed to reflect light differently. It took him a while to realize why: They were all wearing white.

"Duh. It's en blanc," said Maeve, which explained nothing. "How do I look?"

"You look, um, great." It wasn't a lie. She always looked great, but he thought she'd look better if she wasn't wrapped in toilet paper.

"Did you even read the invite, Pres?"

He hadn't. He was wearing jeans—nice ones, but still jeans—and a jean jacket. He'd read as far as *boat* and thought *boat*. Not *yacht*. "Canadian tuxedo?" At least his T-shirt was white.

Waiters poured expensive champagne indiscriminately. It wasn't *drinking*, not the way they usually did it: vodka and Red Bull from red Solo cups in the park at night, wine stolen from their parents' stash in Hydro Flasks, beer procured by someone's older brother. The champagne was barely a liquid. It tasted like light, dissolving in Presley's mouth, making him glow.

He got luminescently drunk.

It made him talkative and he was never talkative. He wanted to talk to everyone about everything. He wanted to *tell* everyone everything. He felt a swell of love for all the beautiful people on the boat, for everyone in the world. He wanted to plunge over the side and float on his back in the water so that he could see more of the sky, which he loved, and feel the ocean holding him up and look back at the boat, receding in the distance, so he could miss it.

And then he saw *her*: a woman, shimmering. Like she had a mesoglea.

He hadn't ever told anyone about the mesoglea. How could he? No one would understand. The mesoglea was Mac, but it wasn't Mac. The mesoglea was what happened to *him* when Mac was nearby: He became held in a thick layer of Mac's *spirit* or ghost or whatever Mac currently was. A gelatinous-looking light that formed an aura.

He beelined right for her.

It turned out she didn't have a mesoglea; she was wearing highlighter.

Her name was Chloe Bean and she was famous for playing a teenager on a show about sex and drugs that everyone was obsessed with. He didn't notice her bodyguards until they were on him, hoisting him right off his feet. They carried him outside, but once they got there, they grunted back and forth at each other and then . . . dropped him like dirty laundry onto the deck. Obviously, they couldn't toss him over the side and there was nowhere else to put him.

Maeve had been *furious*.

Maeve, who'd hoped to ingratiate herself with Chloe Bean, in case Chloe could help her get an audition.

Maeve, who sucked up to Presley's mum just a little more than he was comfortable with.

Maeve, who'd obviously been using him the whole time, which would almost have been funny—who would use *Presley* for anything?—if it hadn't hurt so much. "Everyone else was right, you're *nothing* like Mac," she yelled. Then she started to cry.

He blinked. "No, but he . . . I . . . She had . . . I thought . . ." He stopped. He let the silence fucking *blossom* and waited for her to step into it and blow them up.

Because he wasn't Mac. Because he didn't love her. Because Mac would have loved her and Mac was dead.

The boat rolled slightly on a wave, and he nearly threw up. He lay back on the polished wood deck and waited. The stars sparkled above him, brighter out here than in town, and so innumerable it was like staring at infinity.

She stood over him, silhouetted against the lights on the mast, then abruptly, angrily, wiped her tears away.

"How do you think I feel right now?" She looked . . . furious.

"Uh, incandescent with rage?" He attempted a smile. He loved that phrase. It made him think about how moths loved light bulbs so much they flew too close and died grimly horrific deaths. They were literally helpless to resist. There was a word for it. He frowned. "Phototactic," he murmured.

"What?" she said. "What the *fuck* did you say?" Then, "*You're* the pathetic one."

"I didn't say . . ." He staggered to his feet. He realized he was crying. It had snuck up on him. He wasn't crying because she was dumping him, he was crying at the tragedy of it all. The dead moths. His dead twin. His own inevitable death. Crying was not a good look on him. He got all red-eyed and blotchy, like a toddler. Snot bubbled from his nose. "Shit. No, no, no. No. I just . . ."

Then he heard Mac: *You're flaming out, Bro DiMaggio.*

"Maeve, seriously, I'm . . . sorry. Hey, did you know . . ." Then, because he was drunk and floundering, he tried to explain about moths and flames. And Maeve took out her phone and started filming.

The video went viral, not because of the crying or the incendiary moth speech, which really wasn't that bad, but because of what happened next, which was that while demonstrating a moth flapping its wings, Presley hit Chloe Bean, who'd been coming out onto the deck to vape, right in the mouth, her lip splitting like overripe fruit, crimson blood dripping onto her white silk slip-dress, her vape pen falling overboard like the punctuation at the end of a terrible sentence.

It looked worse than it was, but it was still pretty bad.

Float like a moth . . . punch a celeb like a drunk kid.

There were a hundred memes. More. His blubbery, snotty face. The moths and flames. Chloe Bean's split lip.

That night, after Presley had somehow managed to get home, Mac had stood in the doorway, silhouetted against the hall light, and Presley had lain on his bed, his shimmering hands pressed over his eyes.

"Leave me alone."

That speech was regrettable, Parsley. Social suicide. Why haven't you ever figured out how to keep yourself to yourself, my little green salad?

Presley got up, stumbling, then staggered forward, half-falling over his nightstand, and struck out at his brother's ghost, a mess of self-loathing and drunkenness. "She never liked me. She was into . . . *you.*" He swung again, missed, and broke his finger—the middle one—on the door frame.

Mac wasn't even there. He would never be there again.

Presley stumbled to the floor and cried.

HOW TO
GET BACK UP

PRESLEY

Coach Kat doesn't answer his knock on the orange door, so Presley ducks into the bathroom and sits down too hard on the closed lid of the toilet, his back spasming in protest.

Taped to the door, a flyer advertising "ghost hikes" in the hills stares back at him: MOUNT SOUTHERTON, #1 PARANORMAL ACTIVITY IN THE WORLD! Something seems missing in that declaration. *For* paranormal activity? *Of* paranormal activity? His mum would know. She's always correcting grammar on flyers, signs, and menus with the Sharpie that's always in her purse. He takes his own Sharpie out of his bag and changes the #1 to #199. He crosses out the *Para* and writes *for*.

MOUNT SOUTHERTON!
#199 FOR NORMAL ACTIVITY IN THE WORLD!

He draws a stick figure, falling off the top. He laughs, snaps a pic, then . . . doesn't post it. Mac would think it was hilarious. For a second, he considers posting it on Mac's Insta, which is still exactly as Mac left it, a virtual shrine to Mac's life . . .

He wonders if he should look at it.

He wonders how much that would hurt.

He wonders if it will ever be possible for him to go a full five fucking minutes without thinking about Mac.

He tears the flyer down and crumples it into a ball, tosses it into the corner of the room.

The air conditioner hums.

The pale yellow door is freshly painted, and he runs his hand over its smooth, cool surface. Then he leans forward and begins to sketch . . . not a stick figure, but another sketchy whale. It's a weird thing to do, but it's a totally fitting whale to vandalize El Amado with: The literal translation of *orca* is "of the kingdom of the dead."

"Sharks or whales?"

Presley can practically hear his dad asking with his rolling Scottish burr, then hear Mac, answering quickly, scornfully, "*Duh*, sharks."

And his own voice: "Whales. Sharks are just big dumb *fish*."

"*You're* a big dumb fish."

"Takes one to know one, fish-dick."

And then their mum, interrupting, "Stop fighting, boys. One day, one of you is going to get hurt."

Chocolate or vanilla?

Dogs or cats?

Guitar or piano?

Pepsi or Coke?

Hunting or fishing?

Pie or cake?

They always had opposite answers. It was how they knew who they were, how they defined themselves in contrast to each other. He was: vanilla, cats, piano, Coke, fishing, pie.

Mac was: chocolate, dogs, guitar, Pepsi, fishing, cake. (They both were opposed to hunting.)

But if you define yourself in contrast to someone else, when they die, what does that make you?

Alive, says Mac, from somewhere beyond the stall. *Try not to be such a dick about it.*

HATTIE

While she waits for the skating lessons to need her attention, Hattie opens her email and stares at the list of unopened messages. They seem to pulse, like a beating heart. She blinks, rubs her eyes. There's a 40-percent-off coupon for the Gap. A poem from Poetry.com. An ad for a VW show. The school's Welcome Back! newsletter. An email forwarded from Bug about an LGBTQ film festival in San Diego.

And the message she's been avoiding: Fwd: Fwd: Save the Date.

Until she opens it, it's Schrödinger's email: The cat is both alive and dead. Her mother is both coming back and never coming back. She opens her water and sips it. It tastes like minnows and algae. It tastes like chemicals and disappointment. It tastes like the recycled air on planes. But she's so thirsty. And she needs to pee. It's just more evidence of the terrible fallibility of the human body, as far as she's concerned.

She closes her inbox and opens her messaging app: *Needing to pee and being thirsty shouldn't coexist. How has humanity survived this long?*

CALLIOPE:
You aren't wrong, but you ARE weird.

> **HATTIE:**
> My weirdness is what makes me
> such a delight.

BUG:

clown emoji water droplet emoji dead plant emoji

Someone raps on the counter behind her, and Hattie startles and drops her phone. "Jeez, Rusty. You could have given me a heart attack. Shouldn't you be Zamboning something?"

"We're out of soap in the men's room by the rink." Rusty leans on the counter with both elbows and rests his bushy red-and-gray beard in his hands. "I can do it for you if you want because I'm a prince among men."

"Uh-huh. I'm sure, Prince Rusty. But there's literally nothing to do here today. You can't take away the one thing that's required of me."

"That's fair. You have a terrible job. I, on the other hand, have the best job in the whole goddamn world. I'm living the dream."

"I'm very happy for you. Now good-bye."

She waits while he disappears, whistling, down the hall. The sun shines through the dusty-looking skylights, covered on the outside with a fine coating of ash, and she stares at it until a sunspot forms in her vision. She closes her eyes and examines the shape of it, which is weirdly Australia-like. Australia, where the World Championships will be taking place soon, where she will not be going. There's a deleted email still in her unemptied trash from Nikita Chan, Hattie's old head coach, about Australia. Nikita has four Olympic gold medals in an unlocked glass case in her office and always wears copper-colored lipstick. She's not someone whose emails you ignore, but ignoring emails is Hattie's new superpower.

Once, in sophomore year, Nikita happened to be next to Hattie waiting for the break, and she'd called over, "You know,

Hattie, you're a lot like me when I was your age. You have totally explosive potential."

Hattie hadn't even known that Nikita knew her name.

She'd kept every single one of those words wrapped up in a fireproof box in her heart that she visited, like a museum display, once, twice, three times a day.

Explosive.

Potential.

Those words had propelled Hattie's every stroke, had helped her smash records, had started her move toward swimming stardom, had made her seriously ask herself, *What if I could go all the way?* It was right there, lurking, the possibility of it: a chance she could be good enough.

And there was constantly, always, a magical kid-like belief underlying her need to win: Her mom would definitely show up to the *Olympics.* She would come back. She would remember that she loved Hattie. She would remember that she loved Hattie's dad.

Hattie and her dad used to make up stories, stories that ended with her on the podium and the national anthem playing and her mom and dad seeing each other in the stands and crying and reaching for each other, and the holding pattern that Hattie and her dad had been in would be over. It was a story they told again and again, not always with the same words or in the same way, but they repeated it so often that the idea became *real.* Hattie would win and her mom would come home. Those two things were intertwined, braided into each other. It didn't have to make sense. It was magic. It was a spell with two ingredients: swimming and love. It was a fairy tale that would be the feel-good story of the games, featured on

Good Morning America, written up in the *New York Times*, viral on social media.

The not-quite-totally-deleted email from Nikita Chan says, *Hattie, you've been out of the pool for five months. I can't see how you can still go to Worlds with this kind of gap in your training. I'm cutting you from the roster if you don't respond with a plan for your return before October.*

Hattie is pretty sure she's not going to *return*, when getting within ten feet of the pool makes her heart beat so fast, the only miracle is that it hasn't exploded out of her chest like a hand grenade.

More importantly, Hattie understands fully now that Australia doesn't matter. Swimming doesn't matter. Even if she goes to Australia, keeps breaking records and collecting golds, even if she makes it to the Olympics, her mom won't come. Somehow Fwd: Fwd: Save the Date has finalized that, and she hasn't even opened it yet.

Her mother has officially, permanently, legally moved on. It is Fwd: Fwd: Over.

"I don't care," she says out loud. Her mother stopped being her mother the minute she got a one-way ticket to Bern. The cells of Delilah Hatfield that were Hattie's mother have all regenerated. Some more than once. She's a whole new person. She's been a whole new person for four years, someone who is not Hattie's mother, but that's fine because Hattie hasn't been her daughter for much longer than that, cell regeneration or no.

Delilah is a voice on the radio. She's a stranger who doesn't know or care that Hattie quit swimming, that Hattie threw away her *promising future* and her *explosive potential*.

She's not personally invested in Hattie going for the gold. Or in Hattie going to college. Or even in Hattie going downstairs to fill the soap.

Her dad has long believed that her mom has borderline personality disorder. The *DSM-5* says people with BPD have a "pervasive pattern of instability in interpersonal relationships." Hattie didn't want to believe that, or couldn't believe it, but abruptly, suddenly, she understands that it's true. It's part of who her mother is and why she'll possibly never really know her mother. "Never ever, ever, ever, ever, ever," she says to no one, to the plant on the desk, to herself.

Never feels like shards of broken glass in her throat. Instead of having a taste, it just hurts. She coughs, expecting blood.

Hattie gets up on slightly wobbly legs, goes to the supply cupboard, and hauls out the refill bottle, turning the sign on the counter to a photo of a kitten with a lightning bolt over its head that reads BACK IN A FLASH!

At the door of the men's room, Hattie hesitates, then bangs on it once. Twice. Three times.

Silence.

PRESLEY

Presley's heart jolts in his chest. He drops the pen, and it falls into the abyss, the black tarry depths swallowing it whole.

"Mac?" he says quietly.

But Mac doesn't *knock*.

HATTIE

Hattie opens the door a crack. "Zip your pants," she yells into the opening, "I'm coming in to refill the soap."

She pushes the door open and is hit by a wave of ice-cold air. She pours soap from the gallon-size bottle into the pencil-size opening on the dispenser. More soap drips down the sides of the container than goes in. Bending down to wipe up the puddle, she notices something:

A Sharpie lying on the tiles.

Then, under a stall door, skates.

Skates with feet in them.

"Okay," she says. "Presley? Is that you?"

PRESLEY

Presley tries to think of the right thing to say, the perfect thing, the funniest thing, the only thing. He thinks about it too long. Nothing comes out of his mouth.

HATTIE

"So you're . . . vandalizing the men's room?"

"Um, yeah, no. I mean, yes, it's mine. The pen. I'm in here." A pause. "Are you going to turn me in?" Another pause. "If you think about it, *vandalism* is just another word for public art and everyone loves art, or would love art if they weren't constantly told it was a crime."

"Hmmmm, let me think about that." Hattie lets the silence stretch, trying not to laugh. "What's in it for me?"

"Um, let me think . . . I could draw you your own personalized . . . whale?"

"My own *whale*? Amazing. That's good enough for me. You're safe." She kicks the pen under the door.

"Thanks. Sorry. I'll give it to you tomorrow or . . . later."

"It's okay. Take your time. Make it good. Anyway, I'm glad it's you and not some creepy weirdo. I don't get paid enough to deal with creepy weirdos." She actually earns $16 per hour, which is kind of a lot considering how little she does, way more than this job warrants. She spends her paychecks on renovating Applejack and buying clothes from her favorite store in town, a place called Twig & Arrow that smells like rosemary and mint and sells pretty, pastel, overpriced things, things she feels her mom would have loved: wrap tops and bamboo tees and sundresses that look vintage but aren't. Clothes that make her feel as soft and inoffensive and Instagrammable as a bakery cupcake. They make her pretty. They hide the ugly unlovable truth. Her own mother doesn't love her. Why would anyone else? Suddenly, she wants to smash something: the mirror or her own bones.

"Honestly, being a creepy weirdo sounds like a lot more work than I'm prepared to commit to."

She can hear the smile in his voice. The half-smile. The crooked smile. "That's suspiciously similar to what a creepy weirdo would say while vandalizing a public washroom."

"Um . . ."

"And then when he's caught, he wouldn't know what to say, so he'd say, 'Um . . .'"

"Okay, well, confession: Drawing helps me stay calm because . . . I'm nervous. Not about you. Well, also about you. No! Delete that. Pretend I didn't say that. God. What. No. I'm nervous about teaching. I haven't taught since . . . For a long time. I haven't *skated* for a long time. I'm . . . It's a long story."

"I like stories." She smiles. He's so . . . *cute*. He just is. He's cute and she likes him. She likes liking him. What's happening to her? And he *draws*. Like Topher. Which he's not, obviously. But still. "Maybe you'll tell me yours later? Soon? Someday?"

"Yeah. No. I mean, yeah."

"Okay."

"Okay."

"Well, good luck. Don't let them eat you alive."

There's a silence, then a growl. "I'm a bear," he says. "They wouldn't mess with a bear."

"Godspeed, Presley Jablowski."

She makes herself leave, tripping on the sill. (*Godspeed?* Who says *Godspeed?*) Her face is burning. Her entire body is burning. *Godspeed* is going to result in her spontaneously combusting and melting the floor under her feet, but maybe that's preferable to continuing to exist as a person who says *Godspeed.* (*Godspeed* tastes like ripe blackberries, the kind that used to grow on the out-of-control bush in the backyard before her mom paid someone who owned goats to bring them over. They stayed a week and ate the whole thing.)

She presses her hands against her flaming cheeks.

Yesterday, she didn't even know this kid existed.

Don't make him important, she tells herself, but she's already picturing telling him that his name tastes faintly of orange, like orange-blossom honey and graham crackers, her favorite toddler snack.

PRESLEY

Presley cringes.

A bear?

He *growled*?

She must think he's . . .

His phone pings.

HENRY:

I can only assume if you're sending us
pictures of yourself in wet pants that you're
begging for forgiveness after eighteen
months of ghosting.

Impressive balls you have there. Not to
mention, that is one shameful pic, old friend.
You have no idea if right now I'm submitting
it to r/reddit-embarrassing-wet-pants even as
we speak. Complete with your deets. Prepare
for hordes of redditors, racing to dox you.

Think of it as revenge.

Presley grins. Henry still texts in punctuated paragraphs.
He hasn't changed.

And he's not wrong: Presley is a prick. Who leaves their
best friends on read for a year and a half?

BIG TEE:
Fun fact: The tuberous bush cricket has the largest balls-to-body ratio in the animal kingdom. You got the balls of a TBC, man.

> **PRESLEY:**
> Chirp chirp.

> **PRESLEY:**
> Am braced for internet infamy.
> Bring it on.

BIG TEE:
Says the internet infamous guy . . .

> **PRESLEY:**
> . . . Don't know what you're talking about?

HENRY:
Executive decision: Conditional Forgiveness Granted. You ghost again, you're dead to us.

BIG TEE:
Can't forgive you for wearing that hideous flannel shirt tho—is it a thinly disguised cry for help?

Presley takes out his pen, writes the word *Help!* in a speech bubble above the comic-book style whale—a stick whale?—and takes a photo of his graffiti and hits send.

Then he texts a single word: *Sorry*.

HATTIE

"Hello, young lady." Mr. Stanopolous, who renews his fitness membership once a month, like clockwork, leans on the counter in front of Hattie. "And how are you this fine day?"

"I'm . . ." Hattie doesn't know what she feels, so obviously she can't finish that sentence. She feels too much. Yesterday, she could have just said "Fine." But today is not yesterday. She's something different than fine. She's a kaleidoscope of feelings. "Well, I'm not actively ablaze so I'm doing better than most of the valley corridor, I guess. How are *you* doing?"

"I'm exquisite, my dear."

"Exquisite!" *Exquisite* is a frozen grape, cold and sweet on her tongue. (They always used to keep their grapes in the freezer. Her mom doled them out like candies, rewards for chores and good manners, for keeping secrets and tidying her toys.) "Great word, Mr. S."

"Did I ever tell you that the name Hattie makes me think of vegetables?"

Hattie thinks about this, wondering if it might be an insult. "No?"

Mr. Stanopolous carefully places a head of lettuce on the counter. "This made me think of you. Ninety-nine percent water, you know. And everyone knows you're a water baby!"

"Wow. Well, I'm not exactly a baby, but I'll take that in the spirit you intended. So thanks, Mr. S." Hattie enters his information into the computer and reaches for his credit card. She does not tell him that she no longer goes in the pool or even *near* the pool. He'd be disappointed. She would feel ashamed.

When he's gone, exiting to the parking lot, not even pretending to go to the workout area, she writes *exquisite* down in her red notebook. She's writing about frozen grapes, the specific crunch of them and how she lost her first tooth in one, tainting the flavor with the metallic tang of blood, when the bell that accompanies the doors' opening dings and the swim team comes through in a cacophony of familiar voices, workout bags slung over their shoulders: Trayvon, Gretchen, Cece, Lewis, Grayson, Hannah, and Torben.

"Oh *shit*." Instinctively, Hattie ducks, but she's a full second too late. A second is forever in the pool and also, as it turns out, when you're trying to avoid people.

"Hattie!" calls Gretchen. "Hey!"

"Shitshitshit." Hattie crouches lower, pulling as much of herself as she can into the opening under the counter. She feels stupid, but she can't come out now. There's no way to explain why she's doing what she's doing. She squeezes her eyes shut.

"What's *up*, girl?" Trayvon's question is followed by a drumroll on the counter, directly above her head.

"Leave her." A whisper. Hannah. "She obviously wants to be left alone. She's *literally* hiding."

"Yeah, let's go work out." Torben. "Read the room, man."

Hattie holds her breath, like that will make her smaller, even less visible. A nail pokes her back. Her neck spasms. "The pool is closed," she says, but her voice doesn't really break through the air, which has turned to ice around her.

"She doesn't want to see us *still*?" says Gretchen. "It's been months. I totally don't get it." She raises her voice. "I don't get it, Hattie! I miss you. We're going to scratch the four by one hundred because of you. Don't you feel, like, any responsibility for that?"

"Jeez, Gretch. Too far." That's Hannah again.

"I can see your feet, Hat," Trayvon singsongs. "Looooooove you, girl."

"Let's *go*," says Lewis. "I don't know what's going on here, but it's a whole weird vibe."

Hattie is a heartbeat, a thumping and nothing more, wrapped in a coating of dust and cobwebs.

After she hears the door to the gym open and shut again, their voices receding, she crawls out, the ugly carpet burning her knees. She sits back in Bethanne's chair, her hands shaking slightly, and stares at the empty ice.

Then she digs around in the lost and found and finds a white towel, gets up, and tapes it to the glass. He probably won't know what it means, but . . . he also might. Anyway, *she* knows what it means, and she wants to tell him, or maybe just try the idea on for size.

The first time Jada realized what she felt for Topher might be something, *he was running around the track. Topher was always running around the track, but he somehow did it in a way that transcended the way other people did it. How was that possible? He ran without headphones on, in his own world, like he was a part of it and he was sure of his part in it and he was fulfilling his role. She could see the track from her bedroom window. She wasn't given to watching Topher Gillies working out—that was for pretty much every other girl in school to do—but today she needed to talk to him about the cage-diving options she'd found. She didn't mean to feel something.*

Don't be an idiot, she told herself.

Anyway, she needed to talk to him. Map out a route. Plan the project.

If his parents had signed the permission slip, that is.

She waved at him through the glass, but he either couldn't or didn't see her. Which was fair, so she climbed out her window and onto the roof. When he made the turn again, she waved again. But he still didn't seem to see her, so she went back in and got her pillow and on the next turn, she stood up and waved it in the air like a white flag. This time, he saw her, and ran over and hopped her back fence as though it was barely a slight inconvenience. Then he stood below her, sweat pouring from what seemed like his entire body, and he said, "Oh hey" and there was totally something *about the way he looked up at her, squinting, and the way he caught the pillow when she threw it at him . . .*

She just knew.

It was his face, maybe, his amused expression or the slant of the sun shining on his eyes, but it was definitely something.

Shit, she thought. I can't and won't like Topher Gillies like every other boy-liking person at this school.

Hattie sits back in Bethanne's chair and stares at Lou, the jade plant Bethanne has labeled with a Hello, My Name Is LOU!

sticker. He has five leaves left and two of them are brown and shriveled. "What if this is *something*, Lou?"

She takes out her marker and a Hello, My Name Is sticker from Bethanne's stash and writes *Hypocrite*. She isn't sure this is *love*, but suddenly everything she's ever thought about love and bullshit seems embarrassingly and naively wrong, and she knows for sure that she's in trouble.

She sticks the sticker to her shirt.

PRESLEY

Presley puts his hand on the door handle, expecting to open the door. But he doesn't.

Boo, says Mac, appearing in the mirror.

"Wow, that is *such* a cliché."

Hey, what's a mesoglea? I've been meaning to ask.

"What? Who said anything about a mesoglea?"

He does not tell Mac that the mesoglea is the jelly part of the jellyfish, the clear goo forming its body that resembles the shimmer around him when Mac is nearby. Their dad taught them about jellyfish, back in the days when he explained everything, at least everything to do with marine biology, often in so much detail that both boys glazed over.

It's Presley's favorite word because it's a word that sounds exactly like what it is: globby, spineless, transparent.

You know what my favorite word is? Mac does a spin, then finger guns.

"Dork?"

Wrong. I don't have one. Because I'm not *the dork in this equation.*

"That's what you think."

A dork is a whale's penis, son. The mightiest monster of the sea. He says the last bit in their dad's voice, heavy on the Scottish accent. *Oh man. We should have known he'd turn out to be a shitbag. "The mightiest monster of the sea." What a tool.*

Presley presses his hands to his eyes. "Accurate, but yeah, I also really . . . have to go. Your timing is terrible. It's my first day of work. Please don't fuck this up for me."

Okay, okay. I just miss you, bromigo. Mac grins, revealing the front tooth that Presley broke on the day that he died. Presley flinches.

The fight is why Mac is dead.

It was the broken teeth—Presley can still taste the blood in his mouth, can still viscerally recall the way his tongue kept poking the shards—that had led to the camp counselor insisting their dad pick them up from the end-of-year school campout at Camp Thunderbird, a full three days before it was over.

Neither of them mentioned that, technically, their dad wasn't allowed.

Why *hadn't* they?

Maybe it was just their own impulse to put as much distance between themselves and that stupid fight as possible.

So their dad showed up, threw their bags into the car, hugged them roughly (too roughly) while shouting enthusiastic apologies to the camp staff, and then drove the car, completely shit-faced, off the long, winding road that led away from the camp and into a barn full of dairy cows, killing Mac and two cows (one instantly, one not).

Their dad was uninjured.

"The drunks never get hurt," Presley heard one of the firefighters saying at the scene as he was being strapped to a stretcher. "They're as floppy as newborns."

It was another phrase that was now permanently etched into Presley's gray matter and replayed on a loop.

"Yeah, me too," he says, finally. "Who would've thought it?" He grins at his dead brother, mostly to stop himself from crying.

Whoa, those are dazzling.

Presley's teeth, also broken during the fight, had been crowned, but Mac had been cremated, which was probably better than being left to decompose (but only marginally), and now his teeth—broken and otherwise—are among the ashes being stored in an urn in the tiny house's too-small bathroom cupboard.

"Thanks, I chose them myself. Now seriously, I'm going. Having a job is one of the downsides of being the one who lost the coin flip for the front seat."

You don't need a job. You could be a movie star. Or the star of a toothpaste commercial.

"I'm the better-looking twin, remember? That'll pay off eventually."

Yeah, okay, Ice Princess. Played any hockey lately?

"When did you get funny?"

Ba dum cha. Mac mimes drumsticks in the air. *But seriously, you should have taken it up in my memory.*

"If I wanted to remember you, I'd have bought a commemorative bench." Presley crosses his arms. "Hockey's for dickheads."

Mac laughs and a hollow feeling forms in Presley's chest, the ache of the emptiness that he knows is coming.

Ha! Perfect for you then. Mac's voice is fading.

"You're getting us mixed up. Death must have rattled your brain. *I'm* not the dickhead." Presley presses his hand against the mirror. The glass is damp and cold.

And I'm not the one with the rattled brain. Mac shakes his head, mock sadly, his voice now barely registering. He presses his palm up to his brother's. *Grow green and prosper, Parsley.*

"Get flipped, Big Mac." Presley's own face, now staring back at him from the mirror, is pale, the shimmer still present but barely, like a layer of highlighter on his cheeks and nose.

He takes a breath in slowly and releases it. Then, skate guards tapping on the tile floor, nauseated and a little dizzy, he makes himself get out there.

HATTIE

Hattie watches Coach Kat skating in long slow strokes around the rink while the kids crowd around the gate, waiting for it to open.

Hattie took this exact class when she was five. Her mom stood with the other moms, wrapped in the bright yellow parka that had been her dad's. It was so big and she was so small that it made her look like Big Bird, a tiny blond head on a huge yellow body.

Hattie has the strangest feeling that if she leans on the glass, the theoretical barriers between all possible quantum realities will collapse and she'll fall through time and land on that ice in her five-year-old body, a kid like all the other kids, watched over by a mother like all the other mothers.

But her mother wasn't like them. Her mother was barely out of her teens. Her mother snuck out to drink and listen to music in the van while Hattie skated. Her mother showed up late, laughing too hard and stumbling. Her mother never made friends with the other mothers.

"They're so old," she'd say. "So *boring*, not like us."

Hattie presses her hand on the glass experimentally, as the kids step onto the ice. It's solid. Then she picks up her phone, opens her email and clicks on Fwd: Fwd: Save the Date.

Getting married Saturday!
Weather to be fantastic.

Deets attached.
The cake is coconut, my fav as you know.
His name is Ingo Svensson. (Husband-to-be, not the cake!)
x.

Hattie's mom never signs her emails, as though maybe she can't decide between Mom and Delilah so she chooses x. There's no suggestion that the invitation is *for* Hattie. It's obviously included for informational purposes, to save her the keystrokes needed to type out the material again.

Hattie *knew* it would be this. It's the only thing that Save the Date can mean. But still . . .

She swallows. Tears sting her eyes.

Fuck you, she types in the reply field. She doesn't hit send.

"I'd totally write her letters," Calliope said recently. "Why did you never do that? You love writing. You could have penned long, gorgeous letters that told her everything she was missing and then compiled them, like one of those YA books you love so much. And at the end, when you finally sent it, she'd realize how much she missed of your life and have a massive breakthrough and you'd cry and hug and move to Paris together and start fresh, maybe at your own ad agency or something and later it would be a movie starring . . . Hmm . . . maybe Elle Fanning? As you."

Hattie flinched. "No fucking way." But then she saw Calliope's face. "I mean, I get what you mean. I'll think about it," she'd added, weakly, not meaning it, hating Calliope a little for thinking it could be like that, that her loss was *plot*, that real-life stories could be led like fiction toward symphonic moments of satisfying emotional closure.

If only.

This stupid, terrible email contains more information than Hattie has ever had. *Coconut cake. Ingo Svensson. The weather.*

There's a tearing sensation in her chest, as though all her heart's molecules are forcing their way apart, like water molecules freezing, tiny arms outstretched to push all the others away. She wonders if this is it, an aortic aneurysm or something worse: what it feels like when the truth really *lands*. Her mother is not who she wants her to be. She never was and never will be. Not in this world. Not in any parallel world. She has a mental illness. But . . . a lot of people have mental illnesses and still love people and connect to people and parent people and never let go. Never letting go is what moms are supposed to do. Hattie remembers reading about a whale, an orca, somewhere in Canada, that carried her dead baby around for seventeen days on her back, refusing to let go.

Hattie's mom let her go so *easily*. Like Hattie was nothing. Like Hattie didn't exist.

Hattie puts her hand on the defibrillator, reassuring herself that it's there.

"*Coconut* cake? Seriously?" she says out loud.

It's not like she could have gone to Switzerland anyway, especially not on short notice. She has school. She has a job. She hasn't seen her mom in eleven years. She doesn't even *know* her. Her mom is a couple of emails popping up twice a year: *Happy birthday! Merry Christmas! Hope you're having fun!* Her mom is an abstraction of memory and imagination. Her mom is slipping away from the bleachers in her yellow coat. Her mom is the taste of raw peas grown against the fence. Her mom is in Applejack, lying on the mattress and looking up at the sky through the open moonroof, curls of marijuana smoke unfurling from her nose, a mug of something clanking with ice cubes balanced on her chest. Her mom is putting baby Hattie on the front of her surfboard and kicking out to sea, even while someone on shore shouts, "That isn't safe, lady!" Her mom is holding baby Hattie underwater, waiting for her to swim. Her mom is old records, played too loud. Her mom is passed out on the living room floor while music thunders against the walls and their neighbor calls the police. Her mom is hanging out with the skateboarders in the park, "making new friends," even though they're in high school and she's a *mom*. Her mom is late to pick her up again. Her mom is making angels in the sand in her bikini. Her mom is sneaking her into the neighbor's pool because she knows they're away, or at least she thinks she knows almost for sure. Her mom is apologizing to the neighbors while laughing too loudly. Her mom is on her dad's shoulders, trying to see the band at Phantom Fest while Hattie holds on to his knee, terrified of becoming lost in the shifting forest of strangers' legs. Her mom drives Applejack into a bus stop, denting the front fender into a crease that's still there. Her mom weaves ribbons into Hattie's french braids and tells her she's a little doll. Her mom takes her to the zoo in San Diego and unfurls a banner that reads WILD ANIMALS BELONG IN THE WILD. Her mom forgets her at the mall, where she sits and waits at Orange Julius for three hours before her dad shows up and tells her that her mom has "gone away for a while."

A while which turned into forever which turned into *this*.

This is the ending. This is the closure.

"*Fuck*. Fuck you, fuck me, fuck fuck *fuck* everything."

Hattie's voice echoes in the empty space. All the happiness

and possibility she felt earlier feels like it's turned to charcoal, burned to ash. She rips off the name tag. She isn't a hypocrite. She was right all along. Love is *bullshit*. What does it even mean when you love someone, when you bond to someone, who can walk away?

She had *not* known that coconut was her mom's favorite kind of cake. She can't remember ever having eaten coconut cake. She's always thought coconut looked like dandruff.

She stares at the ice. Only minutes have passed yet she's a different person. She's exhausted from changing so rapidly, from having to keep changing, keep rewriting her own story in her head. An hour ago, she was a person who thought she loved her mom, thought there was room in her heart to forgive. Eventually. Who assumed her mom would want forgiving.

Five minutes ago, she learned she was wrong about her mom.

Now she's numb.

The kids gather around Coach Kat, who waves up at Hattie, gives her a thumbs-up.

"What kind of name is Ingo Svensson?" Hattie says to Lou, pressing the button on the music. Coach Kat waves her arms wildly, shaking her head. Hattie stops the music. The name Ingo Svensson leaves a strange aftertaste in her mouth. Not terrible but a little sour, like something that would be good if only it were ripe: a golden plum, maybe, picked too soon, like the ones they used to steal from the complaining neighbor's tree under a canopy of stars, her mom on a rickety ladder, holding her finger to her lips to hush Hattie, giggling in the moonlight.

PRESLEY

Presley half-runs, half-walks across the expanse of benches toward the rink, throwing off his guards and jumping onto the ice without time to consider what he's about to do. He skids to a stop by the kids and Coach Kat, his skates making a flurry of snow.

"You're late." Coach Kat's expression is unreadable, her gaze unwavering.

He swallows. "I'm sorry." Apologies work better than explanations, he knows. Especially when the explanation involves Mac.

The kids stare at him, anxious and watchful.

"Hey, super-kiddos!" They wobble toward him, bumping into his knees, a flock of unsteady penguins, too bundled up to fully extend their arms. "I'm Presley."

"That's a girl's name," says a penguin.

"Is not," he says.

"Is too," she says. "*My* name is, um . . ." She stops as though she's forgotten. He waits. "Presley," she finishes, triumphantly. "I'm a girl."

"I see your point," he says. "Maybe it's *both*."

She considers this. "No. It's a girl's name."

"Are you famous?" Another voice, solemn, from somewhere behind him. "Coach Kat said you were."

"Yes," he says, with equal solemnity. Coach Kat is now sitting in the stands, writing something on a clipboard. He's on his own. That's fine. This is fine. It's going fine. "Pretty famous. I have a Wikipedia page." He fervently hopes none of them look it up, makes a mental note to ask Henry, now that they're (conditionally) friends again, to edit the TikTok reference out of his entry.

The kid wipes his nose on his crusty-looking mitten. "I have a dog."

"What's Wiggy-pedia?" says another.

"It's nothing. You know what?" says Presley. "I'll show you something. Check this out."

He skates away from them, fast, pumping his legs hard, muscle memory taking over, his skates knowing where to go without him thinking about it, the ice under his blades like a homecoming, his body remembering every angle, every twist. He turns so he's skating backward, looks over his shoulder, then heaves himself up and away from the surface of the ice, already coiled and then twisting, spinning once, twice, a perfect double axel, his blade connecting cleanly when he lands. His body feels heavy and different, but he can still fly, like a concrete bird . . . but still a bird. Then, buoyed by the adrenalin from landing the axel without even warming up, he does a back flip, the ice thwacking solidly against his skates.

"I can teach you to do that," he tells the kids, breathlessly, "but you can't fly until you can glide." He tries to ignore the twinge in his calves, the way his quads are starting to tremble, the strange hollow ringing in his head that hopefully does not preface a seizure. *Breathe.* He shakes out his legs. "So today what we're going to do is learn how to get up, okay? A big part of skating is understanding that you'll fall and that's okay because you'll also know how to get up." One of them falls, as if on cue. Presley picks him up and rights him. "What do you say to a little Chicken Dance?"

The kids look at one another, frowning.

"You'll love it," he promises. "Everyone loves the Chicken Dance." He raises his hands like someone bringing a plane in for landing. The gesture is meant to get Hattie's attention, so she can press play on the soundtrack.

But Hattie isn't looking. There's a white towel taped to the glass.

He nearly passes out, from the sudden exertion, from Hattie, from the white towel . . .

The white towel. Like the one in *The Shark Club*.

Like when Jada wanted to tell Topher that she liked him.

She knows, he thinks, and it makes him feel sick.

But it also means: She *likes* him.

His heart skids and races and slows. He wants to fast forward to the part where they're kissing, which took forever in the book.

But . . . how much does she know?

Nothing?

Everything?

Did *she* look him up on Wiggy-pedia?

He sticks his fingers in his mouth and whistles the way his dad taught him to if he were ever lost in the woods. The sound carves through the air. There's a click and a buzz, then a crash and some feedback, then Hattie's voice over the speaker. "Sorry, Presley!"

He loves the way his name sounds in her mouth. He bends down and adjusts his laces, tries to hide his too-wide smile. *Keep it together, Parsley.*

Coach Kat skates over to him from where she's been leaning on the boards. "Your axel was nice, but the landing was a little . . ." Coach Kat spreads the fingers on her hands and holds them up. "Open. Never jump without warming up. You will be hurt. You know this. Very stupid. Showing off."

Presley nods, wanting to tell her that he can do better, that he can land a *triple* axel, easily, or used to be able to, that he's better than that, or was. He wants to mention all his quads, his formerly promising future! But she must already know. She told the kids he was famous.

He wonders if she knows about the head injury. The seizures. His leg. The reasons why he's stopped.

Instead, he asks, "Does, um, Hattie skate?"

Coach Kat looks at him speculatively and shakes her head. "She was a swimmer."

"A swimmer?"

"*Was* a swimmer. She quit." Coach Kat shrugs, as though that settles the matter.

A kid tugs on his sleeve. "Are we supposed to be . . . ?" she lisps, flapping her arms like a chicken.

"Yes," says Presley. "Right."

Presley flaps his wings, hands tucked into his arm pits so he doesn't accidentally clock one of the kids. They immediately copy him. He looks up. Hattie is watching him making a fool of himself. He flaps even bigger, like an ostrich trying to take flight. She's laughing. Then she tucks her hands under her arms and raises her own elbows up and down. Smiling at him.

He smiles back. He can't help it, couldn't stop it from happening, even if he tried.

HATTIE

Bug opens the small latched gate with a bang.

Hattie jumps.

"Holy aitch, that is *some* hat." Bug hugs Hattie too hard, like it hasn't only been a few hours since they'd said good-bye at Starbucks. She smells like caramel and coffee.

"I'm not wearing a hat, that's my *hair.*" Hattie pulls away, putting her hand on her head.

"I was talking about *that* hat." Bug points at the ice where Hattie can see Presley with the dress-up trunk, wearing a gigantic sequinned cowboy hat.

She smiles. Her mom is getting married, but Presley . . . is *something.* Maybe these two things are a trade-off. *Don't make him important.* But it feels too late.

The numbness is giving way to something sharp, the emotional equivalent of pins and needles. She wants to tell Bug, but she also *can't* tell her. Bug would—accurately—point out that feeling *something* is in direct opposition to her whole brand.

"Whoa. What's going on? Why are you making that face?"

"I'm *smiling.*"

"Well, it's weird. Stop doing that. You're making me feel uncomfortable."

"My happiness is off-putting?"

"Yes. Don't get me wrong, it's a good development. I'm just not used to it, so I find it sus. Are you trying to signal that you're being held hostage? Should I be doing something, like calling nine-one-one or pulling the fire alarm?"

"What? No! God, don't do that. Coach Kat would murder me."

"Well, okay. I guess you can keep doing it. Maybe not quite so . . . big. It's a lot of teeth. Like, of all the smiling emojis, that one is the last." She demonstrates. "Normal smile, big smile, bigger smile, fully committed smile. See?"

"Thank you for the critique, I'll take it under consideration." She taps the glass. Clears her throat. "That's the New Kid. From English? *Mallrats*? Appalachian Trail?"

Bug doesn't answer. She's fixing her eyelashes, which have come unglued, using her phone camera as a mirror, then she hoists herself up on top of the filing cabinets. She kicks the window gently with one of her Doc Martens, these ones hand-painted with flowers. One of them has hot pink laces.

"His name is Presley. Presley Jablowski." She plows ahead, wanting to talk about him. Needing to say his name. "And that isn't his *own* hat. It's from the dress-up trunk."

Then suddenly Calliope is there, vaulting over the orange counter, nearly toppling all the filing and Lou in one fell swoop.

"There's a *gate*," says Hattie. "Jeez."

"The New Kid," says Bug. She points at the ice. "He's here. His name is Priscilla. He's fond of unflattering hats. Hattie is all aflutter."

"Aflutter! Why is he *here*?" Calliope sits down in one fluid motion, cross-legged on the floor.

"I am not *aflutter*. And he's teaching skating lessons to children, Calliope. Obviously," says Hattie, feeling annoyed with them both. "And his name's *Presley*. What's wrong with you two?"

"Presley? Huh. I thought that was a girl's name." Calliope pops a piece of gum in her mouth and starts chewing. It smells like a word Hattie hasn't heard yet, a future word, something fruity, but also faintly like caterpillars.

"That's very gender binary of you," says Bug. "In the future, people will look back on the gendering of names and pity us. Anyway, why is there a white towel taped to the glass?"

"Isn't that from *The Shark Club*? I think that's the part where I quit reading it, it's when Jada's watching Topher and—"

"Bethanne must have done it," Hattie interrupts. She peels it off and tosses it in the lost and found, blushing furiously. "You know how Bethanne is. She's an unsolvable mystery, like how they built the pyramids or why boats sink in the Bermuda Triangle."

"Girl, you're as red as my car."

"Didn't they solve the Bermuda Triangle? Something about tides." Bug picks up Bethanne's binoculars and zooms in on Presley. "Those lips! He looks like Charlie Plummer. Except brunette. And moody. He's a dark and stormy Charlie Plummer. I can see why you like him. Isn't Charlie Plummer in all those movies you like? Some kind of hetero ideal teen?"

"What's wrong with his lips?" Hattie's blush spreads from her cheeks to her hairline. She can feel sweat forming. "Charlie Plummer is cute. Presley is . . . also cute." She feels faint, saying it out loud. She's losing her shit.

"Uh-huh," says Calliope. "I can practically see your hormones stampeding through you." She pauses. "He's a *little* cute. I concede."

"What?!" Bug says. "No. No, no, no. He is *not* cute. *Cute* is baby otters holding hands. *Cute* is puppies in tuxedos or really small versions of full-size things, like . . . tiny toilets." Bug has an impressive collection of tiny things: a tiny Mix-master, a set of tiny vases, a tiny doghouse complete with a tiny dog and a tiny TV, and, of course, a tiny toilet. "That boy has plush lips. Not that there's anything wrong with plush lips. But they look like someone else's lips photoshopped onto his face. His whole face looks like one of those creepy AI compilations of theoretical people who don't exist. That nose is a baby's nose. The more I look at him, the weirder he looks."

"I like plush lips," Calliope says, leaning back against the glass. "But I also agree that tiny toilets *are* freakin' adorable."

"Cuter than that boy," says Bug.

"Actually I'm coming around on the New Kid. There's something interesting about him. Those lips are sexy. I wouldn't kick him out of bed for eating crackers."

"Why do you talk like someone from *The Golden Girls*?"

"Because I love *The Golden Girls*. It's the greatest sitcom of all time. And one day we'll be three elderly women living in a Florida condo, eating cheesecake and delivering pithy one-liners, and it would be a shame if I was the only one who was truly prepared."

"I promise you, I'm not going to grow up to be an old white lady."

"And I *will*?" Calliope takes a photo of herself and passes her phone to Bug. "I don't see it. Do you?"

"Exactly my point," Bug scoffs. "The only one of us who'll be an old white lady is Hattie. Do you watch it, Hat?"

"No. I'm under the age of sixty and it's illegal for anyone without a senior's discount to stream it."

"Yeah, well, your taste is deeply sus so I'm not sure why you're weighing in. Literally the only thing you like is *The Shark Club*. And My Little Pony. Which is for actual children."

"A lot of adults like My Little Pony, but I don't *like* it, I'm just . . . It's nostalgic. Like comfort food."

"Uh-huh. Whatever you say, Sweet Scoops."

"You wouldn't even know that Sweet Scoops existed if you weren't also secretly a superfan."

Another group of learn-to-skate kids wobble on to the ice and the whole thing begins again. Presley waves at Hattie and she presses play on "The Chicken Dance." Already it feels like they have a shorthand way of communicating, a secret language. A *something*.

Still looking at her, Presley takes his hat off, tosses it in the air, and catches it on his head. He smiles. The smile does something to Hattie's insides. Her vision goes funny.

She drops down to her hands and knees.

"What are you *doing*?" Calliope peers down at her.

"I dropped my contact."

"You don't wear contacts." Bug's laugh is a creaky gate, the sound coming from a long way away, crossing deserts and oceans, ricocheting off the burning hills, rolling down the I-5 to get to Hattie.

Hattie lies on her back, closes her eyes. The carpet smells like chemicals. Colors slide behind her eyelids, like some kind of wildly spinning kaleidoscope.

Calliope nudges Hattie with her foot. "Are you being weird?" On the bottom of her shoe, she's written, *If you can see this, you're too close.*

Bug looks down at her and shakes her head. She grabs Hattie's hand and pulls her up. "OMG, you *do* like him," she says quietly. "Like really like him. Well, shocked emoji." She opens her eyes wide and makes her mouth into an O.

"No! I don't!"

"Hattie . . ." Bug is still holding on to Hattie's hand. "I love you. I was only kidding around. It's okay to like someone. It's okay be happy. You're, like, *allowed.*"

"I don't know *what* you're talking about," Hattie says. "Please stop being weird."

But she can't help it, she pictures herself and Presley together in the shark cage dropping down below the boat. In the distance, the shape of the shark, the angle of its body all wrong. She imagines how she'd feel when he swam out of the cage to cut it free of the net.

Bereft, she thinks. Even without saying it, her mouth fills with the taste of whole wheat toast, salty with thick-spread butter, washing it down with sparkling lemonade, an afternoon snack she and her mom ate at Applejack's little table as soon as Hattie's school day was over, illegally parked in the teacher's parking lot behind the school.

"I don't even know him," she adds. "I don't know anything about him."

"*Yet*," says Bug. "But you will."

WAYS TO SAY YES

HATTIE

"Okay, eyes on me, please. Can I just remind you to call me Ana? I feel so old when you call me Ms. Singh!" She smiles at them.

"See?" whispers Bug.

Hattie nods, even though she doesn't. She tries to think of Ms. Singh as someone Bug could have a crush on. She tries to see what Bug sees. Ms. Singh's eyes are beautiful, dark brown and framed by thick lashes. She does look very young for a teacher but she's definitely at least in her twenties. Her cheekbones are high and symmetrical. But she's wearing a T-shirt with Winnie the Pooh on it and there's literally no context in which Winnie the Pooh clothing can be considered hot. Her pale pink hair looks like a faded plastic kitchen scrubber. It makes her skin look worryingly gray.

Hattie looks at the teacher's lips, to see if they're turning blue, the first sign of cyanosis. The last time she did CPR was on Elijah and that didn't end well. Maybe if Ms. Singh keels over, she'll let someone else do chest compressions, let someone else be responsible for whether Ms. Singh lives or dies. Someone else in this room *must* know first aid. She looks around for the other swimmers, and there's Trayvon. Gretchen. Hannah. They've probably got it covered. She drops her gaze before any of them make eye contact and decide to want something from her, an answer or a sign.

She slides down in her seat and tries to focus on a spot past the non-ghost of Elijah, who instantly shimmered not quite into focus like a migraine aura. She blinks. Blinks again. Pinches the skin on her thigh so hard that it'll definitely leave a bruise. Her eyes water. Then her gaze lands on Presley, sitting in the corner, his back against the far wall. He always seems to be hiding in shadows. He looks up just then and they smile at each other.

They've been smiling at each other for days.

Hattie doesn't know what's supposed to happen next. She wants *something* to happen, but she's also terrified of something more happening. She feels like a guitar with the strings pulled too tight, wrong and out of tune. Her mouth twists. *Guitar.* She takes out a piece of gum and chews away the wet green thought of that word.

"Stop making googly eyes at the tiny toilet," Bug whispers in her ear, amused.

"I'm not." Hattie blushes. "Please shut up and return to your regularly scheduled activity of staring creepily at the teacher."

"Laughing-crying emoji," says Bug, tracing a path of tears down her cheeks with her fingertips.

"Soon you'll speak only in emojis. No one will understand you, but you'll lead the nerd kingdom by confusing example."

"I am the nerd queen," Bug says, miming putting a crown on her head. "All hail my crown emoji."

"Stop," says Hattie. "It's too much. The cringe."

"I feel like I'm losing you guys!" Ms. Singh claps to get their attention. "Eyes on me, please!" She widens her own eyes, as though to demonstrate and it works, because of mirroring. People do it without realizing they're doing it, especially if they're with people they like or people they want to impress.

Hattie respects the teacher's use of psychological trickery but wonders if she likes them or is only hungry for approval. She is an actress, after all. Still: One point for Ms. Singh. "Today we're going to do something fun. We're auditioning, but we're not *auditioning*. We're going to turn this thing on its head." She pauses. "I'm going to ask you to write a short paper."

"Paper?" whispers Bug. "What the *aitch*? She's losing her allure."

"Sad for you," says Hattie. "I love writing papers."

"I want you to write down what kind of vegetable you see yourselves as. Then explain your pick. This will give me a sense of who you *are* and how I'll pair you up for your scenes."

"Um, what," says Hattie. "A *vegetable*?"

"Still love writing papers?" Bug whispers.

"Wait, we're being paired up?" Calliope says. "Like all of us are Juliet?"

"Or Romeo," says Bug.

"I'm one hundred percent a dragon fruit," says Calliope, loudly. "Mystical. Different. Delicious."

"That's a fruit," says Hattie. "It literally has *fruit* in its name." She sneaks a glance at Presley. He's already writing.

"Someone is an eggplant . . ." Bug nudges her, pointing at Presley.

"Stop!"

"What's a unique vegetable? I'm thinking . . . durian," says Bug. "I could be a durian. That's the weirdly delicious one, right?"

"It's the one that stinks," says Calliope.

"Am I the only one who knows the difference between a fruit and a vegetable?" says Hattie.

"Girls," says Ms. Singh. "No more talking. Eyes on your own paper, please."

Hattie thinks of Mr. Stanopolous and his lettuce: Maybe he's right. Maybe she *would* be something common, plentiful, easy to grow.

"I know it sounds silly," Ms. Singh says, gently, pausing in front of Hattie's desk. "But just try."

Hattie writes *lettuce*.

She writes about how lettuce is water. Mostly.

She writes about how people are water. Mostly.

She writes about how water, when poured into any shape, becomes that shape.

She writes about how whatever it is that makes us ourselves is like water, poured into the shape our self makes, but that maybe when we die, it flows into something else somehow. She's thinking of Elijah when she writes it. She's thinking of how his Elijah-ness, whatever it was that made him fundamentally himself, flowed into the shimmering image she's always seeing, when it should have flowed further, to wherever souls go when people die. She feels close to understanding something, but she isn't sure what. She chews her pen lid for a minute, then keeps writing.

She writes about why she loves water. And then she circles it back to how lettuce is almost entirely, unbelievably, *water*.

It's only when she's done that she realizes it's the most embarrassing thing she's ever written. She's always writing things down she can't take back. This paper wasn't supposed to be about *swimming*. The teacher didn't ask about Elijah.

But it's too late to write anything else.

She hands in her paper just as the bell sounds.

"Thanks." Ms. Singh looks down at Hattie's paper and smiles when Hattie takes a second too long to let go of it. It's way too personal. Then, like she *knows*, Ms. Singh says reassuringly, "Acting is all about giving yourself away and being vulnerable. Great job."

"Okay." Hattie feels a rush of embarrassment and lets go but also wants to grab the paper back. She wants to yell, "Don't read it!" Or run away. Or set herself on fire. Or all three.

"In conclusion," says Calliope, holding the door open for Hattie, "I think by being a fruit instead of a vegetable, she'll see that I'm different from everyone else. Special. Later, when they interview my old teachers, they'll say, 'I always knew she was a star!'"

"Same," says Bug. "For different reasons. Obvi."

"You aren't both different if you're the same," says Hattie.

"We're different *from the majority*," says Calliope. "Still counts, girl. I bet everyone in this room with a penis put *eggplant*. Every. Single. One."

Hattie looks back over her shoulder for Presley, but he's talking to Javi, and Javi is laughing and she's pretty sure she does see his mouth form the word *eggplant* and they disappear around the corner without looking back. "Lunch?"

"I'm meeting Leo for rehearsal. Besides, I'm not exposing my beautiful pink lungs to that toxic waste outside again, even for you. I can't be coughing on Saturday."

"What's on Saturday?"

Calliope stops abruptly and Hattie bounces off the lockers to avoid hitting her.

"Are you serious? You've forgotten about Saturday?"

"I haven't! Saturday is . . . The best day. It's—"

"It's Phantom Fest, Jerky Pie. Me and Leo are headlining?"

"Oh my god. I totally didn't *forget*. I can't wait. I love Phantom Fest." Hattie does not love Phantom Fest because El Amado's whole *thing* with turning a deadly fire that killed hundreds of people into a party is completely terrible on every level and a pretty terrifying reminder that they're currently in the path of a raging inferno. But she loves Calliope and she'd be lying if she didn't also admit that she loves the fact that maybe, just maybe, Presley will be there.

"Woo-hoo, that smile!" says Calliope. "Is this about Plush Lips? Are you working today? Staring at him starrily while he transforms duck-like toddlers into graceful swans?"

"I work every day," says Hattie, skipping past the first question. "And they're not toddlers. And mostly I read. Mostly I don't stare at anything but my book."

"LOL," says Calliope. "I know. Like you ever stop reading that thing."

HATTIE

"Don't you dare say 'I love you,'" says Jada. "This isn't some kind of teen soap opera and I'm not open to it. I'm already embarrassed for both of us that it even crossed your mind." She lays back in the snow, her hair fanned out, and starts to make a snow angel.

Topher looks down at her. "It's our first date," he says. "It would be terrible if I said that. Even thinking about saying it makes me want to throw myself off this cliff. I didn't think it even. Thinking it and saying it would be so creepy and weird and terrible that you'd be within your rights to have me arrested."

"I didn't mean now, I meant . . . ever. If we keep . . . You know, doing this. Anyway, you said terrible twice." Jada sits up. "And suicide jokes are terrible. And I know it's too soon! I wanted you to know that it's always too soon. For me. And you had a look on your face. And that look made me think, One day, this guy is going to get all . . ." She waves her hands around. "You know."

Topher laughs. "You've been watching too many Hallmark Christmas movies. What actually happened was that some snow got in my eye and now . . ." He winks, then winks again. "Now you think I'm winking at you when actually I'm in terrible eye pain because contact lenses and snow are not a great combo."

"Huh," she says, lightly. "Well, my bad."

He sits down next to her abruptly and leans over so his lips are touching her freezing cold ear, his hot breath making her shiver in a whole new way, and he whispers something she can barely hear. Her brain transcribes each word separately. "You're. My. Reason."

She holds very still for a whole minute, flakes of snow drifting prettily down around them, not even breathing. There's nothing but the muffled sound of the wind blowing in the snow-laden trees and the soft, slow warmth of his breath and every single cell in her body is standing at attention and there's a buzzing somewhere behind her sternum and she wants to say, "What do you mean by that?" or even "I know what you mean." But instead she grabs a handful of snow and rubs it on his face, furiously, and says, "You nerd. Jeez. Who says that? You don't even know me yet. You just think I'm hot, which is different than, you know . . ."

"Wait," he says, "What do you think I said? I said, 'It's snow season.'" What did you hear?" His eyes scrunch up at the corners from the laugh he's holding in. She wants to kiss him so badly that she almost does it, almost tips forward into the few inches that separate them and . . . But she stops herself.

He scrambles away and hurls a snowball that misses her by a mile, and she picks up a whole armload of the stuff and drops it on his head and somehow they still don't kiss, even though the kiss is hanging there in the air between them like the clouds of their breath, biding its time, waiting for the perfect moment.

Hattie is at work, reading.

She feels vertiginous: Bethanne's chair is threatening to toss her onto the floor and the glass windows around her tilt at strange angles. She's just realized that even her best, dumbest lines—blaming her contacts!—she's accidentally stolen from this book.

She used to be a different person. She used to be herself. She used to read a minimum of one new book per week so even if she wasn't exactly herself, she was at least someone new all the time, compiling tiny quirks and bits of personality to form a quilted self out of her favorite YA characters. Her massive collection of novels fills an entire wall of shelves in her room, organized by the color of their spines. She hasn't touched them in months.

All she's read (and re-read) since Elijah died is *The Shark Club*. At first she couldn't read anything. And then . . .

The Shark Club had come along at the *exact* moment she needed it. It had felt like a sign.

When she met Bianca Stark, she was sitting in the tiny El Amado airport, drinking a green tea latte. Bug was working behind the counter at the coffee bar owned by her parents. It's called the Frozen Banana Stand, but they don't sell frozen bananas. Only coffee and tea and tiny, perfect pastries. The entire family found the name so hilarious that Hattie was never able to find out what the joke was because they'd laugh too hard when they told her.

Every once in a while, Bug shouted, "Okay?" in Hattie's general direction and Hattie would wave her hand, nod, and grimace. But she wasn't okay. She hadn't been okay since Elijah's birthday party. She suspected she'd never be okay again. She couldn't get out of her head, and all her head wanted to do was replay that terrible scene over and over and over again, each time from a slightly different angle and she couldn't stop it, no matter how much she drank at beach parties with her friends, no matter how much she lay on her bed and tried to disappear into a place where Elijah couldn't follow her . . . He followed her anyway. Because it was her *fault*, and she deserved to be reminded with every inhale she took, every molecule of oxygen she robbed from the air, that he'd never breathe again.

Hattie and Torben had been in charge of the pool that afternoon.

There were two events: Elijah's birthday party and seniors' water aerobics. They'd done rock-paper-scissors for the party. At the last second, Hattie's hand chose paper. Torben was scissors. She got the party.

In all the parallel worlds where either of them had been rock, instead, Torben would've taken the party: noisy, chaotic, like herding cats.

He would've been the one who had to save Elijah.

Or, more likely, he wouldn't have thrown the mat in the water in the first place. He would've organized a race or lined them up at the pool's edge to teach them a front flip. No matter how it played out, in whatever world wasn't this one, Elijah would live.

But like a butterfly flapping its wings, her paper and Torben's scissors made everything align so that Elijah was dead. And it was no comfort to Elijah's mother that, elsewhere in the multiverse, he was still alive and happy and swimming and smiling and running on the tiles even when he'd been told to stop.

That's what she'd been thinking about when Bianca Stark sat next to her.

Her lungs had been squeezing too tightly, her heart pounding against them, trapped in the cage of her ribs. It was her first real panic attack. She'd doubled over, just enough to be able to breathe, to maybe pass as someone *not* having a panic attack.

("This is the best party ever," she remembered Elijah had told her that when she'd opened the slide and then the climbing wall. He gave her a high five so exuberant, her hand stung.)

If she'd been in charge of water aerobics, she wouldn't have had to do anything. Monica taught that class, jumping around enthusiastically on the pool deck. All Hattie would've done was watch. And Elijah would still be alive.

(When the kids were getting tired, she'd started to wrap things up, had them pulling in the floats, collecting kickboards, finding missing balls. But then Elijah's mother had rushed up to her, looking frazzled, and said, "Please give them fifteen more minutes while I set the cake up?" and she'd agreed.)

If she'd said, "Let them get changed and I'll tell them where to meet and walk them around to the party room!" or just "No," Elijah would still be alive.

(She'd tossed the floating island mat into the water. "The Island in the Lava!" she'd called. "The water is lava! If you fall in, you have to get back up as fast as humanly possible before you boil to death!")

If she hadn't reached for that mat, if she'd instead thrown the basketball in and yelled out the scores for each team that got a basket, Elijah would still be alive.

(The kids climbed onto the mat and fell off the mat and climbed back on the mat and the jumping got more frenzied and the mat was going up and down wildly and . . . She didn't see Elijah fall off and go under instead of climbing back up. It was only when one of the other kids saw his hand, sticking out from under the mat, and screamed, that she saw him. She blew her whistle. Her ears filled with white noise. She dove in, she pulled him out, she compressed his chest, she blew into his rubbery lips. She counted. She never stopped trying, not even for a single second.)

She did all the right things, but Elijah was dead.

(When his mother came to tell them to come for cake, Elijah's tiny body was turning gray on the pool deck and Hattie was being pulled away and the paramedics were bagging him and he was gone.)

Hattie, thinking all these things, didn't notice the woman sitting next to her, instead her eyes were closed and she was wheezing.

(When they carried the stretcher out, with his tiny body on it, she threw up on Bethanne's banana tree.)

Three days after he died, at swim practice, she fainted on the pool deck. The day after that, she quit swimming.

Sitting in the airport three weeks later, her tea clutched in her hand, bent over, she heard a low voice saying, "Breathe, just breathe."

When Hattie felt a hand on her shoulder, she'd jumped, dropping her tea.

"Why are you crying?" Bianca Stark had asked.

And Hattie told her about Elijah. The panic attack had cracked her open, revealing all the ugly truths she'd kept hidden. She took all her pain and passed it to the woman to examine and give back. She told Bianca Stark it was her fault.

She told her how hard she'd tried. She told her about swimming and why she had to swim so her mother would come back and how Elijah was stopping her from swimming, ever again. He wouldn't see his mother again and neither would she.

Bianca Stark had reached into her travel bag, pulled out a copy of *The Shark Club* and a Sharpie, and had written inside it, *For Hattie, who needs this. (Spoiler: It's about forgiveness.)*

The first time Hattie read the book, she fell into it. It somehow felt more real than her own surreal life because it made sense in a way that her life didn't. She felt more like Jada than herself. Jada's story was about forgiving the shark for killing her mother and by saving the shark, she released them all.

Now . . . Suddenly, she just feels confused.

Who is she meant to forgive?

What is she meant to release?

She stuffs the book back into her bag, puts her feet on Bethanne's desk, and plays Taylor Swift's first album on the little speakers. She watches Presley drag a marker over the ice in a circle, drawing a path for the kids to skate along.

Please talk to me, she thinks. *Come up here.*

He pauses, looks up at her, and waves. Then he holds up his pen. He bends down and draws a whale on the ice. She mimes a standing ovation, mimes clutching her heart, but he's distracted by the kids, which he should be. It's his *job*. Her job is not to stare at him and be embarrassing.

"Get it together," she mutters.

She takes a pile of printed photos out of her backpack and uses a pencil to twirl her hair into a bun. Leaning over the desk, she starts snipping, the tiny scissors cleaving out unnecessary backgrounds with satisfying precision. The scissors were her dad's gift to her on her last birthday. They're from Japan. They joke that she could perform surgery with them. She finds the snipping soothing—the clean sound of the blades slicing paper shuts down the swirling part of her brain. She cuts confidently, smoothly, quickly. She puts the clipped photos flat into large envelopes, ready to apply to Applejack's blank spots.

She's collaging the entire interior of Applejack with evidence of herself, glued and Mod Podged into place, permanently lacquered on against a backdrop of collected planets, stars, and outer space from *National Geographic* magazines she found in the basement of the community center. The universe. She's capturing the story of the slice of herself that exists here. Now. And when she runs out of room, she starts layering over the top of the last. Somewhere out there, she imagines another version of her is doing the same thing, but the photos are of different people, doing different things. *Counting penguins in Antarctica*, she thinks. "Hey, Lou," she says. "What if doppelgangers are just tiny folds in the multiverse, layering two versions of you into the same time and place by mistake?"

One of Lou's leaves trembles and drops.

"See?" she says. "Makes you think, doesn't it? Maybe it's true. Somewhere, a version of you has more leaves."

She snips, bent over the photos, until her neck starts to ache, and when she looks up, Presley is crossing the lobby, his skate-guards making his gait awkward, as though he's just received a severe blow to his groin. She startles, blinking.

She willed him to come up here and he did.

He looks like a marionette, legs all akimbo.

"Akimbo," she blurts, just to see: It tastes sweet and waxy, like the handful of red licorice whips her mom bought from the candy jars at the zoo before they were both escorted out by security, her mother's zoo-protest sign shoved unceremoniously into the trash with piles of flattened boxes and broken pallets. They never tried again. Like everything else her mom entered into, she gave up as quickly as she began. Her mom was a quitter. But then again, so is Hattie. She shudders, a shiver with no chill.

"Oh, yeah, hey," Presley says, as though *akimbo* might be a greeting he hasn't heard before but is willing to accept. "Hattie," he adds, like he wants to say her name.

She blushes and the sun blazes fuchsia-bright behind the wall of windows. He takes on an ethereal glow against the yellowish sky, although Hattie is aware that *exaggerating for dramatic effect* has somehow become part of her inner narrative, at least since she met him. But . . . he does look like a hero in a postapocalyptic teen movie.

"Are you . . . okay?" Some of his hair is stuck to his forehead and he smells like boy: sweat, toothpaste, hair gel and french fries, and the ice.

Nothing comes out of her mouth. She nods, shakes her head, nods, shrugs.

"Um, blink twice if you're having a stroke," he says.

She takes a breath. "If you're having a stroke, following an instruction like 'blink twice' might be impossible, depending on which part of your brain was affected." She puts down the tiny scissors, then picks them back up. The picture on the counter is of her and Bug on the beach in front of a fire last winter, their heads tipped back toward a dark sky, both of them wide-mouth laughing, like they're joyfully showing their teeth to a dentist.

He glances at it, then flashes a grin, revealing his too-perfect teeth. "That's a great pic."

"Yeah, thanks. I'm just noticing that it's very *toothy*." She smiles back. She's hyperaware of teeth suddenly. Her teeth are fine, if a little too small, with a gap between the top two that her dentist reassures her is less than a millimeter. *Millimeter* is clean and cold with a mineral tang, like snow. Metric, all of it, is like that and also makes her think of swimming, which is also measured in metric, and she knows she's staring off into space now, looking dazed and disoriented and she needs to bring herself back to the moment. "Anyway, I'm fine!" Her voice sounds too perky, too upbeat, trying too hard.

"Is that an answer to 'How are you?' Because I didn't ask . . ."

Mirroring, she thinks.

"So . . ." he says.

"*So* is generally followed by more words" is how she fills the growing silence, trying not to stare at his plush lips. "Some information or a question or possibly a request."

He laughs. He doesn't seem to be in a hurry.

The silence grows, so she repeats his joke back to him. "Blink twice if *you're* having a stroke."

"Are you a doctor?" he says. "Because I heard recently that stroke victims might not be able to blink twice on command."

"I just play one on TV."

He *is* cute. He's cuter than a tiny toilet. He's cuter than otters holding hands. And she *is* allowed to be happy. She feels *something*. The *something* is happiness. Embarrassingly, tears come to her eyes, so she coughs to hide them.

"Let me start again before this gets too weird."

"Okay."

"Hey, Hattie, I have a request."

"Hey, Presley, that's what I'm here for! Hit me up!"

He names a song. "Do you have it?"

"I have everything." Hattie types the song's title into the computer, her fingers tripping over one another. The computer whirrs sadly, making its burning dust smell.

"Maybe you need to put in the singer, too." He points at the frozen screen. "It's Bonnie Tyler."

"I know. I'm an expert. My mom runs an oldies radio station."

"Oh, that's cool. Which station?" His eyes stray to the window, where the kids are getting restless. She knows it's taking too long.

"It's in Switzerland." They both stare at the computer, like that might speed it up. In the corner of the monitor, Bethanne has stuck a photo of a duck under a rainbow that says, chin UP, rubber DUCK!

"Bethanne," she says, pointing at it. "She's a whole mood."

"Uh-oh. Can I?" He points to the mic. She nods. "Practice your spins," he intones like some kind of skating god, and the kids freeze and look all around, spinning and falling. He waves at the kids, who are now staring up at him and giggling. He moves his arm in a twirl and they stumble, spinning, lifting up their feet: *step, turn, step, turn, step, turn.*

"The kids sure like you," she observes. "You were nervous about nothing."

"Right? We're all old friends now. I should have known. I mean, everyone likes me."

"I'm sure that's not true. Nobody is universally liked." The hard drive grinds to a halt and there it is, the cursor blinking over the choices *play now* or *play later.* "If everyone likes you, it's not because of your taste in music. I don't know if I can play this in good conscience and poison the minds of those innocent kids."

"That's harsh."

"I believe in honesty. Without it, you've got nothing."

"Yeah. Agreed." He tilts his head like he's really *seeing* her.

One of the kids looks up and opens his mouth wide. He might be shouting. He's wearing a yellow helmet and yellow mittens.

"Name one song that's worse than 'Total Eclipse of the Heart' and I'll play it for you and your minions."

PRESLEY

Hattie has five freckles on her right cheek, under her eye, that make a constellation: Cassiopeia. Presley wants to press his fingertips gently against them. He clenches his fingers into his fists.

"'Do You Know the Way to San Jose,'" he manages to say.

She's looking at him like he's lost it. "I'm pretty sure that you just go straight north on the I-5, but I can google it if you like. Why?"

He reaches over and rests his hand on hers, just for a second. What is he *doing*? He jerks his hand back, practically hitting himself in the face with it. "It's a *song*," he says. "A worse song." And then he walks away.

He can feel her smiling, so he turns back. He makes himself do it. Mac would find this easy. Mac wouldn't even hesitate. Mac wouldn't be nervous. Mac would . . .

"So, um, Hattie, I was going to ask . . . Are you going to Phantom Fest tomorrow?"

She lifts her phone and, he's pretty sure, she takes a picture of him.

HATTIE

"I'm definitely going to Phantom Fest," Hattie says, and now she for sure needs that defibrillator because her heart has stopped and she's going to pass out and her vision is tunneling, everything getting gray around the edges. She turns her phone over and puts it down so he can't see that she's just taken a picture of him. A photo of the boy she likes, asking her out.

Sort of.

Maybe.

Is he?

She pokes her finger into Lou's pot so she looks busy, distracted. The soil is damp and cool and reassuring. She wants to climb into it, pull it over herself like a blanket. Lou will save her. Probably.

"Me too," he says, finally. "I'm going to Phantom Fest. So . . . I'll see you there. At, um, Phantom Fest." On the ice, a kid is clearly crying.

"You *really* have to go," she says, pointing.

"Shit. I mean, bye."

Hattie watches him walk away. Her hands are shaking. She's proud of herself for not passing out. What would Jada have done? Jada wouldn't have even been nervous. Jada was never nervous. *You are not Jada*, she thinks. *Jada isn't even real.*

HATTIE:

So . . . Phantom Fest. Plan?

BUG:

Yeah. Our plan is to survive it. skull emoji
ghost emoji

CALLIOPE:

OMG at least pretend to be a fun emoji.

HATTIE:

I'm bringing Applejack. Sleepover?
Will be super fun.

BUG:

I'm in! Yes! All the heart emojis! Mood
turning around emoji!

CALLIOPE:

Welllllll, I might have plans with Leo,
but Applejack with my girls is def
Plan B . . . EGGPLANT EMOJI

CALLIOPE:

Wait, did Hattie just say "super fun"? Who are
you and what have you done with Hattie?

HATTIE:

DANCE LIKE EVERYONE IS STARING

PRESLEY

Javi is late.

Presley leans back against a low rock wall that separates the parking area from the sand and snaps a pic of the surf, sends it to Henry and Big Tee. He doesn't know what he's doing here, or he *does* know, but he can't think why he thought it was a good idea, except he needs friends.

He picks up a handful of sand and lets it run between his fingers. The sand is hot. Everything here is hot. A bright green VW bus pulls into the parking area behind where he's sitting, a wildly painted black-and-white surfboard strapped to a rack on the back. A smattering of surfers dot the horizon, riding the waves casually, smoothly, carving long deep curves into the water. Two kids come running out of the low building that has change rooms and toilets. The ocean looks like something he saw in a nature documentary . . . that definitely featured sharks.

"Yo, Mac?" he says. "Maybe, like, do a shark check out there for me?"

I think you have me confused for a god, which is a totally natural misunderstanding, little bro. But I don't know what's out there any more than you do.

"Oh, you're not one? My bad." He looks around, but there's no visual evidence of Mac's presence. His voice seems to be coming from Presley's backpack.

Being dead is kind of shit, tbh. You'll have to scan for your own
dorsal fins. Worst-case scenario: cup a shark's nose, it paralyzes them.
Or so I've heard.

"Yeah, that's an experiment I don't necessarily want to
attempt in real time." Presley leans his head back on his backpack, using it as a pillow. "You sure you can't take a quick
underwater three-sixty for me? Is there no free will in heaven?"

There's no will at all. But I don't expect your small human brain
to grasp the complexity of my current reality.

"We're identical twins. Our minds are the same size."

Well, actually . . .

"Oh god, no. Please don't well-actually ghost-splain death."

You wouldn't get it anyway. I don't even get it, and I'm the dead
one with the superior, expanded brain. Man, this looks fun though.
Wish I could try.

"Fun? Or potentially deadly?" Presley watches a surfer fall
and then pop back up again, buoyed by the water. A scattering
of seagulls sit puffed up on the beach, feathers ruffling in the
breeze. Presley can taste smoke and salt on his tongue, smell
it on his skin. Mac has stopped answering and his anxiety is
pushing closer to the surface. He tries to picture *golden light*.
He tries to imagine this going well. "You know what? Fuck
it. I'm out of here." He stands up to go, but then his phone
buzzes.

HENRY:
You're living the life. But then again,
so am *I* . . .

Attached to the text is a photo of a car. Presley squints at it.
He can't tell what kind of car it is, only that it looks wildly out

of place in front of Henry's house. At first he assumes it's photoshopped, a joke he should get, but that he can't remember.

BIG TEE:
Tell him that car doesn't make his dick look
bigger.

HENRY:
But it definitely makes me look cooler, right?

Henry's house, where he and his mom have always lived,
is a falling-apart century house with green, flaky paint where
Presley used to sometimes spend the night, staying up until
dawn playing board games and watching movies and eating
the cookie dough Henry's mom always kept in the freezer.
The garden is so full of concrete statues that it looks as though
they must be selling them: an elephant, three clowns, the req-
uisite gnomes, a giant naked baby, a pirate with one leg, seven
different giraffes. In the background, he can see that since he
was last there, she's added a dolphin, a mermaid, and a group of
fairies arranged in a conversational cluster. He exhales, laughing. That house. Some things never change.

PRESLEY:
It's hard to look cool when there's
a half-dressed frog bulging his eyes
at your ass.

HENRY:
This frog is wearing a very dignified smoking
jacket. He can't help what his ocular cavities
look like.

PRESLEY:
One word for that car: Trying-too-hard.

HENRY:
Literally that is three words.

BIG TEE:
I have two better words: ROAD + TRIP. The culmination of every great North American childhood and a metaphor for the road ahead. We're on our way to the future in the future of cars. You in?

PRESLEY:
Two more words: I wish. Gtg . . . Here to hit the waves, not shoot the shit.

BIG TEE:
Over a hundred rad dudes died in surfing accidents last year says Wikipedia, FYI.

PRESLEY:
Thanks. If you don't hear back from me in 24 hours, remember me like this.

He takes a photo of himself flipping the bird. He hits send. Sweat drips into his eyes and mouth. He pushes his soaked hair off his forehead, unzips his new wetsuit—still has that new wetsuit smell!—and lets it hang down around his waist. A hand slaps his back, making him jump, and there's Javi, all smiles and sunglasses, two surfboards under his arm, a streak of zinc on his nose and cheeks. "You made it, man! This is gonna slay! You pumped?" Without waiting for an answer, he tosses the boards on the sand. "Let's do it!"

He shows Presley where to put his feet and how to pop up. They jump up and down on the boards on the sand until Presley's quads are burning and Javi deems his moves "awesome" and then . . . "Let's go, man. Time's wasting."

Just beyond knee-deep, a wave grabs Presley's board, and it smacks him directly on the chin. He tastes blood in his mouth.

"You okay?" Javi hops onto his board and starts paddling. Presley wipes his mouth, spits in the water. He doesn't really have any choice but to climb (awkwardly) on to his own board and start paddling, too.

It takes him ten times, twenty, who knows how many? A million tries, and then he's *doing* it. He catches a small curling wave. He stands up, body crabbed forward and stiff as one of the plastic soldiers he and Mac used to melt in candle flames, throwing them at the ceiling and watching them drop back down on long melting threads of themselves. *Stretch Armstrong*, they called them, cheap replicas of the real thing.

"Yeah!" Javi whoops. "Voi-freakin'-lá, my dude! *Now* we surf!" He spins his board and starts paddling out deeper. Javi wears the ocean like a pair of broken-in jeans, soft and comfortable in all the right ways. Presley is holding his body wrong. Muscles he didn't know he had are trembling from the unexpected use.

Mac's voice: *Just when you thought it was safe to get back in the water* . . .

"Please shut the fuck up," says Presley, but it's too late. He's already imagining a shark beneath him, rising through the depths, and it's not even that deep.

"What's that, Canada?" Javi calls back.

"Nothing. I was just . . . Nothing." He mimics Javi's method of cutting through the ever-growing waves, going under more often than he'd like. He feels pummeled, black and blue under this wetsuit, beaten half to death by the water and they aren't even in real waves yet.

Finally, Javi turns, then sits back on his board, pounds his fist and gestures and points, then paddles with amazing speed into a wave, standing and catching it while Presley, trying to follow and missing, the wave forming seemingly all around him instead of under him, gets spun and knocked sideways, water in his nose and throat. He comes up coughing.

"You missed, dude!" Javi's voice is coming from somewhere, from everywhere. Presley's ears ring.

He crawls back onto his board, tries to face the incoming waves, and stares at his own dangling feet, hanging there like bait. What if he has a seizure? There's no way this is safe. Why didn't Ellie and his mum think of that? He's for sure going to drown. Jesus. This was a terrible idea.

"You gonna just sit there, Canada?" Javi's paddled back out already like it's nothing. He's not even out of breath.

"Yeah, no, yeah. I mean, no. I got it." He goes for it, reminding himself that he has nothing to lose—what even *is* death if you can come back and hang out in a mesoglea of shimmering gel-like light?—waits for the next wave to start to lift him, paddles as fast as he can, the water slipping loosely through his hands, but somehow he makes it, and the wave carries him. He holds himself upright, feet staggered, every muscle clenched so tight, he feels like they might pop. Then, for a handful of seconds, he *gets* it. There's a *feeling*. A surge. A connection: he's part of the wave, the wave is an extension of him . . .

Then he falls.

He tries it again and again, looking for that feeling.

This is why people love it. It makes sense now.

Crouch, relax, fall, swim, wait.

Paddle.

Stand.

Ride.

They're past the end of the breakwater, but the waves are rolling in more slowly, smaller, like the ocean has exhaled a sigh before sleeping. The beach looks a million miles away, dotted with people, a scattering of cars in the parking lot, a lineup at the taco truck.

"No gulls," says Javi.

"Huh?"

"That's why it's so freakin' quiet, Canada. The gulls are all gone. Trippy. Must be the smoke. Like bees. They don't like smoke either."

"Smart. Just say no to . . . smoke, I guess. Go gulls!"

"Just say no . . . You're funny, dude." Javi's laugh is easy and lazy and relaxed, like every other part of him.

"Um, thanks. I used to write comics."

"Yeah? Cool. About what?"

"Oh, it was called . . . *Stwins*. It was pretty dumb, I guess."

"Stwins?"

"Yeah, they were stick figures. Who were twins."

"Gotcha."

They bob in the waves, side by side, staring out at the horizon. There looks like there's nothing coming. It's the first time Presley has seen the water here this calm.

"You gonna tell me your story?"

"My story? I mean, I don't . . ."

"You in witness protection or something?"

He doesn't want to tell Javi his story, but . . . what is Ellie always saying? *You have to open the door if you want people to come in.*

"I . . ."

"Yeah?"

"So my story . . . It's pretty long. We don't really have time."

"Waves aren't going to come until they're ready. That's the great thing about surfing. Like, you sometimes have to just wait, you know? No choice. It's like being a freakin' Buddhist."

"A . . . Buddhist?"

"Right. Like out here, we're leaves on the river, you know? Don't you feel it? No control. You gotta give it all up."

Presley closes his eyes. *Give it all up.* It's not the worst advice. "Okay. So my story . . . Um, the main part of the story is that there was an accident. We were in an accident. A car accident. My brother died." His voice shatters into a million pieces on *died*, tiny shards of the word piercing his eyes, making him blink, distorting everything. "He was killed," he repeats. "My twin brother."

The swell picks them up and lowers them down again, slapping a little against the boards. Presley's guts churn. Grief-sick and seasick feel so similar. He swallows so he doesn't puke.

"Shit, man. That's rough."

"Yeah, it's been . . . bad." His voice cracks. *Don't fucking cry. Keep it together.*

"I get it. *Stwins.* That makes sense now."

Then Presley *opens the door* and everything falls out, like it was a closet stuffed with his entire stupid messed-up life.

When he's done, his mouth feels dry. He looks toward the vast expanse of the Pacific. He looks down at his thighs in the wetsuit and the board and the water lapping gently around the fiberglass. He doesn't make eye contact. "That was a lot. Way too much information. Sorry. Thanks for listening."

"No worries. It's all good. Drop by drop you fill the pot, right?"

"Sorry, I don't know what that means."

"You gotta watch some TikToks about Buddha, man. No offense, but you need it."

"Just please don't tell anyone about . . . everything. Especially about the whole Chloe Bean, TikTok thing, you know? And about my mom. I don't want people to think . . ."

"Sure thing, Canada." Javi mimes zipping his lips shut. "Let's grab the next set."

They turn their boards and . . . "Go!" yells Javi, and they both paddle fast. Then the wave is behind them, lifting them, and even though Presley knew it was coming, the rush of it nearly knocks him sideways, but he somehow hangs on, his body hunched into a crouch, and for a few seconds they ride in parallel, the wind and water an orchestra of white noise rushing past, and then he's wobbling and then there's the messy splash as he falls awkwardly, his board flying up into the air and then crashing back down onto his head. Then he's at the surface, gasping, ears ringing, and the wave is gone, the water smoothing out like it never happened. If he seizes now . . .

Javi is still up, distant now, casually upright, arms dangling loosely as his board slows. He waves, points at the beach.

Presley's alone.

Don't freak out, Parsley. You got this. Look how easy it is. Jeez. Chill.

The waves come at him, bigger than he'd like, and he grips the board tightly. He senses something in the depths below him before he sees it: A shadow. A *movement*.

Bigger than a fish. Smaller than a submarine.

He pulls his legs up instinctively. "No fucking way."

Then, moving fast, it surfaces and there's the familiar black-and-white body and a fin . . .

Yo. Sharks or whales?

He nearly laughs out loud.

It's a *whale*. A goddamn orca. It's a sign. It has to be. He waves in Javi's direction trying to get him to look. "Whale!" But the whale is already in a dive, and when Javi waves back, calling something Presley can't make out, he can't spot it. He puts up his hand, scans the horizon. "Where did you go?" The orca, two hundred yards away now and moving fast, surfaces briefly and rolls, long enough for Presley to see the curve of its belly, the white patch near its eye. It huffs out a fine spray that glitters against the hazy sky, then disappears under the surface again.

"You saw that, too, right, Big Mac?" But there's no answer, no sound, just the low hum of the rising wind.

Presley is the kind of tired that makes it feel like his muscles are pulling him down, flattening him, gravity exerting an impossible force, wanting to drag him to the ocean floor. He misses the next wave, which nearly upends him, but the following one he catches on shaky legs. He rides it most of the way to the beach before his trembling muscles collapse and he ditches, staggers the rest of the way. *Don't puke, don't puke, don't puke.*

"You okay there, Canada? You look wiped, man."

"Yeah. Good. Fine. Hey, did you . . . There was a whale." He's gasping for air, trying to slow his breathing. It's panic mixing with exhaustion and the combination is making him shake. "Did you see it?"

"Probably just a weird wave, dude. They're like clouds. I'm always seeing stuff. That reminds me, do you know Hattie?"

"Hattie?"

"She's totally obsessed with that *Shark Club* book. You should meet her . . ."

"No!" Presley practically shouts it. "I know her. I'm good."

Javi raises his eyebrows. "Chill, man. Anyway, she painted her surfboard to look like an orca a while back, ya know? Like from the book how it says orcas eat great whites? Top of the food chain? She got this idea it would keep her safe from *Jaws*."

"She . . . Wow." Presley's heart is racing.

"Man, that girl is something. She's the whole package. Beauty, brains. And girls who wear glasses . . ." His voice fades and he grins. "My type, I guess. Not that she's interested."

"She painted her board to look like an orca because of *The Shark Club*?" Presley repeats, weakly. It's too surreal to be true.

"Yeah, to repel sharks. She claims it totally works and she's never been bitten. But, like, I haven't been bitten either, so . . ."

"That's really . . . cool. But seriously, don't tell her. Please." Presley closes his eyes. His heart is a squirrel in his chest, scampering, screeching, chattering, clawing. *That* Shark Club *book*. It's too much. Hattie is the first girl he's liked since Maeve or maybe . . . ever.

What he feels for Hattie is . . . Well, it's definitely a *feeling*, a big one with layers and depth. It's as though what he had with

Maeve was an Instagram photo and what he feels for Hattie is a fucking Matisse.

His mind is sifting, the sand is shifting, or the other way around. The sand is hot, that's definitely true. *Be a leaf on the river*, he tells himself, trying to feel how cold that river would be, maybe a river that's the run-off from a winter mountain, water so cold it hurts your teeth just to touch it. He lies back in the sand, trying to relax, but he can't make his jaw unclench. Javi has wandered away. Presley squints and sees that he's talking to a group of kids Presley doesn't recognize. They talk with their whole bodies, all slapping and hand gestures, and ducking. Not his people. His people talk in paragraphs and think too much. He recognizes Roberto. A few others, girls in bikinis, boys in shorts, all of them tanned and highlighted and . . . easy. They are all so chill and smiling and happy and attractive, like an ad for light beer or antidepressants. Boards are sticking up out of the ground like a crop of colorful trees, framing the scene. They're people who seem to have a filter built-in or maybe his eyes are blurring or . . . Shit . . .

The seizure grabs him by the ankles, rushes up his legs, pins him in place. *Click, click, click*. His jaw locks shut. Good thing he's already lying down. *Keep breathing, it'll pass*. He waits. He rides it out. It's like surfing, but . . . flatter. And more painful.

When he unlocks, he blinks until his vision clears, then props himself up on shaky elbows, watches a lone gull chasing the ever-shrinking patch of blue, crying out in grief for something it can't articulate. No one noticed anything. Javi and his boys are tossing a Frisbee. Someone's playing a guitar while someone else sings an old Jack Johnson song off-key.

A dog runs by, full tilt, a bright green ball in his mouth. Out in the surf, a girl in a bikini—she must be freezing, he thinks, in spite of how hot it is out here, the water is still cold—rides a slow rolling wave. From here, the waves look like nothing. Baby waves.

"Hey, man," says Javi. "Ready to go? We gotta pregame. Phantom Fest, we're coming for you!" He beats his fist against his chest. He flings back his head, his long hair whipping against his back. He opens his mouth and howls into the wind.

"Um, yeah," says Presley, a little shakily. "I mean, for sure. Yeah. Epic. Cool."

Triggered Tastes: Lexical-Gustatory Synaesthesia and Childhood—Interview #2
Subject: Hatfield, Isabella G. Interview by Brady R. Finch
(UNEDITED TRANSCRIPT)

BRADY: Part two. Are you ready?

HATTIE: We made a deal, remember? No surfing, no deal.

BRADY: Hattie, you don't have to bribe me to surf with you, I'll surf with you anytime. I need this though. Thesis, remember? So can we please do this first, sitting here in the luxury of your air-conditioned VW minibus? Which, by the way, is looking really great.

HATTIE: Yeah, okay, okay. Thanks. Ask your questions. Hurry up.

BRADY: Are you going to give me your notebooks?

HATTIE: Oh my gosh, I'm sorry. I forgot them. I was totally going to bring them today. My bad, for real. I'll give them to Dad, okay? Are you recording?

BRADY: Yes. I can pick them up if it's easier.

HATTIE: No, yeah, I'll bring them next time. I just . . . Sorry.

BRADY: Okay, let's start. One of the things I noticed when you've told me what you taste is that most of the tastes seem to be things associated with your early childhood. Does that resonate?

HATTIE: No. It doesn't resonate, Brady. It's just food. I like to dress it up . . . Like, I taste lemon and my brain fills in the narrative. I like making them into little stories. It doesn't mean anything. Don't read too much into it except maybe I'm naturally dramatic.

BRADY: They seem like they're all things you tasted before your mom left. And it started when your mom left. Don't you think there's a connection?

HATTIE: A connection? What are you asking me, Brady? I . . . don't know what to say. No. That's not how synaesthesia works. It's neurology. It's neurological.

BRADY: It's a theory. They've found grapheme-color synaesthesia can be associated with PTSD in war veterans. I wondered what you thought of the possibility. The body has ways of somatizing trauma and, although I couldn't find studies with lexical-gustatory synesthesia, it's possible that . . .

HATTIE: I think it's bullshit. *Bullshit* tastes like mint, by the way. *Mint* is not from my early childhood.

BRADY: Are you sure? Like mint chocolate chip ice cream? Toothpaste? Mint Oreos?

HATTIE: That's . . . stupid. Look, why don't we surf now and talk later? I mean, whatever. I agree, okay? Mint chocolate chip! My favorite when I was little! You got me. You win.

BRADY: This isn't a win/lose. You seem not into this today, Hat. Maybe we should finish it on a different day.

HATTIE: I'm into it. It's fine. No, that's a lie. I . . . It feels intrusive. I don't know, maybe I'm in a weird place, but I'm sharing this intimate thing with you and you're . . . you're twisting it. Can we please just surf? We can do this later.

BRADY: I have to hand in my thesis at some point, which means I have to do this research and have this conversation.

HATTIE: Did you ever even think maybe it was a little weird to do your thesis on a person who might not be ready to talk about what you want to talk about? Did I say you could do your thesis on my mom leaving? Did I give you permission to do that? Did *Dad*? Because he won't even talk about her, much less . . . this. I remember saying I'd tell you what words tasted like. I was picturing a list. I didn't say you could do this. Actually, you know what? I love you, but *no*. This isn't fair. I don't want to talk about my mom. It's bad timing. I just . . . Turn it off. Turn it off now. Brady, I swear to god . . .

[RECORDING ENDS]

HATTIE

Hattie pushes opens Applejack's door, slams it hard behind her. She blinks in the bright sunshine, the heat slamming into her, solid and cruel. Her skin is too tight, her ribs clench her lungs into something too small to take in air. She's panicking, trying to inhale, but it isn't enough. *Gasp, gasp, stop, slow down, no.* It's only panic. Panic is normal. People panic. It's only a disorder if she has *maladaptive behaviour in response to the attack* and she's adapting. She's breathing. She's fine.

Fucking adapt *already!* she screams, silently.

Adapt has the rubbery taste of blowing up balloons, a thing she loved to do as soon as she learned how, until one day, she'd blown so hard she passed out.

She holds her breath until her body can't stand being deprived of air for a second longer and is tricked into taking a deep, satisfying, bottom-of-the-lungs breath, one that fills her up and calms her.

In, out, hold. In, out, hold.

Brady's yelling: "Hey, wait! Hang on!"

"No." Her voice is weak and gets lost in the wind. It doesn't matter. The panic comes back, instantly, her throat feels as sticky as cotton candy. Her chest is collapsing, her lungs shrinking again, as small as sour plums. Her pulse races, trying to carry an inadequate supply of oxygen to crucial organs. Her vision goes spotty, her brain needs more. She's panting. *Stop*, she tells herself. *Adapt, adapt, adapt. Slow, deep breaths. It's not that hard.* She fumbles with the clips holding her surfboard to the rack.

Her synaesthesia and her mother are two separate things.

They aren't connected. They just . . . aren't. Synaesthesia is *neurological.* It's not psychiatric. It's a quirk of her brain, not a manifestation of anxiety. It's not somatization. It's just . . . not.

It can't be.

Besides, it's *hers.* It's who she is. It's her thing. It is not another thing her mother gave her, like blond hair and a love of water and pastel dresses and Applejack and forever feeling that she's not worth loving.

Tasting words was the one thing that was hers and hers alone. *Her* weird thing. *Her* quirky wiring.

But . . . *Save the Date!* does taste like a fucking coconut cake.

A memory hovers in her peripheral vision, just out of reach. A song: "Killing me softly . . ." The start of a memory: sitting in the passenger seat of Applejack, her mom singing along with the words, turning to Hattie and saying . . .

Brady interrupts. "Hattie, please wait for me. I'm just going to my car to grab my board."

"Give me *space.* Don't they teach you that in shrink school?"

She runs across the hot sand, her board hurting her armpit, bouncing against her hip. The tide is out and the run seems to take forever, the sand first too soft and making her run in slow motion, then wet and cool underfoot, solidifying, and then finally she splashes into the water, the shock of the cold a welcome one, and she drops her board, starts paddling out, her brain slowing to the rhythm of her long even strokes, only stopping when she's well past the break.

She floats, letting the water hold her and rock her and rock her and rock her. She stares into the depths, a moon jelly floats by, some seaweed, a stick surrounded by wood chips that have fallen off a passing barge, a small school of fish flashing silver near the sunlit surface. When she feels calm and blank and emptied out, she flips onto her belly, paddles her way to a decent spot, then surfs in: slow and easy, nothing fancy, just a clean ride on barely there waves, then paddles back out, repeating it again and again until the sun starts dipping low, painting the smoke-tinged sky deep orange streaked with reds and pinks. Only then does she let the shrinking waves ferry her back to the beach.

Looking at her phone back in the van, she finds missed calls and texts from Bug and Calliope. *Shit.* She won't even have time to go home and change before Phantom Fest. She types quickly without reading what she's missed:

HATTIE:
OMW

CALLIOPE:
Where have you been?!?!?!?!?!?

BUG:
Straight line mouth emoji

HATTIE:
Literally driving! Can't talk! Sorry!

She throws one of her mom's old pastel plaid sundresses (she keeps the collection in the tiny closet she's built in the back) over her drying bikini, shakes the sand out of her hair, and hits the gas.

SPARKS FLY

HATTIE

Hattie raises her phone and snaps a series of quick pics capturing Bug in motion, running toward the van across her brown, dead front lawn, all long legs, denim shorts, a colorful embroidered top with off-the-shoulder puffy sleeves, crisp white Converse that somehow always look brand-new, and a perfectly naked face. When she slams the door, Hattie leans over and hugs her tight, breathes her in. She smells good, like a vanilla-mint candle, but fancy—a $200 candle, not the Bed Bath and Beyond version—like *music*, which is the most delicious word. Bug presses her forehead against Hattie's.

"Okay?" she says, after a beat.

"Okay," Hattie confirms.

"Were you surfing?"

"Yeah, sorry, I lost track of time."

Bug leans back. "And somehow you make that I-didn't-have-time-to-shower look even hotter than the I-spent-two-hours-getting-ready look. Unfair, biatch."

Hattie laughs, rolling down her window, letting hot wind blow over them. She drives right by the community center, where Phantom Fest is already spilling people down the stairs and out onto the lawn, a layer of canned music billowing up into the darkening evening sky. Bug looks at her. "Did you forget to stop?"

"No parking."

"Yeah, because we're late. Cal's gonna kill us if we miss her set."

Hattie puts the brakes on at the town's one red light. It's only when her foot presses down on the pedal that she suddenly realizes why today feels all wrong:

It's *Saturday.*

It's Saturday in El Amado, but because of the time zones, it's *Sunday* in Switzerland.

It's over. It's done. Her mom is now married to someone who is not her dad. The coconut cake is eaten. They've had sex in a fancy hotel or rustic cabin or wherever they went after the wedding. She is Mrs. Ingo Svensson.

It's as if all this time, Hattie has been a helium balloon tethered to her mother by the end of a long string and Ingo Svensson has come along and casually snipped the string and she, the balloon, is floating free, and her mom is not even looking up to see which direction she's headed. It's a good-bad feeling. A bad-good feeling. A disorienting feeling. Terrifying. Or liberating.

Yesterday she didn't have a stepfather; today she does.

Coconut cake. Weather to be fantastic. His name is Ingo Svensson.

"Hattie? What's happening? Are you . . . crying?"

Hattie touches her cheek. It's wet, but she shakes her head. "I'm okay."

"Okayyyyy."

The tears blur Hattie's eyes, smearing the blue-brown sky into a smear of finger-painted art. When the light changes, she pulls over, the gravel shoulder crunching under her tires. She turns the engine off, and it makes its familiar *tick, tick, tick* sound as it cools. She removes her glasses and shakes her head. She feels . . . nothing. She's fine. She really is.

She polishes her glasses on her skirt, then puts them back on. Everything is clear and bright, like an overly sharpened photo.

"You're kind of freaking me out."

"I'm totally fine!" She buckles up and takes a deep breath, putting her hands at ten and two on the wheel. She doesn't start the van. She smiles and it feels real. She feels . . . free. "I'm fine. It's fine. Everything is fine." The cold milk taste of *fine* makes her feel calm. Good. She's . . . free.

"No way, you don't get to *fine* this away. Explain." Bug reaches over and grabs the keys out of the ignition, shakes them in Hattie's face. "We go nowhere until I know what the eff."

"Okay, okay." Hattie picks up her phone from the console, opens the email app, scrolls through, and passes it to Bug. She squeezes her eyes shut so she doesn't have to look at Bug registering what's happened.

"What?" says Bug. "What am I looking at?"

"My mom got married. She married a guy named Ingo. They had a coconut cake. Who even likes coconut cake?"

"Oh. Wow. That's . . . Why aren't you upset?" Bug stares at the message, scrolling. "What did your dad say?"

"I didn't tell him. I can't. He'll be so weird about it. You know him! You know what he's like. It's like . . . There's not enough Taylor Swift in the world to fix that wound, you know?" She swallows. If any part of this makes her sad, it's thinking about her dad finding out. "He's been *waiting*. Her stupid toothbrush is still by his sink!"

"Yeah, god. That's seriously heart-breaking."

"But what's weird is that I don't even know if I *care* about my mom and whoever this guy is. Ingo Svensson. He could be anyone: a doctor, a lawyer, a serial killer. Who knows? I feel like it's nothing to do with me. It *is* nothing to do with me."

"Okay. Good. I think that's good. It's . . . healthy. I'm kind of proud of you. This feels big. Oh, wait . . ." Bug is holding the phone strangely, loose in her hand, like it's something she wants to drop. "But did you . . . I mean . . . Look." She taps the screen and there is Hattie's mom's email, right down to the signatory x. But then Bug scrolls the screen down farther . . . and there's a message from Hattie's dad.

Hattie's dad's message says, *I'll admit this is a surprise, but I'm happy for you, D, if you're happy. I hope you finally found what you were looking for. But did you tell our daughter? She should know, don't you think? I'm not going to do this for you, too. Don't ask me to do that. It's unfair. She deserves to hear it from you. She deserved a lot from you that she didn't get. Don't make this another thing for that list. She's a great kid, D. The best. I'm sad that you don't know her.*

It takes a minute for Hattie to understand what has happened. She reads and rereads what her dad wrote. She thinks about Fwd: Fwd: Save the Date.

Her mom had forwarded the invitation because her dad told her to.

Her dad *knows.*

And her dad wanted her to know, too.

It all lands at once, somewhere in Hattie's gut, something heavy and impenetrable, like lead. No, she corrects herself, like osmium, which is actually twice as heavy as lead, according to

Mr. Kim. "Osmium," she says. *Osmium* tastes strangely flowery, like a nasturtium, orange and salad-y, the kind her mom used to pick in the park and throw onto their frozen peas to make them "fancy."

"Osmi-what?"

"Osmium." Hattie turns the key, hits the turn signal, and pulls out onto the road again in a screech of tires. She shakes her head. Nods. Shakes her head again. Shrugs.

"What's osmium?"

"It's the heaviest metal." Hattie slams on the brakes to avoid hitting Mr. Stanopolous, who's slowly making his way down the middle of the street. She rolls down the window. "Use the *sidewalk*, Mr. S! Someone is going to flatten you."

"You're a good girl, Hattie the Lettuce," says Mr. Stanopolous. "But if I'm in the middle, *everyone* can see me."

"You want a ride?"

"No, I like to walk. Keeps me in fine fettle."

"Fine fettle!" Hattie repeats, rolling up the window. *Fettle* is arrowroot cookies, the kind you barely have to chew, that turn to paste in your mouth. *Baby cookies*, her dad used to call them, but he still eats them all the time. The day her mom left, after the talent show, they ate baby cookies for dinner. *Cookie salad* he called it, breaking them up into bowls, giving her a spoon. "Cookie *soup*," she'd insisted. "You don't eat salad with a spoon."

She turns to Bug and laughs. "You know what? I'm in fine fettle, too," she says. "I think this is closure. This is it. She's never coming back. It's over. Like *over* over. I'm happy. Not *happy* happy, but happy to stop thinking about what it will be like when she comes back. It's like everything I thought about how we'd eventually work it all out is now impossible, and it's actually very freeing." She leans back in her seat, takes a long slow breath. "I'm free." She unrolls the window, she shouts it, louder. "I'm FREE!"

Bug whoops. "Free!" They drive in circles around the block, whooping.

They pass Mr. Stanopolous again, and Hattie beep-beeps the horn, and Mr. S. turns around, widely grinning, and flips them off.

Hattie parks Applejack in the Mount Southerton parking lot. There's only one other car parked there and it's always there: an abandoned eighties sedan, coated with rust and half sagging toward the ground, the windows broken out. The ranger told her that there's a nest in it, a California gnatcatcher, and they're endangered. He won't let anyone haul the car away. There's a sign on it that says NESTING BIRDS, STAY BACK.

"This is far. Too far!" Bug says. "Why are we here?"

"Think about how peaceful it will be to sleep here. No one will know. Your mom will think you're at my house and Cal's mom will think she's at your house and we'll be here. Just us and the nesting California gnatcatchers." Hattie's skin is itchy and tight from the sea and her hair is wildly curling, crunchy from the drying salt and her heart feels too small, her veins too narrow. She takes a deep breath, forcing her lungs to expand. "I just need to walk. I need to like . . . *unfurl*."

"Okay, fine. But . . . *Unfurl*?"

"Unfurl," Hattie repeats. "Before you ask, it tastes cheesy? Like mac and cheese, the kind you get in the box for ninety-nine cents that tastes like it's missing something. Mom used to add a whole pile of American cheese and cream cheese, both. It was so good. Extra creamy."

"That makes sense, weirdly enough. Although I would have guessed Cheetos." Bug pauses. "You know, I bet our vocabularies will never be this big again. Once we take the SAT, all these words will leave us because we won't need to remember them and by the time we're, like, fifty, we'll be reduced to half of what we know now." She snaps her fingers.

"That's ominous. Why are we going to get dumber?"

Bug shrugs. "Brain cells stop regenerating. Don't you listen to Mr. Kim? He knows all."

"Oh, yeah. I guess I forgot. Those cells must have died. It's weird to think about how we're just cells. We're compilations. And if we were compiled differently, we'd be something else."

"I'd be a bird," says Bug.

"I'd be . . . I don't know. A whale, I think." And just saying *whale* makes her think of Presley and she wants to tell Bug about the whale he drew on the bathroom door and the whale he drew on the ice, but somehow they feel like a secret, like something too precious and personal to share.

"Hattie . . . I know we were laughing before, but you don't have to be strong about everything. You don't have to be *fine*."

"I know." Hattie can hear the distant throbbing rhythm of the live music starting. Calliope will be going on soon. "But I really, genuinely feel okay." She goes into the back of the van and closes the curtains—new ones, made from fabric covered with tiny surfers, surfing through a sorbet-colored sea—then she jumps down and slides the door shut after Bug. She grabs Bug's hand. "Let's run?"

"LOL, for real. I'm in track, remember? I'll be there hours before you stagger across the finish line. On your marks, getsetgo!" Bug drops Hattie's hand, starts to sprint. Hattie's flip-flops slap her feet punishingly, but she almost keeps up or maybe Bug is slowing down for her. They run the whole way, hurdling over a low fence, cutting across the vacant lot, Hattie's dress tangling around her legs. They finally slow down when they're behind the community hall, where people are spreading out blankets, lying back, pointing up at the sky, the smoke having the good grace to blow east tonight, leaving the clearest sky they've seen since the start of fire season. Both of them are gasping, trying to look normal. "Sit!" Hattie says, and they drop to the ground, lying back, giggling.

Stars are popping out, freckling the sky with light, the night deepening to a deep velvet blue. People look happy. Everyone's smiling and chatting, from Mr. Kim, who waves at them as they pass, to Coach Kat, who's holding hands with her six-year-old twins, Agatha and Jack.

"I won," says Bug when she's caught her breath. She sits up. "Shorts and sneakers probably gave me the advantage, not to mention my impressive physical conditioning."

Hattie rolls her eyes, getting to her feet, still pressing a cramp in her side. "You weren't even trying! But thanks for letting me feel like I'm not a huge loser. I know I'm out of shape. I hate myself." She reaches out her hand and pulls Bug up.

"It's not how you win that counts, it's *that* you win. And I would have won no matter what and you know it."

Hattie high-fives her, but then her eyes catch Elijah's mother's eyes. She's a tall woman, unmistakable, wearing a colorful dress that the wind swirls around her, making it impossible to look at anything else. She nods once, then turns, and Hattie feels a rush of nausea.

"*Shit.*" Hattie's breath catches in her throat and now Elijah's face is shimmering at her from beside a huge flowering shrub and then she's choking. *Cough coughcough gasp cough.* Gasping for air.

Bug thumps her back. "Are you okay? Do you need the Heimlich?"

Hattie shakes her head. "No. Yeah, I'm . . . I just need . . ." She coughs a few more times, then swallows, leans down, then crouches.

You deserve this, she reminds herself.

It's fine. She's fine. *Fine* is milk. Fine is *fine*. She straightens up, looks around casually, trying to find a place for her eyes to land that isn't Elijah's face. *Be fine.* No one knows she isn't fine. She can act fine until she becomes fine and what's the difference between pretending to be fine and being fine? A tiny hair's breadth. Nothing anyone can see.

The ground tilts. *Focus*, she thinks. *Focus.* There's the swim team all sprawled out on deck chairs around an unlit fire pit. *Nope.* She turns in the other direction. Some of the kids from school are on the roof of the small garage next door, others leaning up against the community center veranda. Javi's lying on a huge red blanket, arms spread, somehow in the middle of everything. One of the popular girls, Mira, is sitting behind him, combing his hair with her fingers. Roberto has a girl on his shoulders and he's galloping around in a circle like a frenzied toddler. "Oh my god, he's going to drop her." Hattie tries to laugh, to sound normal. She nudges Bug.

But Bug is looking somewhere else. "Look! Isn't that . . ."

She points, and Hattie sees her dad. He's leaning toward a woman, who has her back to them. Pale pink hair. "Who . . ." The woman turns: Pretty eyes. Great cheekbones. "Is that *Ms. Singh*?" Her dad holds up his arm, flexes his bicep, laughs, and the woman reaches out and touches it.

"*My* future wife? This does not compute, Hat. Do you think your dad wants to duel me for her honor?"

Hattie pretends to hold her hand up to her ear. "Oh, what's that? The Dark Ages called! They want their misogynistic traditions back!"

"I can't be a misogynist. I'm a woman! Where's my sword? We battle at dawn!"

They're both laughing so hard, tears fog up Hattie's glasses. "You do recognize that you are not a valid option. Because you're a child."

"Oh, eff. Eff it. Eff her! Eff everyone. Eff whatever." Bug sighs. "Where's the alcohol already? I need to be drunk and debauched."

Hattie tears her eyes away from her dad—maybe she'd rather he took up Renaissance music, after all—and they land on Brady and his girlfriend, a lepidoptery PhD candidate named Meka. Brady always talks about Meka like he has something to do with how smart she is, but she was smart before she ever met him. She discovered a whole new species of butterfly when she was doing her grad studies in Alaska. It was named after her: *Hesperia meka*. Hattie can't imagine what it must be like to be that driven, that focused, that *sure* of your own future, to be so important that something is named for you. Last November, Meka drove Hattie to a ghost forest where millions of monarch butterflies were congregating. The area had become rich with milkweed and wildflowers where a wildfire had left a burn scar. Hattie had stood in a clearing and butterflies had landed in her hair, their tiny feet tickling the skin on her shoulders and arms. She has the photo collaged over the bed in Applejack. It's the only photo of herself that she truly loves. She's smiling wide and bright in the photo, her hair lifted up and out by the wind, looking as wild as the landscape around her. It was the last photo of her that was taken before Elijah died.

"Yeah, we need a drink, for sure." She can't think about Elijah. And she doesn't want to talk to Meka because that means talking to Brady, and she definitely can't talk to Brady. She can't ever give Brady the red notebooks, which are now tucked safely into the bench seat in Applejack, locked away and hidden from the world. He would see them as proof that he's right, and he can't be right. "Why did we not bring drinks?"

"Someone will take pity on us. We need to let alcohol impede our glutamate transmissions so we forget everything and just have fun. Don't forget to take a lot of pics, we may not remember anything in the morning."

"That's what I like about you," says Hattie.

"My enthusiasm for alcohol in stressful social situations?"

"No, your ability to articulate things in a way that actually makes them seem like science and not just a dumb choice that will end with one or the other of us vomiting into a shoe."

"You're wearing flip-flops." Bug points at Hattie's feet.

"Well, then we know for sure it won't be me," says Hattie. "Too bad about those nice white Converse though."

PRESLEY

Presley isn't the kind of incandescent drunk that makes him love everyone, it's the other kind, the kind that seems to have slammed into him out of nowhere, the kind that makes his heart race and slow in fits and starts, nausea prickling the back of his throat, regret thudding through his veins, but he's not sure why or what, exactly, he's regretting, except maybe the drink itself. He's not even sure he *is* drunk; he may just be having an extended panic attack or the residual hangover from his seizure this afternoon. It's all jumbled together into one hot, uncomfortable mess, and he should leave, but he doesn't want to leave because he wants to see Hattie. He said he'd be here, so he'll be here.

He shakes his head, hard, like he's trying to dislodge the alcohol from his system. The big, soft sky spins above him, blurry with stars trying their hardest to shine through the smoke, which, like so many things he's noticed lately, feels like a metaphor for something, although he's not exactly sure what. He sits hard on the ground. He just needs a few minutes, that's all. The ground around him is covered in clover he realizes now that he's up close. He starts looking for a four-leafed one, combing his hands through the green. Finally finding one, he holds it to his nose, breathes in the green smell of it.

Dorkus Maximus, in the wild, sniffs his surroundings, intones Mac.

"Ha-freakin'-ha," Presley mumbles. "Since when did you talk like Henry and Big Tee?"

Hey, they were my friends, too.

"As if."

I liked those guys! Maybe I'll go visit them. They could figure out what the hell is even going on with . . . this. With me. They're geniuses, right? Maybe that can be, like, the plot of Stwins 2: The Return.

"Yeah, I don't really do that anymore." He's not sure if he's saying it out loud or if it's just in his head or if it matters, if anyone would care, if anyone is listening. He clears his throat, looks down at the grass, which is moving disconcertingly. He's drunker than he thought, drunker than he wants to be.

Across the field, someone has built a makeshift dance floor, and his mum and Ellie are dancing even though the music hasn't started yet. His mum looks happy. Her head is tipped back, and she's laughing and he feels a familiar flash of fury. "Mac is *dead*!" he wants to scream, but he knows that's unfair. Maybe he's jealous that she's happy. Or maybe he just doesn't understand how she did that, how she's put Mac into a separate room, one that she doesn't have to live in all the time.

He wants to be happy, too, but he doesn't deserve to be because a goddamn coin flip got him the safety of the back seat.

"Macaroni?" he says. "Still there?"

A girl next to him tips her head down, her long, purple-dyed hair brushing against Presley's cheek. "What's that?" she says. "I'm heeeere." Then she giggles, twirls so her hair is suddenly all over him like an octopus's tentacles, then disappears into the crowd. He wishes he was more sober. Or sober at all. He takes a deep breath, tries to breathe the alcohol out, clear his head.

He catches sight of Mr. Stevens walking around the periphery with a big orange cat on a leash. Mr. Kim doing something with a flashlight that looks like a magic trick. And then there's Javi, in a small crowd of girls, all with nearly identical wavy hair.

Are they all happy? Is everyone happy except him?

Presley is suddenly thirsty, cotton-mouthed; his throat is as dry as the Sahara. Raspy. He has a Slurpee cup next to him, full of a slushy mess of something that burns his nose and hurts his mouth and makes his stomach lurch. Javi whipped it up in Roberto's blender before they came here, laughing while he poured it into old 7-Eleven cups, saved for just this reason. Mountain Dew and gasoline, that's what it tastes like.

You know, you don't actually have to drink that.

"I'm not really. I'm just . . . holding it."

It's a bad look. You're never gonna get the girl if you're wasted. You want to be another meme? Let me save you.

The drink flies out of Presley's hand, lands hard on the ground next to him, liquid exploding everywhere, splattering his pants. "Whoa, I thought you couldn't do that. Good one."

I didn't do it, fish-dick. You did.

"Neener neener, dork."

"You talkin' to me, little dude?" Roberto crouches beside him, looking confused, although he has resting confused face, so it's hard to know if it's about Presley or just a coincidence. Roberto is enormous—almost seven feet tall and proportionately gigantic all over. He lets out a huge belch.

Presley gets a strong whiff of the disgusting drink and something else—garlic and Doritos—and has to swallow so he doesn't gag. "Yeah, no. Nothing."

Roberto nods, punches Presley in the arm—why do they all do that? "No worries, man. You okay?"

Presley tries to say something, but Roberto is already rising up, towering over him and blocking the light from the building like an eclipse. Presley manages to nod, or thinks he does.

"I'm good," he says finally to the spot where Roberto was. "Thanks." He's moving in slow motion, or everyone else is sped up. The night is passing like time-lapse photography and he's missing bits, blanking whole seconds.

He picks up the cup and dumps the dregs of it out, splashing most of it onto his shoes.

Sober up, trash-hole, he tells himself, hoping to find water, hoping to find the coordination to stand up.

HATTIE

On the stage at the front of the crowded hall, Calliope stands in front of the mic. She taps it once, twice, three times.

"It's time!" Hattie pulls Bug into the crowd, both of them holding tight to soda cans emptied and refilled with pale pink wine, poured from a bottle hidden in the backpack of a kid who plays the trumpet in the marching band.

"A great big booo to you, El Amado! Welcome to Phantom Fest!" Calliope's voice ripples through Hattie like water, floating her up and away. Her total confidence, the way she owns the stage, makes Hattie want to explode with pride. Leo picks up his guitar and twangs a few strings and Hattie tries, unsuccessfully, not to think *guitar*—steamed spinach!—but then he starts to play a riff that slices the night cleanly like a knife through butter. The crowd falls silent, instantly. Hattie gasps. "So good," she murmurs. Fleetingly, she understands what Calliope sees in him.

Then Calliope starts to sing. Her voice commands the stage, overrides the guitar, asks for everyone's attention, the attention of the stars themselves. It rises and falls, wrapping them in a long scarf of music that pulls silkily over their skin, raising goose bumps, making them shiver.

After half a dozen songs, she's done and the crowd stays hushed for a whole minute, then erupts into whistles and applause, which gradually fades into the sounds of a party: whooping and laughing.

"I could *easily* be in love with her," says Bug mournfully. "I'm sort of joking about Ms. Singh. Cal is my one true love." She points at her chest, sadly. "I have a broken heart, but at least it's still beating."

"You can *love* your friends; you just can't be *in* love with them. It never ends well. Have you never read a novel?" Hattie puts her arm around Bug. "Even on the off chance that love isn't bullshit, Calliope would a hundred percent for sure destroy you. You, you are a fragile . . . something. And you *know* what she's like."

"I . . . guess so. But you know what, Hatfield? I might be a little drunk, but I have something to tell you. It's, like, super important. Here it is . . ." Bug gestures wildly, nearly falling over. "You're *lying*. And I know you're lying. But I don't know if you know you're lying. I just don't think you think what you think you think you think, you know? And if you do think it, you're wrong: People are always falling in love with their besties and living happily ever after or dying or whatever in books. And, like, in life. No one has read more books than you and the best friend thing is for sure a thing. And I think you want to think you think love is bullshit but . . ." Bug's voice is blurry with wine. "Wait, that might have been too many think-thoughts." She giggles. "The point is . . . I forget the point. I love you. It's not bullshit. You're loved. You love." She grabs Hattie's face, kisses her first on one cheek, then the other. "Now go and love loving love." She hiccups dramatically, then spins Hattie around and points her toward Presley, who's sitting cross-legged on the ground, staring up at them, that half-smile making Hattie's heart stop and start, start and stop.

"Oh, hey," he says. "I was looking for you."

In one move, she drops down to the ground next to him, her drink slopping stickily onto her hand and onto her dress. Her heart darts around in her chest like a slippery fish. She takes a deep, slow breath and the party falls away. There's no one here but her and him. "Dana Vollmer travels with her own defibrillator," she says.

"Sounds like a good idea," he says. "But I don't think you can defibrillate yourself."

"You're right." She laughs. "Do you know who she is?"

"Nope."

"She's an Olympic gold medalist. She has long QT syndrome."

"Sport?"

"Duh, swimming. There are no other sports."

"I could argue, but I won't."

"Okay."

"Okay."

"This is good," she says, aware that she's a little bit drunk, that everyone here is at least a little bit drunk, that the evening itself: the darkening sky, the stars, the moon, the shadows of the buildings and trees and shrubs and people, all of it is blurry and maybe, too, a little bit drunk on everything that's happening here, all the happiness and dancing and music and . . . this.

"This *is* good," he says back, and touches her arm. Both of them jump slightly from the tiny shock of static electricity.

Zing, she thinks.

PRESLEY

Presley is aware of how his heart is pumping oxygenated blood around in his body, how that blood in his arm is warm, how the blood in Hattie's arm is warm, how he is intensely weird for thinking right now about how warm their blood is, pulsing in their veins, how alive they are and the mechanisms of that—he blames Mr. Kim—the way their hearts are ferrying oxygen to their brains and hands and feet. Since Mac died, he's thought a lot about the biology of being alive, the impossible-but-true mechanics not just of breathing but of the sodium-potassium pump that makes his heart keep beating, the way his nerves pass messages around his body like a million tiny texts, the way chemical reactions in his brain make him feel his feelings and remember his memories.

Hattie leans into him, her bare arm against his bare arm and he feels her skin and his body is all synapses and nerve endings and fast pumping blood and breathing too hard and he's possibly losing his fucking mind.

He doesn't move. The wind pushes her hair into his face, and it tickles his chin.

She turns toward him. "Did you say something?"

He shakes his head, smiles at her. "Nothing." He reaches out and presses the pad of his thumb against the freckles on her cheek. "Cassiopeia," he says. "Constellation of freckles."

She raises an eyebrow. "What if I told you they were fake?"

"*Are* they?"

"No."

He laughs. "That's a relief. I was wondering if you were maybe a little weird."

"I'm *totally* weird as it turns out. You're in luck." She presses her hand to his good cheek and then, with the other, traces his scar with her finger. "Is this fake?"

"Embarrassing, but . . . yes."

"Good. So you're totally weird, too."

They're both laughing now, leaning more into each other. *Synapses*, he thinks. *Nerve endings. Things that add up to more than the sum of their parts.* He reaches for her hand, and she lets him. He flips it over and starts tracing the lines in her palm. Her skin is so soft. He begins to trace her veins up her wrist toward her elbow, aware of the fact his breathing is getting shallower, and god, he wants to kiss her.

Then, suddenly, she pulls away. She says something he can't make out.

"What?"

She points. "I have to pee. I'll be back." She stands up and before he can stand, too, she's gone, which isn't really how he'd imagined that whole scene playing out.

HATTIE

There's a line for the bathroom and Hattie leans against the concrete-block wall, which is solid and cool, and watches Presley looking around for her. He looks surprised, like he can't believe she's gone. She never knew anything could feel like this, liking someone and having him like you back and . . . just liking each other. It's so simple.

She raises her phone, zooms in, takes a picture of Presley looking *for her*.

She smiles, moving up a spot in the line. The door opens and closes.

Someone bumps into her, hard.

"Whoa. Sorry." Javi is looming in front of her. "Hey, Hatfield. Wanna dance?"

"Two things: (a) This is the line for the bathroom, and (b) no."

"You with Canada, then? Saw you two together just now."

"Maybe. So?"

"Taught him to surf today. It was rad. I like him. He's good people."

"Thanks for your stamp of approval, I guess?"

"No worries." He leans against her shoulder, a thing he does with everyone, a thing Hattie is 100 percent not in the mood to entertain.

She steps sideways so fast he nearly topples. "Have you never heard of personal space?"

Javi looks hurt, shrugs. "Sorry."

He looks so pathetic that she feels bad, wants to explain about how she promised Bug she would never like him, how pushing him away is just habit now, but just then Mira Sinclair bounds up to them. "Javi!" she squeals, jumping up so he's forced to catch her mid-leap, like a *Bachelor* contestant. He whirls her around, nearly smashing her into the wall.

"See ya, Javi." Hattie ducks inside the swinging door to the washroom, where there's still a line, but happily a shorter one, and one that doesn't contain Javi or any of his fangirls.

In the mirror under the harsh lights, she looks wild and nothing like herself: all curls and faint evidence of crying—smudged mascara, a redness around her eyes maybe nobody would notice but her. Her glasses are smudged so she takes them off, polishes them on her dress, which has a big pink sticky stain spread over her hip.

She ducks into a stall when it's her turn, pees, but stays sitting there. She leans against the cool metal partition. It's blank and fresh, desperate for graffiti. Maybe a whale, she thinks, smiling, because *Presley*. He's waiting for her. She needs to get up and get back out there. She wants to. She flushes, goes out to wash her hands. There are two girls by the sink, one blond and one brunette, but otherwise weirdly identical, laughing at something on their phones.

"OMG," says Blond. "That's Chloe Bean!" She squeals. "I love her!" Hattie doesn't recognize the girls—they're maybe sophomores, young and giddy and drunk—but then . . . "What kind of name is Jablowski, anyway? This is hilarious."

"Hang on," says Hattie, but they ignore her. *Presley Jablowski*. She frowns, steps closer. "What is that?"

"Like, the new kid?" says Brunette. "The senior with the scar? He's a meme." She's giggling so much she can hardly get the words out. "It's so funny!"

Hattie leans closer and Blond holds her phone up and Hattie watches Presley, half laughing, half crying, delivering a speech about moths. "Phototactic," he says. She's holding her breath and she doesn't know why, but then there's Chloe Bean and Presley's hand, flapping like a moth in love with a light, his crooked trying-too-hard kind-of-drunk determined smile, and then there's Chloe Bean's lip bursting like a ripe plum—what happens when you hit a lip that's full of fillers is something she's wondered more than once, and now she knows—and there's blood and someone has added words to the video, *BIF BAM POW!* like a comic book, and a laugh-track and then a word bubble above Presley's head saying *OOPS!* in huge capital letters, and a zoom-in on Presley's horrified face. Then the video returns to a freezeframe of Presley's hand and Chloe's lip and the meme writing: *Float like a moth, sting like a drunk kid*, which doesn't make much sense, but whatever, since when do memes make sense?

She feels stunned and then confused and finally, mostly, she feels sorry for him.

"Thanks," she tells the girls. She wants to grab the phone and throw it away, like that will stop them from spreading it, from turning him into the Meme Guy and making him a punchline, but even her drunk-brain knows better. It's out there. She can't stop it. Poor Presley.

She heads for the door, then turns back. She's not ready to see him, not quite. She doesn't want to accidentally tell him that she's seen it. She doesn't want to embarrass him or have him think she's laughing at him or even tell him that she knows at all. If she just reads for a few minutes, she'll feel normal. *Regulated*, her dad would say. Reading helps her regulate.

She goes back into a stall, stepping past the girl who was next in line who says, "Hey!"

"Sick! Sorry!" she yells, too loud, too awkward.

She opens the book at random, standing in the stall, leaning on the graffiti-free wall. She's breathing strangely, hyperventilating maybe, so it's fitting that she lands in Chapter 8.

When Mr. Hanks left the classroom, Jada and Topher were alone. Jada was hyperaware of the sound of her breathing, the squeak of her sneaker on the floor when she swung her leg back and forth. She stopped swinging. She held still.

Topher was thinking about breathing, too. By thinking about breathing, he made his breathing weird. This used to happen to him when he was little, he'd get stuck in a trap of thinking about breathing, which made him lightheaded, which made him pass out if he didn't get to a bag fast enough. It was a medical mystery for a while until his mum took him to the doctor and the doctor explained it. Topher had been an athlete his whole life. He'd run a million miles, even back then, he was always running. Cross-country, track, around the block, whatever. He was a runner. When he was running, the breathing thing didn't happen. It happened when he was holding still. It happened when he wasn't busy doing something else, when he started listening to his breathing . . . Kind of like now.

He fell off the stool, just missing smashing his head open on the corner of the bookshelf they were meant to be sorting.

"Holy shit," said Jada. "Oh my god." And then: "Please don't be dead." And: "Are you dead?" And then she slapped him.

PRESLEY

Presley is watching Hattie's friends, Calliope and her boy-friend, Leo, who was playing the guitar, and the other girl, the one they call Bug. *Estrella*, he remembers. *Ms. Rodriguez.* He knows they're considered the nerdy ones, the outliers, the ones who don't care about school teams or spirit week or wear-ing the right clothes or driving the right cars, but they're also almost comically good-looking, like movie stars playing nerds in a movie, but not quite pulling it off, slouching up against the side of the building, talking and gesturing and touching each other. If he holds his phone up, looks at them through the camera . . . they'd make a perfect aspirational Instagram post: #friends #AllAmerican #livingthedream. The boy is waving his hands around, telling an animated story, laughing, and the girls are falling into one another, passing a bottle. As he watches, they, too, suddenly burst into uproarious laugh-ter. They're all well-dressed and have prominent cheekbones and good hair and together, they look like catalog models for Abercrombie and Fitch.

He misses Henry and Big Tee. Javi is fine, in small doses, but too . . . chill, too outgoing, too much like someone Maeve would be all over, too much like someone who'd like Mac more. He misses feeling like he belongs, like he's part of something, so he's going to try. He has to try. He needs to try because . . . *Hattie.*

"Here goes nothing," he mutters. He stretches his mouth into a casual smile. He tries to look like he doesn't care, which is impossible, because he does, which in itself is a disorienting feeling. How long has it been since he's genuinely *cared*? About anything?

He makes his way over to a tub full of ice and bottled water and grabs one, gulps it down. It's so cold, his throat spasms, making him cough, jolting him back to a place part-way between sobriety and pain.

This is easy, he reminds himself. *What would Mac do?*

"Yo," he practices. "Yo."

Or you could, you know, be yourself. I can see why being me would be your first choice, but you're okay, too, Parsley.

Presley flips off his brother, the ether, nothing. "Yo," he says, approaching them. He tries again, more normally. "Um, I'm Parsley. Presley, I mean. Hey."

"Priscilla!" Bug squeals and hugs him like they're old friends and it's easy, it's so much easier than he'd ever imagined, and he's pulled into their circle, he's leaning against the wall, he's laughing, too, and from a distance, he probably looks like he's exactly where he belongs.

HATTIE

Hattie, coming out of the bathroom, walks smack into Torben Pekkanen.

"Shit. Sorry, Tor." She tries to step around him, dropping her eyes to the ground. Her heart skitters and stalls. *Don't talk to me*, she thinks. *Please don't talk to me.* She squints at him, suddenly almost unable to see him. The shivering glow of Elijah's face is hanging between them. His smile. His missing tooth. "Shit." She closes her eyes, waves her hand around like she could brush him aside like a curtain.

"Hattie." Instead of stepping out of her way, Torben steps to the side and blocks her. Then she sees behind him: *everyone.* The whole team: Trayvon, Gretchen, Cece, Lewis, Grayson and Hannah. "Hattie. We need to talk to you."

"Um, what's going on?"

"I told you this was stupid," says Grayson. "This is not going to work."

"It's an intervention?" says Hannah, helpfully.

"Yeah," says Trayvon. "We're intervening."

"Okay, I'm a little drunk, so can you intervene some other time? I'm also kind of in the middle of something." *Intervene* tastes the way a Christmas tree smells, all green and oily, specifically festive and somehow cold. Snowy. A winter trip to Lake Tahoe, a cabin with her grandparents, her mom sledding down the ski slope and getting stuck at the bottom, necessitating a call to mountain rescue.

"Nope," says Lewis. "Sorry."

Hattie shakes her head, trying to center herself here. Now. "I . . . can't. What is this?"

"Hattie, it will take five minutes, I swear."

"I . . ." Hattie can feel the panic rising in her throat. *Adapt!* She wants to claw a hole in the wall like a cartoon character, escape from her old team and from Elijah and from whatever this is. *Fight or flight.*

Torben leans into her, whispers in her ear. "Please. Hannah worked really hard on this." Then louder: "Come on. We have a whole thing set up. Five minutes." He grabs her elbow, steering her down the stairs and into a room she didn't know even existed. Stacks of green plastic chairs, some tables. A laptop set up with a projector.

He presses some keys and the screen lights up.

"Very funny, guys, please can I . . ." She lets her voice fade into the music. There she is. On the screen. She finds herself leaning back onto a pile of chairs for support. Hannah squeezes her shoulder. Then:

An upwelling of music

Hattie on the blocks

Hattie diving into the water

Hattie mid-stroke

Hattie at the finish, looking up at the scoreboard

Hattie with her fist in the air

Hattie waving the flag

Hattie at the medal ceremony

more music

more swimming

more *Hattie*:

Hattie with trophies,
Hattie with the team,
winning and swimming
swimming and winning
and all the time:

Elijah, staring back at her from the light illuminating the screen, nodding, his shimmering face, his perfectly imperfect smile, his tooth gap, his wide eyes, wanting . . . *something*.

"Not *now*," she says. She is almost, but not quite, crying. Her heart is pounding hard. She thinks she might be panting. She covers her face with her hands, tries to breathe like a normal person, peeks between her fingers to see the video frozen on a frame of her own face, practically unrecognizable with a too-wide smile, eyes almost shut from smiling so hard, and she remembers that feeling, the rush of winning, the first scan of the audience, thinking she saw a yellow puffer jacket even though she knew her mom left it behind, that fleeting split second of *what if* . . .

She swallows. Hard. A scream or tears or both.

Someone flicks on the lights.

"We really love you, Hattie," says Hannah, her arms hanging awkwardly by her sides. "We miss you. And we really, really want you to come back." She reaches up like she's going to hug Hattie, but Hattie ducks.

"Um, yeah, and we can't win without you," says Gretchen. "That's the bigger picture? You owe us."

"Shut up, Gretch." That's Trayvon. "We also care about her, don't be an asshole."

"Where did you get all this . . . footage? This video?" Hattie's voice is a whisper. "Where did it come from?"

Then Gretchen's face is in front of hers, looking worried, her familiar always-smiling kind face. "Your dad. Is that okay?"

"My dad?" Hattie repeats. She closes her eyes. Does he want her to swim? Why? She isn't going back. She's never going back. She thought . . . She had thought that's what it was about. She'd always thought swimming was about her mom, coming home. But that's so *dumb*, she sees that now. That's how a kid would think and she's not a kid. Not really. Not anymore. Her dad just wants her to be happy. That's probably all he ever wanted. For him, her swimming was maybe never seriously anything to do with her mom. How could she have thought it was?

"Hattie?"

"Sorry, I was just . . . That was amazing. Thank you."

Then they all start talking to her at once, making Hattie think of the seagulls on the beach when they see someone's left their french fries unguarded. *Squawk!* "You have to come back." *Squawk!* "We want you to come back." *Squawk!* "You're too good to quit." *Squawk!* "You have to try." *Squawk!* "Please come back." "Come back." "Come back." "Come back." *Squawk! Squawk! Squawk!* And like the seagulls, they're relentless. They aren't going to give up. They might never give up. She has to go.

She raises her voice. "I'm sorry." She stands up, pulling away from their hands and their words and trying to not think about the video, that feeling, the pull of the pool. Where Elijah *died*. It's all mixing together, nightmarishly, twisting around and sticking to her ears, her brain: his face and their words. *Come back come back come back!*

"I *can't*."

She runs out of the room, trying to unstick everything that's clinging to her like thick webs. She's barely outside when her stomach starts twisting and roiling, and she has to bend over, her throat too tight, her mouth watery. One dry heave and then puke splashes out, all over her mostly bare foot, her stupid flip-flop drenched.

"Just think about it, Hat," yells Trayvon from somewhere behind her or from inside her head or from everywhere.

PRESLEY

Presley is playing a drinking game, bouncing Ping-Pong balls into empty Solo cups. He flips the ball into a cup and Calliope claps. He's really good at drinking games because they're the same games, minus the drinking, he and Mac played when they camped with their dad, who didn't need games to drink, who slowly got wasted and passed out without any pretense of having fun. They had Solo cups. They had good aim. They had lots of practice.

The two girls are leaning into each other, playing with each other's hair. Leo's wet mouth hangs open as he stares at them. He tries to take a drink but pours it on his lap. Behind him, Mac shimmers.

"Yo," Presley says out loud without thinking.

"Yo, yo, broself," Leo slurs, then swings around. Leo is not good at drinking games, and so Leo is falling-over wasted, about-to-puke wasted, sloppy-and-loose wasted. "Oh, hey, weren't you just . . ." Leo turns again. "Whoa, twins, man." He loses his balance, falls directly on top of the game, the red cups crumpling under the weight of his body.

"You *saw* him?" Presley says urgently.

Leo laughs. "I saw 'im," he repeats, but Presley can't tell if that's an answer or if he's just repeating what Presley asked. "Saw 'im," he says again, his eyes rolling, then closing.

The ground tilts under Presley's feet and a wave of tingling rushes through him, like a seizure, but not a seizure, like the opposite of a seizure, a rush of something good: validation or sort-of validation or *understanding*, like he understands something he didn't before about Mac, about what's real and what isn't.

He's got validation from a passed-out drunk, so it's validation that's not really validation at all, but it's also . . . familiar.

"Just like Dad, right, Mac?" he says, but there's nothing beyond the table where Leo lets out a guttural snore, nothing between Presley and the empty place where Mac should be, should always have been, where Presley thought he'd be forever.

HATTIE

Hattie runs back outside, putting as much distance as she can between herself and her old team. She has to get out of there. Fight or flight. *Flight* is definitely her pick.

"Presley?" She doesn't care who hears her. "PRESLEY!"

PRESLEY

Presley sees Hattie. He hears her. Everyone else seems to fall away, disappearing into a blur of noise and nothingness.

He waves.

HATTIE AND PRESLEY

"There you are," they both say at the same time, crashing into each other somewhere in the middle.

"Ready to go?" says Presley, like it's obvious they're leaving together.

Hattie's eyes are red. She's been crying, he can tell. "Yes." She grabs his hand and pulls.

Hattie's dad and Ms. Singh are sharing a single lounge chair. Ms. Singh's head is on Hattie's dad's chest. Hattie's mother's toothbrush is still by the sink, her boots by the door, her wedding invitation in their inbox.

Hattie's head spins. She hates being drunk. She wishes she hadn't touched the wine.

Ingo Svensson. Weather to be fine. A coconut cake. Fwd: Fwd: You tell her.

"What's wrong?" says Presley.

"Nothing."

Hattie drags Presley across the vacant lot, avoiding the groups of teens setting up to drag race down the old farm road, past the intersection with the one traffic light, up behind the activity center, and toward the long gritty single-lane road to Mount Southerton. They cut across a field, stumbling in the pits and ridges left by kids joyriding, then they jump across the ditch. The gravel scuffs under their feet and there's the sound of distant crickets chirping, but other than that, the night is almost unbelievably, magically quiet, the party fading to nothingness behind them, the noise of the crowd pushed by the wind toward the sea. But the wind is also moving the smoke over them, shoving the fire in the direction of the Pacific (in their direction, too) and the stars are sliding in and out of focus, behind the screen of black, toxic-smelling air. The stench is still not overpowering though, still playing a quieter note than the pines and the dry grasses and the asphalt, still hot from the day's intense sun.

Hattie's hand fits in Presley's like it belongs there.

Presley squeezes her hand just so she squeezes back. Their hands have a whole conversation. *I like you. I like you, too.* His thumb brushes her wrist. Her whole body shivers.

You're allowed to be happy, Hattie repeats to herself. *You're allowed to be happy.*

PRESLEY

Hattie unlocks Applejack's door and slides it open, gets in, and turns on the camping lamp on the table, throwing a yellow glow around the small space. The inside of the van is something Presley might have dreamed. Every surface is collaged with photographs of Hattie and her friends and her dad, going back to when she was little. Layers of photos, tiny and large, overlapping and cut into shapes and patterns that somehow have become one cohesive piece of art: arranged by color so that it gives the effect of an ombré rainbow.

Everywhere: Hattie.

He thinks of the question his dad used to ask when he was feeling philosophical, which meant he was drunk. *How can you even prove that you exist?*

The inside of this van is proof that Hattie exists.

He has to bend a little so he doesn't hit his head. He runs his hands over the varnished walls. "Proof that you exist," he says.

She closes her eyes. "Please don't make fun of me. I know it looks weirdly vain. This . . ." She indicates the walls. "I swear, I'm not a narcissist."

"No. I get it. It's . . . evidence. It not only proves you exist, but it proves you're *happy*, that you've been happy. I'm blown away. This is incredible. This is . . . *you*."

"Thanks," she says. "Let's not talk about it. I feel totally naked right now." She shakes her head, blushing. "I mean, it's pretty personal." She clears her throat. "When my mom left, she took all the pictures with her. Like every single picture, no joke. After that, Dad always asked me to take pictures with his phone, everywhere we went. And we went everywhere. Like we were proving we were okay without her, we had evidence of us being happy. I've always taken pictures, ever since. It's like I need them or I feel like . . . maybe I'll disappear, too. I know that's dumb. She didn't disappear. She's in Switzerland. She's fine."

"It makes sense." Presley thinks of the box he has beside his bed, printed-out photos of him and Mac, hundreds of them, just in case technology fails or his cloud gets wiped or who knows what, he just needs to have them. He kneels on the mattress so he can look closely at the photo of her with the butterflies. "I just . . . Wow. You're so fucking beautiful."

"Okay, okay, okay! Stop. Compliments freak me out." Hattie cranks the old-school moonroof and it slowly opens, revealing the blurry stars, the smoky sky, the shadows of the skinny trees blocking the hazy moonlight.

"This is like a dream," says Presley. "It's art. It's a dream about art. And about you. About the whole universe." He gestures at the stars.

"Are you drunk? You know you sound like a huge dork when you say stuff like that, right?"

"Yeah, I don't care. I embrace my inner dorkiness. Did I tell you I wasn't a dork? Because if I did, that's my bad. I'm totally a dork." He laughs. "Hey, did you know that a dork is actually a whale's penis?"

"What the fuck? Is that *true*?" He's laughing too hard to answer, but he's nodding and she's laughing, too. She lies down on the bed, and he lies down next to her. She rests her head on his chest. "Is this okay?"

"This is more than okay." He wraps his arm around her. "This is great. This is perfect." Her hair smells like the sea. And coconut. And like *her*. He breathes as deeply as he can, he pulls it all in.

"Are you sniffing my hair?"

"Um, yeah. Is that weird?"

"It's totally weird! God, did no one ever give you lessons in this?"

"In hair sniffing?"

"In how not to be weird! You're supposed to hide your weird. Haven't you heard?" She laughs, leaning over him so she can smell his hair. She breathes in deeply. "Oh, wait. You're right. This is . . . Your hair smells good, too."

"I know, right?"

"You nerd."

"I thought I was a dork!"

"I can't call you that now that I know what I know, that it's a . . . penis." He can feel her blushing, the heat of her face against his chest, his heart pounding against her cheek. "Let's just promise to never hide our weird from each other."

"Deal," he says. "I'll show you mine if you show me yours."

"Eventually," she says. "I promise. I think. I think I promise."

"Okay," he says. "I think I promise, too."

HATTIE

Don't kiss me, Hattie thinks, and he doesn't, and she's disappointed and relieved, both.

"Um, can we . . . Let's go for a walk," he says. "I'm going to fall asleep, and I don't want to fall asleep. I don't want to miss . . . this."

"A walk?"

"Yeah, it will be romantic. Weird *and* romantic."

"Okay."

PRESLEY AND HATTIE

Hattie puts on her mom's running shoes—vintage white Nikes with a pale blue swoosh she and her mom found in a Goodwill bin on one of their shopping adventures, shoes her mom *loved*, shoes her mom had declared she'd "die for," shoes her mom left behind. The shoes are too small and give Hattie blisters, but she loves them in the way you love an abandoned teddy bear or the last Christmas tree in the lot, things that were meant to have been loved but weren't.

She and Presley set out, with flashlights they took from under the passenger seat, following the reflective trail markers leading up to the summit. Nighttime sounds hum around them, louder now than before: the whistles of unseen night birds, the low hooting of an owl, the wind sighing through the trees and scrub, the background hum of freeway traffic, their feet thumping gently on the path, kicking rocks out of the way, slipping a little in the dry dirt, their breathing getting heavier as the path slopes upward.

"You know, I hear this place is number one for paranormal activity," says Presley. "In the whole world. Amazing, right?"

Hattie laughs. "Have you been reading the bathroom wall again?"

"Well, yeah. It's where I get my best information."

"So, *do* you believe in ghosts?"

There's a long pause that stretches between them.

"Yes," Presley says.

And there he is and there are all the stars coming into and out of focus and all the night sounds and . . .

Mac.

"I'm a twin," Presley says, and his voice catches already, like he's going to cry, which he knows he will. "I *was* a twin."

She feels herself holding still on the inside, like she's holding her breath, but she isn't. She doesn't know what to say or maybe she knows that if she says anything, the spell will be broken, so she nods.

She keeps nodding.

He talks and she nods and her heart beats faster and harder, partly from the exertion and partly because it's so much, his pain and his loss and his twin who's now his ghost. When he's done telling her about Mac, about the accident, about the mesoglea, they're nearly at the top of the trail. It's been an hour. Maybe more. She can't tell. Time held still while she listened, while she tried to take it all in, while she tried to form a response.

"Oh" is what she says. "Oh, Presley."

"Yeah," he says. He feels emptied out. Empty, but good. Light.

They've stopped walking now, so they're standing side by side, looking at the sprawl of hills, the ocean, the lights of El Amado, and looming in the east, the glow of the fires, the huge swathes of flames and billowing smoke that seem too close, too imminent, far too real.

"So . . ." He clears his throat. "You have a ghost, too. Right? I mean, I thought I saw that you . . . Well, you have a mesoglea."

"Mesoglea," she repeats, tasting the grape-jelly-ness of the word. "Do I?" She closes her eyes and there's Elijah, so she opens them, but he's still there, between them, and she swallows because she doesn't want to . . . She can't . . .

"Yeah, you do," Presley says, gently.

Suddenly, she feels angry. She doesn't want this. She doesn't want a ghost or a mesoglea. She wants to be alone on this hill with a boy she likes. Is that so wrong? "I don't actually believe in ghosts."

Presley flinches. Not a lot, but enough that she sees she's hurt him, and she feels mean, wants to take it back, wants to not wreck this night. "You don't, huh?"

The path feels wobbly under her feet, and she looks around for a flat spot to sit. She climbs up on a boulder, still warm from the day in a way that makes it seem alive, waits for him to sit, too. He does, tentatively nudging her arm with his. She leans into him slightly. She wants to apologize. She wants him to know she understands. She wants to believe in ghosts. She wants to not be haunted. She wants to know him. She wants him to know her. She wants him to *want* to know her. She wants to . . .

"What's your favorite color?" she says. "I feel like we've skipped too many of the first things. Like the getting-to-know-you things." She's talking too fast. She's saying it all wrong.

"Hattie," says Presley.

"Presley," says Hattie.

"Green," he says.

Their legs are touching, pressing against each other. The wind stirs the wildflowers and the dust and pushes even more smoke into their faces, stinging their eyes. "We should go down," Hattie says, but neither of them move. "It's getting kind of hard to breathe up here."

Then suddenly, a flash of green-lit eyes, watching them. She lets out a small scream, but it's only a deer, as scared as they are, leaping back out of sight.

"What the fuck?"

"Paranormal deer!"

"Ghost deer!" He pauses. "Not that you believe in that kind of thing."

"I definitely don't believe in ghost *deer*. I didn't mean . . . I don't mean . . . I just . . . I know Mac is real. To you. And . . . I don't know. I don't know what I mean. I'm sorry."

He stands, takes her hands, both of them, pulls her up, and turns her to face him. The breeze lifts her hair, blows some against her lip, but she doesn't pull away to fix it. "Hattie, this is . . . I believe that ghosts are love. And love is real. It's the most real thing. So ghosts are real, but maybe not in the way people think."

"I . . . don't think I get it. I want to! I just . . ."

He lets go of her hands, puts his hands in his pockets. She wishes he hadn't let go. He looks up at the sky, takes a deep breath. "I think ghosts exist because we're not ready to stop loving the people who died, and that kind of love doesn't have a form to take, so it takes the shape of the person who was lost."

"Oh," she says. She swallows, so she doesn't cry. *Elijah*, she thinks. *Elijah, Elijah, Elijah*. She should tell Presley why his explanation makes perfect sense. She should let him know that of course she gets it, that she *knows*, that she feels the same way.

He adds, lightly, or in a way that's meant to sound light but actually doesn't: "So maybe that deer's mother loved them. Maybe that deer . . . had a twin brother." His voice cracks.

"Presley," she says. "Oh my god. I'm sorry. I . . . get it. I do."

Their eyes meet.

He reaches out his hand. She takes it. They're almost perfectly matched in height. He steps closer, then closer again, and stops, just short of kissing her, and they stand there, breathing each other's exhalations, lips nearly, but not quite, touching.

"I believe in your ghost," she says. "I know you love him so much." Then: "Do I really have a mesoglea?"

"Yes." He pauses. "Ghosts might not be *real*," he says. "But what is real? Is there a difference between perception and reality?"

She frowns. "I . . . guess I don't know. Like if you believe a thing is real, then it is because you believe it is, so it's real to you?"

"Yeah, like that."

Later, in the van, lying under the open moonroof, Presley says, "There's something I have to tell you. It's about . . . well, me. And fame, or infamy, or both."

Hattie yawns. "You've told me so much already."

"Is it too much? You can tell me to shut up."

"Shut up."

"Okay."

"I was kidding!" She raises herself up on her elbows, looks into his eyes. "Look, I know about . . . her . . . and the . . ." She makes a vague flapping gesture. "I don't want you to think it means anything to me, because, like, it doesn't. It doesn't change who you are. It's not what's important. You're what's important. You're important to me." She closes her eyes.

"Are you sure it doesn't change things?"

"I'm sure," she murmurs.

Her eyes stay closed.

PRESLEY

Presley watches her fall asleep. He memorizes the curve of her cheek, the downy fuzz on her skin, the salt dried into her hair. The twinkling lights of his headache aura fall around him like the stars he knows are there that are now totally obscured by the thick haze exhaled by the rising smoke.

He only drifts off when the sun starts to creep up over the horizon, painting the now oddly brown sky with yellows and oranges, a chorus of birds chirping all around them in perfect harmony, like a gospel choir singing about the end of the world, and he dreams they're swallowed by the flames but somehow he isn't afraid, he's wrapped around Hattie and he's a question that's been answered and she's the answer and everything is *fine* and there's no sign of the abyss, the darkness is gone from beneath him, and there's nothing there now but the gritty path they walked on, stones that up close are a beautiful shade of orange and gray and everything in between.

HATTIE

Hattie's mouth is as dry as the ground.

She groans, untangles herself from Presley, staggers up, and brushes her teeth at the tiny sink.

"Hey," says Presley sleepily from the bed. "That's not fair." He sits up. "Is it . . . tomorrow? Are you going to get in trouble?"

Hattie shakes her head. "My dad is the most laidback father of all time. He's a big believer in letting teenagers make bad choices so they can figure out who they are. He was a teen dad, so . . ."

She takes out her phone.

> **HATTIE:**
> Slept in Applejack. Rate party on a
> scale of 1 to Taylor Swift?

Her message stays unread.

"Everything okay?"

"Yep, probably." She scrolls up and down her messages. There are dozens from Bug and Calliope: memes and emojis and selfies (with increasing blurriness) and: *Hattie and Presley, sittin' in a tree, k-i-s-s-i-n-g* . . . and *Don't worry about us, Hat. Heart emoji love emoji eggplant emoji Wear a condom!* and *OMG Leo was just caught be-dicking Mr. Stevens car again!*

Her phone buzzes.

DAD:
On the Taylor scale, definitely . . .
The Lucky One.

> **HATTIE:**
> Dad, that's no info at all and also
> way too much info if you're saying
> you . . . got lucky (and please say it
> is not that). See you later. Taco . . .
> Sunday?

DAD:
Sounds like my kind of perfect. I'll be there.

Later, when it gets too hot to stay in the van, Hattie drives Presley to Secret Cove, a tiny pocket of beach at the bottom of a steep trail protected by the jutting land from the rolling surf, a shallow lagoon of calm water and pale sand. They strip down, backs to each other, and dive into the cold water, coming up spluttering. Presley floats on his back, the water beading off his face, and to stop herself from leaning over and licking it, she swims out as far as she can, the stroke coming back to her as easily as breathing, her body leaning into it and remembering how it loved to move this way. She swims out forever and looks back at the beach and sees that Presley is sitting on the sand, watching her. He's tiny. A speck. She's in deep, her legs kicking over the vast nothingness of the ocean and she thinks about sharks because she can't not, because *The Shark Club* is as much a part of her as anything. They're just fish, she reminds herself.

She goes under, then down, diving until she can touch bottom, sits on the sand for as long as she can, comes up gasping, then swims as fast as she can past a short reef where waves are breaking in smatterings of white foam, then back to shore. She's breathing hard.

"You're amazing. I don't know anyone who swims like that. You look like a sea creature or something. A dolphin."

She shakes her head. "Thanks. But lots of people swim like that."

"Not really. You're good and you know it. Like especially good."

"I guess. I mean, I know I am."

"It's funny how we're both athletes. Were. We *were* both athletes."

"Yeah."

"It's almost weird, isn't it? That we'd both be really good. That we'd both quit. That we'd both end up . . . here. Like, together."

"I guess." She's shivering, her muscles cramping from unexpected exertion. Elijah's face shimmers briefly against the cliff and evaporates, like he was never there.

"Why did you quit swimming, Hattie? You never said."

She shrugs.

"Hattie? There must have been a pretty big reason because you belong in the water. At least, it looks that way to me."

She can't bring herself to form the words: *I killed Elijah. Or I didn't save him. Which is the same thing.*

"I can see your mesoglea. It's real. Look." He grabs her hand. Shows it to her. "Do you see it?"

She nods, because she can, a light glow, then closes her eyes because she doesn't want to.

"So?"

She shakes her head. "It isn't. It's just . . . PTSD. It's syn-aesthesia. I have synaesthesia." She explains *synaesthesia*—the word itself tastes onion-y and sharp like the diced onions her mom put on egg salad or hot dogs or burgers or tacos—about how she tastes words, literally, a short-circuiting in her brain that sends a communication about something unrelated, how it brings up memories.

It's easier than telling him about Elijah.

"That's pretty wild. I've never heard of that."

"Yeah, I guess it's rare. My dad's grad student is doing his PhD about it. About me. Sort of. About . . . PTSD. About how screwed-up brains sometimes physically change after some-thing terrible happens." She shrugs, like it doesn't matter, tries to make light of it. "Some words are delicious!" She laughs, doesn't tell him that his name is one of them. "Like the word *abracadabra* totally tastes like candy corn."

He makes a face. "Candy corn is the worst candy!"

"If by *the worst*, you mean *the best*, then yeah, I totally hear you."

"Ha-ha," he says, nudging her. His skin is warm against hers and she shivers. She wonders if he'll kiss her or if she should kiss him or if . . .

"But all that doesn't explain your mesoglea," he says quietly.

She doesn't want to tell him. She digs her feet into the sand, piling more and more sand on them until they disappear. She runs more sand between her fingers and watches it fall like salt.

"Hattie?"

She shrugs. "I guess . . . I don't know. I think it's related. My mesoglea, or whatever. It's a PTSD thing. I'm sure it is. It's not the same as you and Mac. Elijah doesn't talk to me. He's just there, like a still photo, so I don't forget. It's my own brain, not a ghost."

"I'm pretty sure you can't see someone else's synaesthesia, like, *literally*." He touches her hand, and it's like touching phosphorescence, the sparkle shimmies away from his touch. "Elijah," he repeats. "Who's Elijah?"

She closes her eyes. Elijah's face is so close to her, she could touch him if he was real, which he isn't.

She starts to cry. Presley pulls her into his chest, rests his chin on top of her head. They sit like that for a long time, long enough that something finally cracks inside her, ice thawing, molecules moving closer to one another, allowing themselves to feel warm and to start moving, liquefying, becoming something that can *flow*.

She tells him the whole story.

It takes a long time. The tide edges closer to them and farther away. The sun burns their exposed skin until they move into the shade of a sprawling low-flung tree that looks for all the world like a person, bending, trying to touch the sand or maybe trying to protect them. She tells him about Elijah and swimming and how much it mattered and how it can't matter anymore because she didn't save him. She tells him about her mom and about how she's been waiting, all this time, for her to come home.

She tells him everything. Then waits for him to say something.

He presses his cheek against hers. He wraps his arms around her.

"Say something!" she says.

"What's your favorite color?"

"Blue," she says, and she points at the patches of blue sky spreading above them, the wind having changed direction, pushing the smoke back to where it came from, the beautiful perfect blue sky, the beautiful perfect sun behind the leaves of the bending tree, throwing patterns of shade onto their skin.

SWEETER THAN FICTION

HATTIE

"So are you going to give us the details of what happened with you and Plush Lips the Tiny Toilet?" Calliope makes a kissy face.

"I think I liked it better when you called him the New Kid." Hattie fishes an ice cube out of her peach iced tea. "Plush Lips sounds terrible. See also: Tiny Toilet."

"Tell us everything. I want to know if he made you see"—Calliope fans her hands wide—"stars."

"Literally, yes. The whole Milky Way. We hiked up Mount Southerton. We climbed and we talked. It was nice. It was dark. There was a terrifying deer that was possibly a ghost. Then we slept. The End."

"Girl, you slept? That is so . . . *wholesome*."

"Gee, thanks."

"You're welcome. I'm going to assume there was no hot action, which, as you know, is a disappointment to me and probably all of humankind."

Hattie makes a face and blushes. "No hot action. And I doubt all of humankind is as invested in my sex life as you might think. New topic?"

"Uh-huh."

"Literally any topic except this one."

"Okay, how about this: Bug told me your mom got married. So . . . That's a thing that happened? Like a *big* thing. One: Why didn't you tell me? And two: Why do you seem fine?"

"Good questions. I would have told you, I guess I just . . . I don't know."

"You don't know?"

"No, I do know. I feel a great vast nothingness where feelings about my mom used to exist. That sounds weird because it is weird, but it's also true. I feel like in another world in the multiverse, I'm smashing tables and screaming into the void, but in this one? Nothing. It's like space. Empty. It's probably diagnosable, but for now it's liberating so let me have it without questioning it." *Liberating* tastes like strawberry yogurt, but not real yogurt, the stuff that comes in tubes. Hattie's mom once packed her an entire box of strawberry yogurt tubes in lieu of lunch in kindergarten, and she handed them out to the class and pretended it was her birthday. "Anyway, here . . ." She passes Calliope her phone with the wedding invitation email open. "All the deets."

"Bug! You did not mention that Hattie's mom married a piece of Ikea furniture! How did you overlook this?" Calliope starts typing. "Look! An *Ingo* is this super ugly pine table." She holds up the screen.

"Aw," says Bug. "Your new stepdad is so budget-priced." She barks with laughter. "Even better, he's . . . sixty-nine dollars."

"Sixty-nine!" Calliope howls. "That's too good."

"Ha," Hattie manages, but suddenly her heart has turned to osmium in her chest, and she can't catch her breath. *Stepdad.* It's not quite true that she feels *nothing*. Her feelings are all physical and nothing else, but the physical feelings are real. A very heavy heartbeat sends a wave of pain reverberating through her whole body that she feels in her teeth. "The only thing I cared about in this equation was Dad getting hurt and he's not hurt if he's all heart-eyes over Ms. Singh, so I'm over it. It's fine. I'm fine." She stands up, slinging her backpack over her shoulder. "And we're going to be late."

"No one says *fine* twice if they're actually fine," says Bug, hugging her, and Calliope blows her a kiss.

When Hattie opens her locker at lunchtime, Calliope has stuck a photo of a blond, bearded, Swedish-looking man with a penis drawn on his forehead, a printed-out picture of an Ingo table in the foreground. Across the top, she's written, *This Collage Sucks: Stepfather Edition.*

"Why a penis?" Hattie calls across the hall to where Calliope is fishing around for her lunch bag.

"Well, he's obvi a dickhead. If he wasn't, he would have, like, flown you out for the wedding or at least Zoomed with you so you could know who he was before he married your mom. Do you like it? I seriously don't know how you collage so much. All that cutting out! All that glue! I have a cramp in my hand in a part I didn't even know existed, and it took all of my spare period and it's a mess. I'm starting to truly respect your work, Hannah Höch. Lunch outside in the choking remnants of fresh air?" Calliope slams her locker with a bang.

"Who's Hannah Höch?"

"What? You don't know? Only the most famous collage artist ever."

"Did you just look that up, Twinkle SmartyPants?"

"Duh, yeah. So, lunch?"

"Affirmative." Hattie leaves the art taped to the inside of her locker, slamming it shut. "Stepfather," she murmurs experimentally, but it still feels wrong and terrible in her mouth, like the time she was three and reached into the back of the attic closet where they stored clothes they didn't wear often—ski stuff and her mom's wedding dress—and found a mothball and, thinking it was a marshmallow, pressed it against her tongue.

All day, Hattie is aware of Presley. She's never felt this before: so *aware* of another person, alive and existing and breathing the same air.

Where he is in the building.

Whether or not he's looking at her.

How often he smiles when their eyes meet.

He's watching her, too.

She feels *observed*.

She doesn't take *The Shark Club* out of her bag once all day, not even when Mr. Stevens leaves the room to walk a student to the principal's office and forgets to come back. She stares out the window at Mount Southerton, where they walked and talked. She looks at her hand and thinks about how he squeezed it. She presses her fingers to the freckles on her cheek. *Cassiopeia*. She looks at his profile, her eyes tracing his scar again and again. *Look at me*, she thinks, and he does, and their eyes meet and it feels seismic, like the earth will crack open from the intensity.

"What are you doing?" Bug says, amused.

"I'm just thinking," says Hattie, but before she can even try to explain, Leo gets up and draws a giant penis on the board, complete with hair, and they're both too distracted to remember what they were talking about.

HATTIE

Hattie can hardly look at Ms. Singh, knowing what she knows, which is nothing, but also something. On Sunday, over tacos, she'd tried coming right out and asking.

"Dad," she'd said, trying to sound casual. "Are you hooking up with Ms. Singh?"

He'd totally given himself away by saying, "Who . . . *Ana?*" and then pretending to choke on a shrimp, going so far as to mime self-Heimliching over the back of the chair.

"First-aid jokes are rarely funny, Dad. Plus, I would have saved you if you needed saving." She stole the last shrimp from his plate. "For your own safety."

Then Elijah's face appeared over the kitchen island, and she'd pretended to have a headache so she could go lie down, which then turned into the truth: a headache and a deep, dreamless nap and next thing she knew, her dad was hoisting his suitcase into his smart car and waving from the driveway. He was going to a psychology convention in San Francisco. He was gone before Hattie even had time to make a dumb joke about psychologists—*How many psychologists does it take to change a lightbulb?*—and she still didn't know if her dad and Ms. Singh hooked up and still didn't really want to know.

After he left, she walked over and stared at the photo on the fridge, trying to see something in her mom's face that wasn't there. The air in the house felt different when he wasn't home. Air-conditioned and still and lifeless.

"They can't change the lightbulb, they can only ask it to consider if it wants to change or if it's getting something out of the darkness," she said out loud. If her dad had been there, he would've laughed, but her mom's face remained unchanged and the toddler version of herself was still crying. She took the photo off the fridge and put it in the cutlery drawer. Then she went to her room, found a photo of herself and her dad, printed it out, and stuck it on the fridge over the discolored square.

"Live in the present," she said to her dad's smiling face. "Let go. You're free." She waved her hands in the air like she was casting a spell. "You're allowed to be happy."

In the new photo, she's wearing the same dress her mom wore in the original. She's looking away from the camera. She's laughing. Her dad is making bunny ears behind her head and he's laughing, too. They're happy without her. The two of them, Hattie and her dad: They're a complete family. They're enough. They're *happy*, or at least, getting closer to happy every day.

"I had a chance to read your essays this weekend!" Ms. Singh is saying, "And I'm both surprised and not surprised by what a large crop of eggplants there are in the room! It's okay, you can laugh, I should have known! My bad." She laughs, as though giving them all permission to laugh, but only a few people do and it's awkward. Hattie feels an empathetic cringe, then laughs too loud and too late. Ms. Singh makes grateful eye contact and Hattie's face burns.

"I've paired you all up according to your vegetables, and your task will be to take a scene from *Romeo and Juliet* and change it up. You can do that by setting it in modern times or making it queer"—Hattie nudges Bug so hard with her elbow that Bug lets out a muffled shout—"or by changing the outcome or . . . Surprise me! I want you to take the essence of R and J, the driving force of a love that sweeps in and changes everything, and turn it into something that's both new and timeless. If that's too much of an ask, then . . ." She pauses, and Hattie can practically hear her thinking, *The teacher's eyes twinkled! She was in on the joke! She was beloved by her students!* "Make it funny. Comedy is a valid form of theater, after all." The class watches her as she takes a piece of paper out of her notebook with a flourish. "The list!" She pins it to the board. No one moves. "Go see who you're paired with," she prompts, and only then do people shuffle forward.

Hattie and Bug stay seated until the crowd has fallen away. Hattie makes eye contact with Presley, and he winks. Then he points to himself. Then he points to her. Her heart snaps, cracks, pops like cereal in milk. What is wrong with her? She coughs, blushes, smiles.

Calliope whoops from the list. "I got *you*, Bug!"

"There you go," says Hattie, breaking her gaze away from Presley's. "You can do *Juliet and Juliet*, after all. Dreams do come true, Rainbow Dash."

Bug taps Hattie's name on the list, attached to Presley's. "But you and Priscilla shall be the love story of the century! Plush-lip emoji!"

"I don't think that's an actual emoji."

Bug sketches something quickly on a piece of paper, holds it up. It's Hattie, smiling, her lips in a pucker.

"Oh, stop it. Also, how are you so good at that?"

"I practice."

Hattie glances at Presley's seat, but he's not there. She looks around. He's standing behind her. He grins. "Juliet? I'm Romeo." He bows. She giggles, stopping abruptly when Ms. Singh knocks on her desk.

"Sit, please! You will have a few classes to work with your partners and figure out your scenes, which we will start performing for each other after midterm break. For now . . ." With a flourish, Ms. Singh presses play on a video of different takes on *Romeo and Juliet* and the class settles in to watch, still muttering to each other. Presley reaches out and touches Hattie's shoulder, once, then retreats, to his corner seat. She reaches up and presses the place where his fingers were. While the video plays, she watches Presley watching the video, then she watches Ms. Singh, texting on her phone.

Texting and smiling.

Smiling and texting.

It's only when they're leaving the classroom, Hattie sees that behind Ms. Singh's desk, under her coat, there's a suitcase, a carry-on bag sitting on top. She stops in her tracks.

"Hattie?" says Ms. Singh. "Do you need something?"

Are you going to San Francisco to meet my dad at the conference? Hattie wants to ask, but she lets the question die on her tongue and shakes her head instead. Her dad is coming home on Friday. If Ms. Singh is gone for the rest of the week, she'll know. "Um, have a great time," says Hattie. "Wherever you're going. If you're . . . you know, going somewhere." She points at the suitcase.

"Oh!" says Ms. Singh. "Yes, I . . . Thanks, Hattie."

Hattie shrugs. She doesn't really mean it, but she wants to, which is close enough.

PRESLEY

In art class, Presley makes Hattie an invitation using a series of stick figures in seven boxes. It's Hattie and him.

Or maybe it's Jada and Topher.

He hates that book so much, but she loves that book so much, and these two diametrically opposed forces somehow equal him wanting to . . . needing to . . . Well, he doesn't want to blur the lines, but he thinks blurring the lines might make Hattie happy. It's pretty simple, wanting to make her happy. He wants her to feel seen and known, and he knows she loves *The Shark Club*, and it shouldn't matter that his feelings about it are so big and complicated and . . . negative. She doesn't know anything about that. And he can do this for her. He wants to.

Sort of.

He takes a pic of himself and one of Hattie and he prints them a whole bunch of times and then cuts out the faces and glues them onto the empty ovals of the stick figures' heads. He's so engrossed that he doesn't notice the time passing and barely finishes before the bell rings.

On top, he writes the title: *The Seven Dates.* Then he adds two boxes. Check one: Yes ☐ No ☐

In the first image, the stick figures are skating. In the second, they're eating ice cream. In the third: a roller coaster, their arms in the air. The fourth one features five different kinds of pie. In the fifth, bike riding on a beach. In the sixth, a picnic in the moonlight under towering trees. In the seventh, they're stepping off the side of a boat, into the water, into the cage. It was art imitating life imitating art, or something like that.

His heart is beating fast when he slides the paper into a brown envelope at work and asks Bethanne to leave it for Hattie. It feels like both the right thing to do and the wrong thing to do. He doesn't know which. He'd ask Mac if Mac was here, but Mac isn't here.

You're the one with the big problem, bromigo. To me, it's just a book.

"It's not just a book!"

"What?" says Bethanne, and Presley blinks. He'd got disoriented. He'd tripped out of his reality and into one where he could debate with Mac whether *The Shark Club* was the problem or not, whether he could blame *The Shark Club*. He does. He blames the stupid book for everything. He shivers.

"Can you give this to Hattie?" he repeats.

"No problem," says Bethanne. "I'll put it on the pile of filing that she'll never see because she never does it." She smiles sweetly. "How are you liking the job?"

"Oh, it's good. Yeah, thanks," says Presley. He wants to snatch the envelope back but is also a little too scared of Bethanne to try. His face is so hot he's sure she can tell what's in the envelope, how much of a dork he really is.

"I saw your Wikipedia entry," she says. "You've had a real interesting life, hon."

"Oh . . . Have I?" says Presley. "I guess I have. Um, thanks." He leaves before she can say anything more.

"I never liked that Chloe Bean!" she calls after him. "She looks mean!"

He holds up his hand to his ear like he didn't hear her and shrugs, then waves, stumbling a little on the stairs in his rush to get away before she says anything else.

HATTIE

Hattie is looking down at the ice where Presley spins, then spins more, faster and faster. She doesn't understand how he doesn't fall, how he can spin so fast, how his legs look like rubber, bent and contorted yet still beautiful.

The pool has reopened, so the place is busy, or as busy as it gets. Kids need change and goggles. They need a towel or they found a towel. Their parents want to sign up for lessons. Hattie has to keep looking away from the ice. When she looks back, Presley is leading the kids around an obstacle course of traffic cones.

She's walking a mom of seven through a lesson schedule for all her kids when the phone rings. It's Bethanne.

"Don't forget to do the filing," she says, in a singsong voice. "I know you love filing. Look at the pile of filing. Just look at it. Filing! So much filing!"

"Bethanne, it's super busy. Stop repeating the word *filing*. It's weird. And I don't think I'll have time." Hattie hangs up, but she glances at the pile, and she sees it: a big envelope with her name on it. She can tell without opening it that the envelope is from Presley. She recognizes the blocky writing from the *Help!* above the whale on the back of the stall door in the men's room.

She's almost afraid to touch it.

When the mom has finally gathered up her kids and left, Hattie picks the envelope. Puts it down. Picks up her phone.

Puts it down. Picks up the envelope. She runs her finger around the edge of it, around and around. The corners are sharp. She sniffs it, not caring how weird that is. It smells like paper and memories of mail, the exciting kind of mail: brown paper packages from distant grandparents or books ordered from England that she couldn't wait for the US release date to read.

Finally, she tears it open and pulls out a single sheet of paper. She looks at it carefully, letting the phone ring without picking it up. She barely takes her eyes off it to give someone a locker code, to accept a swimming pass, to push a brochure across the counter about skate rentals, to give Mr. Stanopolous change for the coffee machine.

It's the sweetest and best thing she's ever seen, but it's not the first time she's seen it.

This is a dream. She's asleep and this is a dream. She's dreamed her way into her favorite book. Or maybe she's slipped between worlds, but the one she's entered is fiction. It can't be real. It's too *implausible*. "Bullshit," she says, but she doesn't believe it. She slides her minty-tasting tongue against her teeth. "Bullshit," she repeats, drawing it out.

But . . .

She carefully examines each frame, tracing the stick figures with her finger, feeling the shallow divots made by his pen, the cut edges of the photos he used of their faces.

It's the same one that Topher made for Jada.

She grabs a piece of paper and using a sharpie writes *YES* in big letters and holds it up against the glass.

"It's an invitation to a goddamn musical montage, Lou," she tells Bethanne's plant. "And everyone knows that every good YA adaptation has at least one musical montage."

Rusty knocks on the counter, passing. "You know that talking to yourself is the first sign of dementia," he says. "Want me to make you a tag with your name and address on it in case you wander away and get lost?"

"I'm seventeen," says Hattie. "I think it's low risk."

"On the plus side, dementia isn't the worst thing. You don't know what you don't know," he says. "Sounds okay to me! I mean, think about it. Would you rather die knowing you'd forgotten everything or die not even understanding anymore what death is all about?"

"No one is dying in this scenario," she says. "And you shouldn't eavesdrop on private convos. Rude."

"Private conversations between you and . . . your plant?"

"It's *Bethanne's* plant," she says, and is relieved when the phone rings and she can answer it and escape.

At the end of her shift, Hattie shuts off the computer and flips the phones to the recording that says they're closed. She's aware of her breathing, of her sweaty palms, of how her breath smells. She takes a piece of gum from Bethanne's stash. It's fruity, not her favorite, but better than stale breath.

Finally, footsteps on the stairs from the rink and there he is. Presley Jablowski. She says his name so she can taste it, even though he can't hear her from that far away. He looks . . . shy. Adorably shy. He still has his skates on. His hair is damp. She wants to touch him. She wants to wrap herself around him. She doesn't understand all that she wants; it feels bigger than *wanting*. She knows she's smiling too widely, that the smile is pouring out of her, unchecked, like a spotlight.

"Hi," she calls.

"Hi." He smiles back, coming closer. Their smiles illuminate the entire space, the world, everything. It's corny. They're corny. This is real.

"I have to lock the doors." She stands too fast, sees stars, then goes and drops the locks into place, flicking off the entrance lights, and then they are alone in the low-lit lobby, her heart beating so hard she's sure he can see it, even in the half-dark. His eyes bore into hers, *seeing* her.

"Hi," she says again, helpless to this whole thing.

PRESLEY

When Presley took the job, Bethanne told him he was free to use the gym and the rink, if it wasn't in use. "You know, for whatever," she'd said.

This is *whatever*, he thinks.

It's so much better than the *whatever* he'd imagined when she'd said it.

"Ready?" he says. Hattie is wearing a sundress he hasn't seen before, this one light green. He glances at her feet, white sneakers and socks. Up close, he can see that the fabric of the dress has a pattern of tiny smiling people, drawn in black.

Stick figures.

"Ready for what?"

"Your first skating lesson. You said yes, right?"

"Now?"

"Unless you have something else you'd rather do."

"I definitely don't." She turns on the computer again and taps the keys, and music starts pouring from the speakers. It's muffled from here, but he's pretty sure it's Taylor Swift.

HATTIE

Presley finds Hattie some skates in the rental area. "Size nine?" he calls.

"How did you know?" she calls back.

"I'm great at guessing people's skate size. It's my superpower. One day, I'll use it to save the world."

"From ill-fitting shoes?" She laughs. She slips off her sneakers, flexes her toes.

Presley reappears with skates and a huge puffy jacket. "From the lost and found," he says. "They won't come back for it tonight."

The jacket is yellow because that's how the universe works, and the universe wants her to think about her mother so she does, then wishes she didn't have to think about her all the time. She isn't free. She was wrong about that. She puts the jacket on. "Do I look ridiculous?" She knows she looks exactly like her mom and it's a strange feeling, another slip through layers of time and place.

Presley's dark eyes take her in. "Not even a little ridiculous," he says. "You make that coat look better than it knew it could look. You could sell that coat. You look perfect." He ducks his head. "Um, was that too much?"

"Yes. No one looks perfect in a puffy coat, and a *yellow* puffy coat is a whole other level. There's a reason why no one claimed this coat. Also, it weirdly smells like horses. Help me with these?"

"What do horses smell like?" He laces the skates for her, pulling them tight around her ankles. She can feel his breath on her legs, and it makes her skin tingle. She closes her eyes, remembering how Coach Kat kneeled in front of her and showed her how to thread the laces around the hooks. "So you never have to wait for your mom to help again," she'd said.

"Um, horses smell . . . warm. Like fur and hay. You've never smelled a horse? Sad. You, a professional sniffer of hair, are really missing out." She watches him fumbling her laces. "I *can* do it myself. I'm not totally helpless."

"I've tied hundreds of skate laces in my life. Maybe thousands. I'm an expert. You can't do it nearly as well as I can, guaranteed."

"Wow, that's two major life skills! Size-guessing *and* skate lacing."

"You'll want to hitch your wagon to this shooting star." He points at himself and winks. Then he laughs, shaking his head. "Pretend I didn't do that. Embarrassing myself is actually my third specialty and I'm really, really great at it. Just waiting for my Most Embarrassing Person Alive world record certificate to arrive in the mail."

"If your theory is right and ghosts are real and not just *DSM-5* symptoms, you'll probably also be the most embarrassing person dead."

"Hardy-har-har."

"I haven't skated since kindergarten," says Hattie. "You have no idea what embarrassing is until you see me try. I'm going to fall on my ass one million times, no exaggeration. You should have an ambulance on stand-by."

"I'll catch you," he says, looking into her eyes in a way that makes her shiver.

She swallows. "Thanks. I'm heavier than I look."

"Seriously, you won't fall. I'm a great coach, or so Presley Jr. says, and she's got shockingly high standards."

He pulls Hattie to her feet and leads her to the gate. She takes a deep breath of refrigerated air—such a *specific* smell, such a rush of memories—and steps out onto the ice for the first time since she was six.

Presley skates slowly in a circle, shaking out his legs, smiling at her. He's even cuter on the ice, more confident. He moves differently, stands straighter, looks happier. He does a few quick fancy steps.

"Show-off," she says, holding tight to the boards, her body bent awkwardly to lower her center of gravity.

"Oh, you're impressed? Well, check *this* out." He skates away fast, then jumps, his legs making the sound of a whip through the air, his blades carving sure lines on the gleaming surface.

"What's a stronger word than *show-off*?" She wavers, then falls in slow motion, her hands landing first. "Ouch. Why is it so slippery? And cold?"

He skates over to her, pulls her up, supports her under her arms. The soundtrack starts the next song. He's smiling.

"Don't laugh at me!"

"I'm definitely not laughing at you."

She smiles back. Her cheeks hurt. She's so aware of his hands. His hands, his hands, his hands.

This is our musical montage, Hattie thinks. She's living it. It's happening. She can't believe it. No one gets this, not in real life, yet here they are, his hands strong and certain, moving her around the ice like a puppet. She's playing the part of herself in a movie that's better than her actual life. The song that's playing is her first ever favorite song, the song she sang in the only talent show she was ever in.

The one when she played her mom's blue guitar.

The song is "Love Story."

"Did anyone ever tell you that you look a little like Taylor Swift?"

"Yes, literally everyone. My dad used to call me mini-Tay." She closes her eyes remembering, nearly falling over.

"You're prettier."

"As if, but thanks." She's knock-kneed, her ankles collapsing inward. "Taylor Swift would never let her hair do this." She points to her head, her mop of unruly wavy curls.

"Straighten!"

"My hair?"

"What? No, your ankles, silly." He reaches out and grab both of her hands in his, and he skates backward, pulling her along, watching her feet. She hadn't known you could skate *gently*, but he's doing it so it must be possible.

"Slow down!" She's wobbling, slipping.

"I'm barely even moving! Here . . ." He turns around. "Put your hands on my hips."

"Oh, sure, now you're making me touch your butt."

"Those are my hips, perv."

She grabs him, scared she's going to pull his pants down when she falls. But she doesn't fall. She's doing it: skating. Or sort of skating, sort of stepping. He swoops around so he's beside her. "Stop moving so fast! You're making me dizzy!"

He spins around and around, and they're both laughing so hard that she does fall and so he falls beside her, and they sit on the ice, leaning on each other, laughing helplessly until the song ends.

"The secret," he says, "is to keep your eyes focused on something that's not moving."

"Like I could *spin*! I can barely stand!"

The next song starts. He gets to his feet, holds out his hand. "Total Eclipse of the Heart" blasts around them, too loud in the echoing empty space. When she's standing, he guides her to the boards and then he holds up his finger.

"This is going to be really rough. Don't judge."

He takes a breath, shakes out his arms, skates to get into position, and she's aware of how she used to think skating wasn't a real sport and hates her former self for being such an asshole. His athleticism is unmistakable. It feels *intimate*: the sound of his breathing and the *oof* when he hits the ice, that puff of breath. At the end, he swoops low in a bow, and she raises her hands above her head.

"Standing ovation!" She claps and claps. "Wild applause!" She whistles. "The crowd goes wild! Ten from the California judge!"

PRESLEY

Presley catches his breath, skates slowly back to her, shaking his legs out in turn, trying to stave off the inevitable cramps. "What's my prize?"

He's sweating. He tries to catch his breath without looking like he's struggling and then gives up, bending at the waist, taking long pulls of air. He's still not back in shape, not even close. "Aren't your legs cold? We should stop. Not because I'm dying right now." His lungs are searing with pain, his legs trembling slightly.

"As if I can even feel my legs. Legs are overrated. Teach me something else first."

He shows her how to skate backward and how to do a spin, just like how he teaches the little kids, and when she falls over, he plucks her up and then he steps toward her and pulls her into his arms. They stand there, staring at each other's eyes, and it's not even a little awkward. Time freezes. Then the music changes to "Do You Know the Way to San Jose."

"I made a playlist," she says, and he can feel each word touching his lips, small puffs of air. "I know it's kind of cringey." She glides forward a little and hides her face in his shoulder.

"We have to do a lot more things with a lot better music playing so you can add to it," he says. "It could be so much better. We'll make it so much better."

HATTIE

Hattie can feel every beat of Presley's heart, *fast fast slow fast slow fast fast*, like Morse code.

"This is good," she says, her voice muffled by his jacket.

"This *is* good," he agrees. "But this is the worst song in the entire universe."

"I kind of like it now," she says.

PRESLEY

"Hattie," says Presley.

"Presley."

They look at each other, eyes locking and holding. Something shifts and changes in the air, something visible, a swathe of colors, a glimmer of light.

Then he leans slightly closer, and she leans slightly closer, and it *happens*. They're kissing. For a minute, an hour, forever, their lips, tongues, and hands explore, gently, then more urgently.

He touches her and touches her and touches her. His hands move under her jacket, finding skin, the shock of it is an almost unbearable ecstasy.

Her hands reach for his face, soft and cool against his burning cheeks.

The soundtrack loops back to the beginning.

HATTIE

Every part of Hattie responds to the kiss.

She *wants* this.

There are parts of her that she'd never thought about before that want this.

There's something ancient and biological and evolutionary that wants this.

Her body curves into his, finding the ways they fit together. She kisses him back.

The kiss is a wave that's pulling her under, a rip current that she's allowing to take her as far as it wants out to sea. Her legs are shaking. She can't breathe, but she doesn't care that she can't breathe because this is something different from breathing and better.

They kiss and kiss, and his hands move, and her hands move like they know where they're going, like she knows what she's doing, and she would have thought she wouldn't, but she does.

She's never been so aware of her body and aware of his body, the way he's pressing against her . . .

She's not scared.

She's nothing but the hunger that's cracked open inside her. Everything is different, changed, and can't ever be unchanged: her organs, her blood, her cells. She *wants*.

Biology wins, overrides everything.

She's pressing back so hard against him that if their cells were to push apart, even slightly, the two of them would merge, every part of her finding space in the gaps between every part of him until they're one person.

They keep kissing.

Then . . . suddenly,

a pause that lets her think too much,

then the pushing of his tongue against hers,

his hand touches her breast . . . And there's practically a screeching of brakes she can hear and feel.

A split second.

An I'm-not-ready feeling that crashes through her.

Like stepping off something high and landing too hard.

She feels *jarred*.

She feels disoriented.

She's feels too much, and it isn't good anymore, it's terrifying, or it would be if she could articulate what it was, but she gets only fight-or-flight, specifically *flight*.

Adapt!

Adapt!

But she can't, it's too late. She's thought it. She's over-thought it. Her brain is spinning, out of control.

She wants . . .

She doesn't want . . .

She doesn't know what she wants.

If she stays here, she won't be able to stay in her skin, that's how it feels, like something is pulling her out of herself, re-arranging her body so it's inside out and she's all heartbeat and adrenalin and a rush of cold sweat and she manages to pull away, to skate back, drops her arms away from his body, one hand reaching up to wipe her mouth.

"What?" he says. "Wait, are you okay?" He looks dazed. "Was that . . . I thought . . . What's wrong?"

"It's not you," she tries. "I'm just . . ." She shakes her head, then nods, then tries to smile, but she's also crying. She doesn't know what's happening, it's like she's feeling every emotion, all at once.

Hattie's mouth isn't working. Her voice won't come out. Absurdly, she wonders if he swallowed it, swallowed all the parts of her that could talk. She puts her hand up, touches her lips.

"Oh my god. I thought you wanted . . . I'm sorry, that's a shitty thing to say. I'm sorry. I should have asked before if it was okay. What can I do?" He reaches for her shoulders, her arms, her hands, like he's trying to hold her in the moment, pull her back into the feeling.

She totters away, her legs and feet now frozen and numb, gets to the gate, and wobbles again when her blades hit ground that feels too solid and too still after the ice. Every part of her feels strange. Too heavy and too light, empty and full. She can't explain what she's feeling. She knows this is unfair; she has to say *something*.

She likes him! She liked kissing him!

She's gulping at air.

Hyperventilating.

Adapt.

"Shit." She tears at the skate laces. None of this makes sense. This isn't in the musical montage. She's ruining it. She's ruining everything. "I'm sorry," she mutters. "Sorry, sorry, sorry." She wants to get into Applejack and drive. She wants to park and take out *The Shark Club* and read until her heart stops racing. She wants to hit pause.

"Hattie? I don't want to have messed this up. You're freaking me out. Tell me what I can do."

She wipes her nose on the sleeve of the stranger's horse-smelling puffy jacket, shaking her head. *Be normal!* She shoves her feet into her sneakers, not bothering to unlace them. "It's fine." Her voice is crackly, like tissue paper being consumed by a flame. It comes out unsubstantial like that, thin and wispy. "I'm being weird." She shakes her head. Nods. "I warned you. I'm weird. I promise it's not you, it's me."

He looks so worried. She likes him so much.

She leans over and kisses him on the cheek, her lips brushing his stubble and his scar, and it makes her knees feel weak. She wants to press herself against him again. She wants to lie down and pull him on top of her, feel his weight pinning her to the earth. The instinct is so strong, it's like being in a rip. *Swim to the side*, she thinks. Or is it *Let the current take you?* Either way, she's not ready. In another world, yes, but not this one, not right now.

"Hattie?"

"I'm not *upset*. I know I look . . . This was really fun. I'm okay. I can't . . ." She waves her hands. "I'll see you tomorrow at school, okay?"

"Um, okay. But, Hattie, can we just . . . talk about it, please. I really like you. I feel like this is . . . not good."

"It's good. This is good." She grabs her backpack and half-walks, half-runs to the exit. Fight or flight. *What would Jada do?* She turns around and flips him off, her heart in her throat—he did the Seven Dates, so he *must* know that's how Jada communicates, he has to be able to interpret this. But she doesn't know how to be *Jada*. And he isn't Topher. She curls her hand into a fist. He's brought *The Shark Club* into this, but now it feels like pressure, like it has to be *love*, like it's already written or something and she feels like . . . She has to . . . She doesn't want to be . . .

She doesn't know.

She doesn't know why she doesn't like this.

She likes him. She does!

She is so *confused*.

Then she's in the parking lot, unlocking the drivers' door of Applejack, climbing in, not starting the engine, just sitting there, waiting for her heart to stop racing, breathing in all her favorite things, all her mom's old things, the always-present smell of Mod Podge used to varnish the photos into place, the galaxy she's glued to the ceiling above her. She picks up the stuffed Fluttershy sitting on the dashboard and tucks it under her chin, inhaling the sleep-smell of it—she always slept with it when she was little—until she feels better, steadier, okay.

Through the windshield, she can see Presley walking in the opposite direction toward the cliff road, swinging his bag. She knows he's hurt or confused or both. She wants to undo it. She wants to explain, but how can she when she doesn't understand herself?

When he's out of sight, she starts the van with shaky hands and heads home.

> *"We need a code," says Topher. "If you don't want people at school to know we're together—which is weird, by the way—then we need a signal. Like if I'm suddenly thinking of you in art class and I want you to know, I'm going to tap my nose."*

"Tap your nose? Like you're knocking off the cocaine you were snorting at recess?"

"Yes, exactly like that."

"Okay, weirdo, you do you."

"So, what's your signal going to be?"

Jada thinks about it. She's lying on a blanket at the beach. The blanket is green and soft with one big hole in it that her foot keeps finding and tangling in. Above them, the stars are peering down, also curious about what she'll choose. Lazily, she lifts her hand and flips him off.

"You're going to flip me off to remind me that you like me?"

"Yeah, it's perfect, right? No one will ever guess." She leans up onto her elbows and then she's on him, straddling him, lowering her face to his, and he's laughing but also kissing her and he doesn't deserve his life to be this perfect and if it ends tomorrow, he won't mind, because this.

He kisses her back. And kisses her and kisses her and kisses her. And the kiss takes both of them somewhere else, underwater to a coral reef alive with fish, darting in schools like rainbows all around them, and it's the corniest image in the world and also the most real and they're in it, they're not breathing, they're letting the magic drown them instead.

It's so easy in the book. No one is panicking or running away. Hattie's mad at herself for making it complicated. She's mad at herself for feeling swept up in a current and even more mad for being terrified of drowning. She shouldn't be afraid of drowning. There's one thing she understands well, and it's what drowning feels like. She's never drowned. Obviously. But she's looked on the internet until she's found people who have, people who almost did, people who survived it. She knows what happens. The way people can't breathe for about eighty-seven seconds before they inhale, whether it's safe to or not. She thinks about that eighty-seven seconds a lot. She also knows that after breathing underwater, you lose consciousness, but right before you do, lots of people report feeling euphoria. People say they hear singing. Just like in *The Shark Club.*

She hopes Elijah heard singing. The singing feels important. Stupid, but important.

Anyway, you can't drown in a *feeling*, so she doesn't even know why she's thinking about it, except Elijah and *The Shark Club* and Presley and his Seven Dates comic and what she's feeling . . . It somehow all adds up together to be *drowning.* Her, underwater, unable to breathe.

She smooths out the Seven Dates paper and then folds it and tucks it into the back of her red Moleskine notebook.

"Well, shit," she says out loud, and her voice is too loud in the house without her dad there. The air feels different, too: too cool and too still. She picks up her phone, texts him.

Hattie: *You still up?*

Dad: *I sure am. This hotel is amazing. This is a hotel room for royalty.*

He attaches a photo of himself, wearing the *Fearless* T-shirt and his pajama pants. The room has two huge beds and a wall of windows, the city illuminated and alive behind him. She can see the Golden Gate Bridge, traffic like tiny fireflies humming in both directions.

HATTIE:
Wow, this is what happens when
you keynote, Big Guy. You're a star
in your field. In the sky! A shooting
star!

DAD:
We'll see. I might still forget my speech
and pass out at the podium and have to be
airlifted home where I'll change my name to
Mike Michaels and resume an alternate life as
a professional golfer to avoid ever speaking
of it again. Did you have a good day?

HATTIE:
I did. Yes. It was good. Are you
having a good day? Do you even
know how to play golf?

DAD:
I don't, but that's why it's a great disguise.
My day on the Taylor scale is definitely The
Man. There was a fruit basket! I ate it already.
Delicious. Rate your day?

HATTIE:
Jump Then Fall. I tried skating.
I'm not cut out for ice.

Hattie puts down her phone and spins it on the counter.

DAD:
You've always preferred your water at a
perfect 80 degrees.

HATTIE:
True fact. Dad, can I ask you
something?

DAD:
Anything.

HATTIE:
Are you alone?

Three dots appear in a bubble on her screen. Then they
stop. Then they appear. Then they vanish. This goes on for
long enough that Hattie has time to change into pajamas,
brush her teeth, climb into bed. Finally, to put him out of his
misery, she replies.

HATTIE:
Happy for you, Dad. Turning off
the phone to go to sleep now.
Untouchable!

The dots start again.

DAD:
Untouchable!

DAD:
Let's talk when I'm home, okay? I love you
more than you loved Shake It Off when you
were twelve.

HATTIE:
I love you, Dad . . . . but let's be
real, slightly less than Shake It Off.

PRESLEY

When Presley gets home, his mum and Ellie are sitting on the outdoor sofas. Ellie is petting the goat.

"Seriously?" says Presley. "That goat is a pest. Don't encourage him."

"What are you talking about?" says Ellie. "This goat is our pet. He's lovely. Look at him! He's an old soul. His name is Howard. Say hello to Presley, Howard."

"We have a pet goat named Howard? Maybe you should start writing a newsletter, keep me up to date." Presley doesn't know if he's happy or sad or thrilled or devastated or ecstatic or broken. The way she kissed him. The way he felt. The way he kissed her. The way their bodies fit.

"Honestly, Pres." His mum laughs. "How do you live here and not know anything that's going on?"

"I genuinely don't know." He sits down in the small chair, suddenly dizzy, puts his feet on the arm of the sofa where his mum is lying. He wonders if he ever knew what was going on. Ever. He definitely doesn't know what just went on tonight with Hattie. He closes his eyes against the spinning stars in the bottomless sky, trying to stop the feeling that he's falling upward.

What is the opposite of the abyss? Heaven?

But he doesn't believe in that, obviously. If heaven was real, that's where Mac would be, and Mac's still here, a voice in his ear: *Just try to keep it together, Parsley. Shit is only as weird as you make it and you're making it WEIRD.*

Maybe it's just that the abyss is all around—up, down, sideways—threatening to pull him in from unexpected angles. He clears his throat. "Do we have any other pets I should know about?"

"Just the one," says Ellie. "But we're thinking of getting some miniature horses. So where were you?"

"Miniature *horses*? Sure. Of course. I hear they smell . . . good." He smiles because he can't help it, opens his eyes, stares up at the stars until they start popping through more and more, poking their dot-to-dot pictures into the velvet darkness. "I was with Hattie. Skating. You'll like her, Mum." He laughs, then stops, stifling the laugh because *is* it funny? He still isn't sure if it is or if it's terrible or if it's neither, just an uncomfortable coincidence. "She's a *Shark Club* superfan." Haltingly, he tells them about her, leaving out the more personal details, leaving out how it ended, leaving out the *kiss*.

"Superfans make me nervous," his mum says mildly.

His heart thuds. "Nervous?" He's mad. Why is he mad? Of course superfans make her nervous. Stuff happens. People go too far. But . . . "Hattie makes you nervous? You've never even met her. You've literally never even heard of her!"

"I didn't say anything about her, sweetheart. I'm sure she's lovely."

"Whatever."

"Oh, it's *whatever*!" She laughs. "You're such an American teen now. Like a sitcom."

"Ha-ha," he says. "Hilarious."

"Pres," says Ellie. "What's she like?"

Presley shakes his head. "She's . . . funny. She's nice. She's pretty? I don't know. I'm just getting to know her. I just like her, that's all. I want to *like* her without it being about the stupid book. Is that so wrong?"

"No one said it was, Presley." His mum sounds worried, and he hates that she sounds worried, and he hates that he's going off about her book, and he hates everything that's happened after the kiss. "I'm sure she's a lovely girl."

"She has good taste in books!" Ellie adds.

Presley rolls his eyes. He wants to shout or scream or something. Run, maybe. Or punch something. He grits his teeth, tries to reset. He doesn't want to be a person who wants to hit anything. Ever. His heart is beating too hard, too fast. "Can we talk about something else?"

"It might be a *good* thing, love," his mum continues, like he hasn't spoken. "If she loves Topher, then of course she'll love you. He has so many of your qualities: your stick figures, your sense of humor, your kindness, your way of speaking. How could that be bad?"

"God, Mum. She doesn't *love* Topher. Or me! I just met her. Can we just . . . not? Can we leave it?" In the silence, he stares at the goat, who blinks at him slowly, like he knows something. Or she. Whatever. He doesn't know how you can tell with goats, and he's not going to look closer. "That goat smells terrible," he says, and his mum and Ellie laugh, even though it wasn't even slightly funny, and the subject moves on to the building of the big house and the plans and the architect and a mistake in the size of the upstairs bathroom and he tunes out, letting his mind wander. Topher *is* a little like him, which is weird because when his mum wrote the book, he was just a kid. Was he always the way he is? Besides, Topher is as much like Mac as he is like Presley. He has Mac's love of hockey, his weird laugh, his love for grilled cheese sandwiches, burnt on the outside and dripping with American cheese on the inside.

He hates that Hattie loves that goddamn book, but maybe he can make that add up in his head to something okay. Something better. She likes *him*. She likes him without knowing she likes him. It takes him a second to realize he feels jealous, kind of. Jealous that she might love *Topher*.

Presley's head is buzzing with static, the numbness running in channels down his cheeks. He presses them with his hands. "I'm going to bed," he says.

"I love you to the moon, kiddo." His mum stands, giving him a quick hug. His face is lost in the cloud of her hair. It smells like perfume. It smells like peaches.

"Goodnight, honey," says Ellie.

Presley lets the door slam behind him.

He feels sick from the headache, from the book, from the wave of anger, from everything he doesn't understand.

Hattie *knows* he isn't Topher.

But he made a huge mistake by playing into it.

That was so stupid.

But maybe he knew. Maybe he subconsciously thought . . . she would like him better if she thought he was like Topher. She hasn't seen him seize yet, but it's going to happen. It can't *not* happen. And then she's going to see him for what he is: Broken. A cheap, broken replica of a character she's in love with.

He swallows his pills. He wants to fall asleep and to make this day be over. This wonderful, terrible day. This best, worst day of his life.

I'm actually pretty sure Topher is 80 percent me and only, like 20 percent you, says Mac, from somewhere behind the clothes shelf, but when Presley drags himself up onto his elbows to look, there's nothing there at all. He falls back onto his pillow and sleep crashes over him like a wave, pulling him out of consciousness and into the relief of the tarry abyss.

24 HOURS AND
6 MINUTES,
EXACTLY.

HATTIE

"What's going on with you today?" Bug slips into her seat next to Hattie's. "No one is this happy about English, ever. *You* are definitely never this happy about English. Or anything, for that matter. Spill the tea."

"Who said I was happy?"

"You are. I can tell. I have a sixth sense. It's a gift. My grandmother was a psychic, you know."

"Well, then ask her." Hattie is smiling. She's smiling too much. She looks across the room, and Presley smiles back at her. A half-smile. An uncertain smile. She wants him to know it's okay. She smiles wider.

"Was," says Bug. "She's dead, you heartless monster. Also, I've literally never seen you smile like that. Something is going on. Something happened."

"You're imagining it," says Hattie. She feels her stomach cramp sharply. She's not sure she even knows what happened or if it was bad or good or both or if he understands why she freaked out or even if *she* understands why she freaked out.

"Why is your face doing that?"

"I'm thinking. I'm expressive. I can't help it."

"You can probably rule out a life of crime," says Bug. "You look one hundred percent guilty."

Hattie groans and drops her head to the desk. "I am! I mean, I'm not. I don't know what I am."

"That sounds like true love then," says Bug.

"True love is confusing and painful?"

"Exactly."

"Well, it's not love," says Hattie, definitively, but maybe it is. Maybe that's why she feels so sick. Or maybe she has food poisoning.

"The Tiny Toilet is . . . coming over here," says Bug, taking out her phone and staring at it intently.

And it's true, Presley is in front of her. He raises his eyebrows.

"What?" she says, smiling, smiling, smiling. She tries to stop.

"Um, I was thinking, we should talk?" he says. "I'd like to talk."

She nods. "I'd like to talk," she repeats.

He smiles, his eyes squinting at the corners in a way that makes her head feel light. "We both want to talk then. That's good. After school?"

"Sure. Yes. We both . . . we'll talk. We want to talk. I'll meet you in the parking lot." She's saying too many words, but she can't help it. She avoids looking at Bug, who she can tell is making a heart with her hands.

"Okay," Presley says, after a beat.

"Okay. *Are* you okay?"

"Yep." He smiles, a real smile, the scar pulling at one side of his mouth. His smile is like an answer. He puts a folded piece of paper on her desk, then goes back to his own. She unfolds it carefully. It's two stick figures, eating ice cream. Topher, but not Topher. She shakes her head. *Presley.*

"What is it?" says Bug in a singsong. "A love note? You have a phone! He could text you like every other normal human being. You two super-nerds were made for each other. This is the love story of our generation. Move over R and J."

"I don't think he's ever even asked for my number. That is a little weird, now that you mention it. But weird is good. It's better than normal. Normal is boring."

"Have you asked for *his* number?"

"No."

"Why not, you weirdo?"

"I don't know!"

But she does know: Topher never texted Jada because Jada was worried her phone would give her a brain tumor, a thing that actually hadn't occurred to Hattie before she read the book that she's low-key worried about now, too. There are so many ways bodies can fail to function: missed heartbeats, rogue cells, lungs full of water. She tries not to think about Elijah and so thinks about Elijah, who appears, hazily, on the other side of the window, staring at her.

"I love-hate this for you," says Bug. "I hate-love it." She pauses. "But for eff's sake, give him your number. And I mean this with nothing but supportive love, but you're at perilous risk of being *too* My Little Pony, you know?"

"Noted," says Hattie, pretending to write it down. "Solid advice. Thanks."

She slides down in her seat and opens *The Shark Club* but doesn't read it. Everything feels like too much. Too much Topher. Too much feeling. Too much . . . confusion.

PRESLEY

Presley is waiting for Hattie in the parking lot after school when a black Mercedes-Benz pulls up in a screeching of brakes, a cloud of dust. It parks practically on his feet, forcing him to step backward.

"What the fuck." He coughs. His eyes sting from the dust. "You dick."

His phone buzzes.

HENRY:
Sorry about that.

> **PRESLEY:**
> ?

> **PRESLEY:**
> NO way.

The doors of the Mercedes swing open, and Henry and Big Tee jump out, grinning, then they're beside him, hugging him awkwardly. "*Yes* way."

"Oh my god," says Presley. "Holy crap. What are you doing here?" Embarrassingly, he feels tears welling up in his eyes. He coughs again, both because his lungs are full of dust and to hide the fact he's crying.

"We took the ultimate test drive." Henry looks around. "It's uncomfortably hot here."

"It's Southern California during a heat wave," says Presley. He feels like he's dreaming. "What did you expect?"

"That's valid."

"Um, what are you *doing* here?"

"Epic Road Trip™." Big Tee does a dance, that mostly involves hip swivels. "I told you! This rite of passage has now been officially checked off the bucket list."

"You have a bucket list?"

"Duh. Everyone has a bucket list, even if it's not written down, even if it's just fantasies you think of as goals or dreams. It's all a bucket. It's all a list. Bucket lists are metaphorical, son."

"Um, okay. Right. Obviously. I'll take your word for it. This is . . . This is wow. This is a surprise." Then, worried he's being unfriendly, he punches each of them in the arm.

"Ouch, jeez. What was that for?"

"Surfer greeting," says Presley. "Trust me."

"You know, it's legal to put her into auto and let her drive herself in California. It's very progressive here or maybe it's just that everywhere else suffers from a failure of imagination." Henry stands up straighter. "It was necessary to come down to test the feature properly, and we could hardly come here without seeing you. You provided us with a destination. The self-driving feature is incredible, and it's not even at its full potential. Regulations keep it in check." He pats the car's roof. "It doesn't fly, which you'd think would be the case by now, but one day it won't even need a driver."

"It's rad," chimes in Big Tee. Henry raises his eyebrows. "What? I'm translating it to Presley's new lingo."

"Um, hey?" Hattie says, coming up behind Presley.

He grins. "It's you!"

"Yeah, it's me."

He can't believe Henry and Big Tee are here and he's so happy they are, but their timing is terrible. Mostly all he wants is to talk to Hattie, make sure everything is okay. But she wouldn't have come if it wasn't, right? He doesn't know. He wishes he could just look into her eyes and understand all of it, right away, but that's not how it works, or maybe it is, but only in unrealistic romance novels like *The Shark Club*, not in real life.

Chill the fuck out, Parsley. Just talk to her.

"Um, well, I . . . Hattie, this is Henry and Big Tee, my oldest friends who are here from Canada for a metaphorical bucket-list road trip. Big Tee and Henry, this is my . . . Um, Hattie."

Hattie raises her eyebrows, then nudges him with her hip, leaning against him briefly before pulling away. "Are you guys coming for ice cream? We were just . . ."

"Get in," says Henry. "Is there a Dairy Queen here? I prefer to eat ice cream from franchises where quality is assured and standardized between the US and Canada."

Hattie and Presley climb into the backseat and Henry says, "Dairy Queen," and the car heads out toward the highway, and Henry and Big Tee lean back with their eyes closed, arms folded behind their heads like they're starring in a commercial.

"Slay, you slayers," says Presley, and then he laughs. "Forget I said that. I don't know why I said that."

"Sure, Slayer," says Big Tee. "Slay on, you crazy diamond, just like Pink Floyd said."

"Oh, shut up," he says, cuffing his friend affectionately on the back of the head.

He glances at Hattie, puts his hand down, flat on the seat beside him. She hesitates, then puts her hand on his.

"Is this okay?" he whispers. "We can talk later or after or . . . I'm sorry, I didn't know they were coming."

She squeezes his hand. "It's good. I'm sorry about . . . what happened. It wasn't anything. I don't want you to worry. It's just me. I'm a little . . . weird. Honestly, I can't even explain myself to myself most of the time." She looks sad, like maybe if Henry and Big Tee weren't here, she'd cry.

"Forget it," he murmurs. "It really doesn't matter."

HATTIE

"So, you've known him for a long time, huh." Henry and Presley are getting ice cream at the counter. Hattie's sitting in a booth with Big Tee, the refrigerated air-conditioned air laced with something hospital-like, antiseptic. Big Tee is the tallest human she's ever met, taller even than Roberto, but as skinny as . . . She can't think of what. A flamingo maybe. A giraffe. A giraffe's heart weighs twenty-five pounds and is two feet tall. She thinks about telling him this. He looks like someone who would appreciate random information, but she bites her lip.

"We've been friends since kindergarten!" He raises his hands in the air, then pushes his glasses up his nose, except he isn't wearing glasses, a gesture that's totally familiar to her. She pushes her own glasses up in empathy. "We were drawn together by fate and a shared interest in trying to break a world record for LEGO construction. We chased world records our whole lives, but never got one. Doesn't matter. It's the journey, not the destination, right?" He laughs, a strange donkey-braying noise that makes the other two look over. She laughs, too. She can't help it. He continues. "After his accident, Pres kind of . . . vanished on us. He was all Maeve, all the time, you know? We didn't blame him. Not really. She wasn't in our league, you know? We were major DMBs."

"DMBs?"

"Dorkus Maximus Boys."

"Oh . . . right."

"I guess Pres always had a bit of an edge 'cause being Mac's twin elevated him a little. But he just wasn't into the same stuff as Mac, hockey, partying, all that. He didn't like Mac's dude-bro posse either. He'd rather figure out how to maximize his total for blindfolded bottle flips, you know? We've been Nerdfighters practically since birth. Well, Henry and I have, but Presley's an honorary capital-N Nerd, too. Anyway, when he texted us a few weeks ago, we were like, *whoa.* It's not like we forgot him, we just took for granted that he'd advanced beyond us on the social hierarchy." He pauses. "We *were* a little surprised he left without saying good-bye. But to be honest, we hadn't talked to him since Mac died."

"Gosh," she says. It tastes like the warm gush of fruit inside a Fruit Gusher, her mom's substitute for actual fruit on days she was especially manic. *Maeve,* she thinks. *Who the fuck is Maeve?* The idea of Presley with someone *out of his league,* whatever that means, makes her flinch. "Sorry. That's . . . I . . . Um, how long are you here for?"

"Oh, we're leaving right after this." Big Tee looks at his watch, taps the screen.

"You're going back *tonight*? To *Canada*?"

"We have . . ." He looks at his phone, then punches a few keys. "Forty-five minutes. Exactly."

"How long is the drive?"

"Twenty-four hours and six minutes." He holds up his phone. "All the stats you could ever want to know and then some." He lowers his voice. "You're better for him than Maeve."

"Oh . . . Thanks?" She's not sure how to take that. "I'm probably much nerdier."

"Exactly." He brays again. "She was zero percent nerd."

"Here you go," says Presley, sliding in next to her, holding out a large chocolate-dipped cone. "Ice cream as promised."

"Thanks." All she can think is: *Maeve? Maeve? Maeve?* over and over again until it's indistinguishable from the low murmur of the boys' voices, their laughter, the scraping of spoons in cups, the sound of people ordering, and the cash register beeping in the background. She can't be jealous of his past . . . But she is definitely jealous of his past.

"Maeve," she murmurs when no one can hear, just to see, and it tastes like marmite, a dark brown paste of vitamins and yeast that her mom used to spread on toast in the morning in a nod to self-care. Hattie had snuck a spoonful of it once, thinking it would taste like Nutella, and then had been so scared to admit that's why she was sick, so instead of confessing, she'd quietly snuck into the hall closet and thrown up into one of her dad's baseball hats.

"Are you okay?" Presley whispers to her as they head back out to the parking lot.

"I'm good," she says as quietly as she can. She doesn't sound like herself. She sounds like she's lying. She tries again. "It's nice to meet your friends. I'm sorry I'm socially awkward. Or just you know, *everything* awkward." She squeezes his hand again. He's the only boy she's ever held hands with, but she isn't *his* first, which is . . . Well, obviously. He's eighteen. He's *normal*, or at least way more normal than her. Most kids didn't spend the majority of their teen years rejecting the concept of love. She knows that. But she isn't his first anything. He's had a girlfriend before. Which is fine! Fine. "I'm fine," she says, again, letting the cold milk taste of *fine* wash away everything else. She raises her voice so Henry can hear over the thrumming music pouring from the speakers. "Can you guys drop us off at work?"

"Of course," says Henry. He punches in the address as she dictates it. "She'll get you there in twelve minutes."

"Hattie has a VW bus," says Presley. "She's a she, too."

"All vehicles are she," says Henry. "It's from ships in olden times. The ship was perceived as something that took care of the sailors, kept them alive, nurtured them. Like a mother. So ever since then, all vehicles are female." He glances in the mirror at Hattie. "Sorry, I'm kind of a living, breathing AMA." He pats the car's front dash. "We call her Mother," he adds. "To distinguish her from Mum, who obviously I call Mum."

"Mum," repeats Hattie. She giggles.

"What?"

"I don't know, it's cute. So . . . Canadian. We say Mom."

"British, actually. That's why Presley and I get along so well, all our blue blood, right, mate?" He says the last part in an over-the-top British accent.

"'Xactly, mate," says Presley, his accent even worse. It's possibly the cutest thing Hattie can imagine. She squeezes his hand.

The car pulls into the parking lot of El Amado Activity Center, and Hattie and Presley get out.

"Twenty-four hours and six minutes starts now," says Big Tee. "Right on schedule."

Henry reaches out the open window and gives Presley an awkward handshake. "So . . . come up and see us sometime?"

"Yeah," says Presley. "I'll do that. I'll come one day when I have twenty-four hours and six minutes to spare."

"Well," says Henry, "it will likely take longer in an inferior vehicle."

"Got it, mate," says Presley, punching him in the arm.

PRESLEY

Presley looks up at Hattie's booth as he skates off the ice.

Don't stare, he tells himself. *Don't be weird or desperate or needy.* But he can't stop looking up at her booth, hoping to meet her eye.

Coach Kat is sitting on the bench. She slides her pen into the clip on her clipboard. She looks at him thoughtfully, appraisingly. "You are really not a bad skater. You have qualities."

"Thanks? I used to be . . . better. I could have been . . ."

She shrugs. "Maybe you will think about skating again when you're ready."

"Oh, yeah, I . . . I don't really . . . I'm not . . . I don't skate anymore. I can't be ready. I won't . . . ever be ready."

"Oh?" She raises her eyebrows and looks first at him and then at the ice. "You are skating right now."

"Yeah, but I'm injured. I have a . . ." He points to his head. "I have a . . . head injury. I can't, anymore. I don't do it, like, for real. I have seizures."

"I know. But there are many ways to keep skating without competing. You are a good coach. The kids like you. You know the sport. You love to skate." She makes it a statement, not a question, so he doesn't disagree.

"Yeah, sure. I mean . . ." He pauses. "That's different."

"You thought you would go to the Olympics?"

He shrugs. "It wasn't, like, impossible. It was *possible.* I wasn't *not* good enough." He doesn't tell her that he really, truly believed that not only would he make it, but he'd win, and then keep winning, until he achieved the ultimate world record: most gold medals, figure skating, men, currently held by Gillis Grafström, with four (three golds, one silver).

"You might have. You are the kind of skater people like to look at. The kids like what you do. They don't bother to pretend. You have what they call the It factor. But now . . . So." She shrugs.

He nods. "Yeah, exactly. Doesn't matter now."

"Well, you are a very good coach. If you want to teach more than Learn to Skate, there are courses you can take. You can be a coach. If you want to be. Maybe you want to be a cook or an archaeologist. I don't know. Are you going to college?"

"Maybe," he says. "I hadn't really thought about it. I don't know."

"No? You haven't thought about your future?"

"A lot's been going on, I guess." He shrugs. "I'll figure something out. Coaching is . . . I like to coach. Maybe." Fleetingly, he wonders who the winningest coach has been, if there's a record for that.

She looks at him, shakes her head like she pities him. "The Olympics are only one event, Presley. What do they measure? Your worth? Or how good you were on one day? Everyone who gets that far is very good, but they are also just young people with a life still ahead of them. Your whole life's worth boiled down to one single moment in time is dangerous, too. Because is anything else enough after that? You are young and quite stupid—not your fault, all young people are quite stupid—but maybe you will figure it out."

"Figure what out?"

She looks at him, through him, that's how it feels, like she can see everything inside him and knows what he's thinking and feeling and . . . everything. "How to live a life. Your life. The life you have."

Presley traces his blade around in a circle on the ice. "I used to be a really good skater."

"You might be good at other things, too. Has no one ever told you that?"

She walks away, and he thinks, *Wait, what things?*

He pushes off again, skating harder and faster and faster and harder until he's all sweat and heartbeat and breathing, nothing else, flying around the ice, the boards blurring as he goes.

HATTIE

Hattie takes people's money for classes, makes change for the vending machine, writes words in her red Moleskine notebook, and watches Presley skating laps. He's skating fast, carelessly, almost without looking, careening around the rink.

Come up here, she thinks, focusing on the back of Presley's head, then his face, then his knees, his flashing blades, his livid scar, his white teeth.

Come up here and see me.

Come up here and talk to me.

Come up here and tell me what you're thinking.

Her notebook is almost full. She assumes Brady still wants it. That he still needs it. That he hasn't changed his mind about his thesis because she freaked out on him.

Freaking out seems to be her thing lately.

But whether he wants her notebooks or not, she still feels compelled to keep them. She writes smaller on each line, so she can fit more in. The notebooks are like a part of her. The notebooks are her. They're how the world tastes to her, how her whole life tastes. What's more personal than that?

Tingle is a crisp apple, sweet and fresh.

"Tingle," she says out loud. It's good. A memory surfaces: her mom carving an apple with a sharp knife into slices so thin, that when they hold them up to the light, they can see right through them. Hattie, with her front teeth missing, putting the slices on her tongue and letting them dissolve like candy. Her mom, laughing, "One day you'll be able to bite an apple again! I promise! Don't cry!" But she left before Hattie's teeth grew in.

Hattie stares at her hand, holding the pen—chipped green nail polish, one ragged hangnail, a perfectly round scar on her left palm where Calliope stabbed her with a pencil in second grade, before they were friends. A chill runs through her, a shiver that feels like a realization, but one she can't quite put her finger on.

She scribbles out *tingle* and the story about the apple and puts the book back in her bag and piles everything else on top of it, like she can hide it from herself, whatever it is.

What is it?

She shakes her head, then she turns off the computer and straightens out Bethanne's desk, getting ready to leave for the night, still aware of Presley, going around and around on the ice.

When she gets to the parking lot, Presley is leaning on Applejack's bumper, smiling at her.

"There you are," he says.

"Weren't you just . . . How did you get out here so fast?"

"I told you, I have *many* secret skills."

Hattie takes a deep breath. "Okay, get in," she says. "Do you have somewhere you have to be? I know where we can go."

"Are you kidnapping me?" He grins.

"It's not kidnapping if you consent," she says, which is from *The Shark Club*, the thing that Jada says to Topher when they leave for their road trip at the crack of dawn, the sun spilling golden light all over his face. It's one of her favorite scenes.

She glances over at Presley. His face contorts into something between a smile and a frown. She waits, but he doesn't say, "Consent granted." Instead, he forces a laugh. "I'm in," he says. She tries not to be disappointed, but she is. Just a little.

Hattie parks Applejack at the Point, an outcropping of land, narrow and steep on each side, which stretches out into the Pacific, a natural breakwater that's as flat and wide as a single-lane road extending almost its whole length. It isn't a road.

"Is this *legal*?" asks Presley when she's carefully made it to the end. "This feels like it shouldn't be allowed. Are you good at driving in reverse?"

"So good. And we won't go to jail. Probably. Depends how you define 'legal.'" Hattie cranks the handle that opens Applejack's moonroof. *Legal* is strange in her mouth, slightly wood-flavored, like the flat paddle spoons that came with ice cream cups on hot dog day at school. Suddenly, she's tired of the taste of everything. She swishes her tongue around in her mouth, looking for the taste of something else.

The wind pushes hard against the side of the van, and it rocks slightly. "Seriously, is it *safe*?"

"Depends how you define 'safe.'" She cracks a grin and sits down on the bed, looking at him, then she lies back, her eyes not leaving his. Tentatively, Presley perches next to her, then, when she doesn't freak out, he lies down, too. He doesn't touch her.

Through the open roof, it's apparent that the sky has been blown partially clear again by the wind coming in off the ocean. The stars freckle through the darkness, a faint scattering of distant light, more and more stars coming into focus the more he stares until he's sure he sees the whole galaxy. The air smells like *California*. He breathes it in. He's never felt more love for the place, or maybe it's just her: coconut and bougain-villea and the sea, all layered under something sweet. Up until this moment, he's felt *dislocated*, but suddenly he's in the right place, exactly. Then, he looks up: a massive shooting star.

"No fucking way! Did you see that? Or did you *plan* that?"

"Ha. I did plan it, actually. This is the best place to watch meteor showers. No light pollution."

"This feels like a scene from a movie. How is this my life?"

"You got lucky?"

"Yeah. Or . . . maybe *you* got lucky." He pauses, letting the silence pool around them. Then: "But can I . . . Can we talk about . . ."

"Um, no. I mean, yes, but . . ." Hattie gets up, opens the cupboard, and presses some buttons hidden inside it. Joni Mitchell starts singing softly. "My mom's," she says. "It's this or Fleetwood Mac." She sits down at the little table, looking back at him on the bed, then she stands, pulling her hair for-ward, then back, pushing her glasses up her nose, taking them off. Crossing her legs.

"Hattie . . ."

She shakes her head. "Just give me a sec."

"Okay."

She gets up and carefully lies back down next to him, but she's different, less relaxed. "Let's . . . talk."

And suddenly he knows she's going to tell him she just wants to be friends. "We don't have to!"

She doesn't seem to have heard him. She's staring up through the moonroof. "Do you believe in the multiverse?"

There's another shooting star, then another. "You mean like the idea that we all exist in an infinite number of possible versions of ourselves?"

"Yeah, like that."

"I guess I never really thought about it. I like the idea of it, I think. Do *you*?"

"Yes," Hattie says. She turns her head to look at him. He looks sad or scared or anxious or some combination of all three, and she feels terrible for being so *weird*. But she wants to explain. She wants to make it make sense out loud, how everything is random, but every random thing is simultaneously co-occurring somewhere else with a different outcome, which means that tragedies are only tragedies in one of an infinite number of realities. But if she explains it wrong, or if he asks questions she can't answer, it might fall apart. He'll find plot holes. He'll expose flaws in her theory. And she needs Elijah to be alive, somewhere, so he is. She squeezes her eyes shut.

"Did you see that?"

Hattie opens her eyes. Presley is pointing at the sky.

"Oh yeah," she lies. "That one was amazing."

He reaches over and touches her arm lightly, his hand brushing her skin, her skin jumping in response. "Is this okay?" he says, and instead of answering, she turns her face to his and kisses him again and again and again until he kisses her back. "Are you sure?" Her entire body screams *yes*, the stars still falling but forgotten, while Joni sings and sings, her voice quietly filling the van with something validating that makes all this a perfect scene. "We could still talk," he says, his lips still touching her lips.

"I don't want to anymore," she says back, and then they're both giggling from the vibration of each other's words.

"Kiss-talking should totally be a thing," Presley says, pulling away.

And, kissing him again, Hattie laughs and lets go. She stops trying to think so hard and so much. "Kiss-laughing, too," she says.

"*The Guinness Book of World Records* longest kiss was fifty-eight hours long," he says.

"You are *such* a dork," she says, kissing him more, no longer able to tell which are her own words she's tasting and which are his.

PRESLEY

The wind rocking the van and the music and the velvet sky hold them together, and Presley is half-floating and half-aware of Hattie's body and her skin and her smell and her taste. He doesn't know what it all means, but he thinks it means everything is fine and he's fine and she's fine and this is as fine as he's ever been or will be again. He hopes his breath doesn't smell like meat or garlic and that he smells as good to her as she does to him and that he's kissing her right and he's aware of the ocean, roaring around them in a way that feels disorienting, as though they're on a ship, and he's aware of her lips and her tongue and what it's doing to him and he wants to tear off all his clothes and her clothes, but instead he kisses her and kisses her and he lets that be enough (more than enough) and he's never wanted anyone like this before and he's also aware of how he's an animal and she's an animal and their bodies are animals doing what animals do, both of them wanting more, flooding with hormones and wanting, wanting, *wanting*.

Up close, her blue eyes are flecked with amber and in her left eye, there's a small slice of brown cutting through the blue, and it's so beautiful to him, she's so beautiful to him, he wants to cry. And her skin is so cool and soft and her lips are everything and he wants to stop kissing her so he can stare at her but he also never wants to stop kissing her. He wants to make her feel good and to make her feel seen and loved and wanted because he's never seen or loved or wanted anyone like *this*.

It's different than sex, it's so much more and better and bigger than just that, but it's also that, his body wanting what it wants, and he wants . . .

"Hattie." He exhales into her ear, and she shudders.

"Presley."

She flips herself up, onto him, straddling him, suddenly looking shy, she tucks her hair behind her ears. He reaches up for her, pulls her down, doesn't even remember to feel embarrassed by how much of him she can feel now. She grinds against him, and he nearly lets go, it's too intense, but he doesn't want to stop, he wants this to keep going and . . . Then the wind gives the van a bigger-than-possible push, and she rolls off him and starts to laugh, and he laughs, too, trying to regroup, his brain all white noise and elation and ecstasy. He feels high. He feels like maybe he loves her. He thinks he might *love* her! He *definitely* loves her.

A wave crashes so close to them that it splatters the windshield. He lets out a scream. "Shit, we're going to get blown into the sea."

"Probably not," she says. "But we should go." She presses her palm against his cheek, then kisses him gently.

The wind whips against the van again, and this time it does feel like the wheels lift off the ground. "I don't want to, but I'm also a terrible swimmer. Sad we didn't break the kissing record though."

"We just need practice."

"Practice and an official judge. I spent a lot of my childhood on this exact thing."

"You spent a lot of your childhood imagining setting a kissing record?"

"Ha, well, no. A LEGO record. But close enough."

"I think a judge would make it weird."

"But weird is good, right?"

"Mostly," she says, starting up the van, which sputters reluctantly then coughs to life. "But sometimes my weirdness is . . . a lot."

"I like your weirdness," he says.

"You say that now, but it hasn't got really weird yet," she says.

"How weird is it going to get?"

"I like to shroud myself in mystery," she says. "You'll probably find out, but last night was kind of a taste of it."

"Oh *that*," he says, as though he's forgotten already.

It's only after she's dropped him off and he's falling asleep that he realizes in all that happened today, he didn't see Mac.

Not once.

He dreams of the abyss, of standing over it, looking down and *there's* Mac, his outline visible in the bubbles.

"There you are!" he says, and suddenly Mac pushes through the surface, his mouth spilling tar, his eyes desperate, and he's choking and gasping and clawing at his face and then, struggling, he's sinking down into the darkness, and Presley is reaching for him, calling him, grabbing him, but it's too late. Mac is gone.

"No. No. Mac, Mac, MAC." He wakes up shouting his brother's name, sweating and exhausted, staring up at the Post-it note that reads *Mac is dead*, with the stick figure with x's for eyes, tears leaking down his cheeks, a hollow aching burn in his chest.

HATTIE

Calliope is waiting at Hattie's locker in the morning. "There's something you're not telling me, and I demand to know what it is," she says. "I won't let you go to class until you've spilled your secret."

"Who says I have a secret?" says Hattie. "I'm an open book."

"So you say, but speaking of books, where is your book? I haven't seen you reading it at all this week, and that makes me nervous."

I don't need to read it, I'm living it, Hattie wants to say but doesn't. Instead, she pulls it out of her backpack, triumphantly waving it in the air. "You think you know things, but you know nothing! I was reading it just this morning, over breakfast." Which is actually true. Without her dad at home, everything feels lonely, and at least with *The Shark Club* she feels less alone.

"Mmmmm-hmmm. Okay, My Little Fluttershy, you're blushing so much right now I could fry an egg on your face, but I'll let you have your secret. Just not for long. Promise you'll tell me everything there is to tell about Plush Lips the Tiny Toilet later, and I'll think about letting you live."

But before Hattie can answer, everyone's phone goes off at once, a wailing screech that makes Hattie nearly jump out of her skin.

"What the . . ." says Calliope, looking at her screen. "Oh, holy heck. It's happening."

"*What's* happening?" Hattie wants to press her hands over her ears to block out the sounds, but instead she puts her fingers to her pulse, which is racing. She can't remember how to make her legs move or which direction she should go. There's a defibrillator in the office. Is her heart beating wrong? Unevenly? She coughs and pounds her chest with her fist, hard. She squints at her phone, trying to read it, but the text is all blurry and seems like it's moving.

Just then, the principal's voice over the PA: "Please stay calm. Everyone has received the fire evacuation alert, and we will now proceed as practiced. Please make your way to your homeroom class. Your teachers will be waiting to sign you out if you have your own method of transportation, or to guide you to the gymnasium to ride the bus home. I'd like to emphasize the importance of staying calm. As you know, there is only one road out of town, and due to the risk of that road being blocked by the fire and El Amado being cut off from access to the freeway, they're evacuating the town as a precaution. It's *only* a precaution. You have go-bags and you know what to do. Remember: There is time. Stay calm. Be safe. *Don't panic.*"

The speaker goes silent; the halls erupt in chaos.

"So much for not panicking," says Calliope, who seems amused.

"Do you need a ride?" Hattie says to Calliope. "Let's go! Let's go. We have to go."

"Breathe." Calliope shakes her head. "I'm going with Leo. We'll drop Bug at home. Are you okay? You look weird."

"I'm not panicking. I'm not! I'm totally not."

"If you could say that in a less panicky way, I *might* believe you."

"It's fine. Panic is my natural state. I'm adapting to the panic. It's only a problem if you can't adapt." *Panic* tastes like the stale, hard gingerbread of a collapsing Christmas gingerbread house, a failed craft, the one her mom got frustrated with and threw in the sink before storming out to the van, leaving Hattie alone with the mess, which she cleaned up, because that's what she did. She fixed things. She was *five*.

"Hattie?"

"Seriously, I'm fine." Hattie takes a deep breath and lets it out slowly, then another and another, until it makes her light-headed. "I'm breathing deeply, see? I'll be fine. I know what to do. Breathe. Et cetera." She stuffs some books into her backpack and grabs the Stepfather collage, folds that, and puts it in, too. She fits in as many of her locker snacks as she can, in case she gets hungry on the drive to wherever she's going to go. San Francisco, where her dad is? She hoists her bag onto her back. She's aware that her heart is still doing all the wrong things. It would be ironic to die in a fire before the fire even starts and she doesn't want to die ironically. Or at all.

"You're literally shaking. I don't want to leave you like this, but I have to go."

"It's adrenalin. Fight or flight. Go."

"Are you sure you're okay?"

"I'm pretty sure this is like a crashing plane and you're doing a terrible job of saving yourself first," says Hattie, with all the conviction she can muster.

She looks around, standing on her tiptoes to see above the crowd of teachers with clipboards and students, all opening and slamming lockers, some laughing and jostling, others looking scared and sad.

"Bye," says Calliope, and grabs Hattie in a hug. She kisses her on the cheek. "I love you. Text me when you're somewhere that's not here."

"I will," Hattie promises.

The fact that she doesn't have Presley's number now just seems stupid, and not charming and quirky. He doesn't drive! How will he get home? She starts moving through the hall, waves her car keys at her homeroom teacher, who nods and scribbles on the clipboard, until she gets to Presley's locker, and there he is.

"Hey," she says. "Hi."

"Oh!" He looks happy to see her. He holds up his phone. "Texting my mom's wife. My stepmom. For a ride. Already let the teacher know."

"Is she coming? Tell her not to come. I'll give you a ride. I can drop you off at your place. We just have to stop at my house and grab something. I think there's time. I thought everything I needed was in Applejack, but I forgot one thing that I really need." She tries to slow her breathing, but she's hyperventilating even thinking about the picture on the fridge, the flames reaching for it, the edges melting in the heat before catching and blackening.

Presley glances at his phone one more time. "I'll go with you," he says, typing something. "It's a better plan. I want to go with you."

PRESLEY

Anywhere and everywhere is in his mouth, but he stops it from coming out, even though it wants to be said.

"You ready?"

"Ready."

He grabs her hand.

"Run?" she says.

"Run," he says.

And they do, hearts racing, hair flying, not quite believing that it's happening, that the fire is coming, that any of it is real.

Presley enters Hattie's room and sits down next to her on her bed. Out the window, he sees the smoke thickening, becoming more real every second. There are sirens that seem closer than they should, and the roar of low-flying planes and helicopters. The air buzzes with urgency.

It's like a war zone.

He puts his hand on her shoulder, traces a circle on her bicep. He thinks about trying to breathe in all that smoke, how the cells in their bodies carrying all that oxygen are going to struggle. "We should *really* get going," he says.

"I can't believe this is happening," she says.

"Yeah."

She leans against him. He kisses her hair. Maybe neither thing is real: this or the fire. Then finally, he says, "It's just *stuff*, right?"

She picks up a framed photo, shows it to him. "Look, it's me and Elijah."

He stares at it. "He's cute."

"Yeah, he was." She shoves it into a bag. "I want this. I'm glad we came back because I would've forgotten. I needed this. And I want to bring the map. Just in case. It was a lot of work."

He looks and there's a huge collage that takes up most of the wall. It takes him a minute to realize what it is . . .

"It's Topher and Jada's road trip from *The Shark Club*," she says. "I maybe didn't tell you just how into that book I am? I know you know I *like* it. But I . . . really like it. It's sort of embarrassing."

"Holy shit." His words come out like an exhalation. A chill runs down his spine. He traces his finger along the velvet ribbon. The details are intricate and perfect and so detailed and it's almost too much to process. "Wow."

"I told you things would get weirder," she says.

"Yeah, well, wow." His heart pounds hard against his sternum, and he feels light-headed. Sick. He knew she was a fan. A superfan, even. But . . .

This is a lot.

"You hate it," she says.

"I . . . Can I take a picture for my mum? She *has* to see this."

"Sure. But . . . why?"

"Why what?"

"Why would your mom care about my map? Does me being Queen of the Nerds somehow make me more likeable to her or something?"

The room spins around Presley. "You don't . . . know? I thought . . . you said . . . you knew?"

"Knew what?"

"After the party, after Phantom Fest, you said you knew. You said it didn't matter." He feels a flare of anger. "You said it didn't change anything, but . . ." He looks at the map. "I kind of find it hard to believe." He sits down on her bed. "I'm getting a headache," he says. His body prickles with pins and needles. "Shit, I'm going to . . ." He lies back, closes his eyes, *wills* the seizure away. "Make it stop, Mac," he thinks or says, he's not sure.

I'm not a magic genie, Mac says, sounding far away, gravelly, but getting stronger. *You don't get three wishes.*

"I wish for more wishes," he says, relieved and sick all at once. Mac is *here*. Everything's fine. He's fine. Mac's fine.

Or, more accurately, the ghost of Mac is fine. He squeezes his eyes shut more tightly.

"Presley? You're scaring me. What's going on? What the fuck? Presley!"

Presley's body clenches.

"Presley!" Her hands are on his face, his chest, his arms. She's pressing her fingers to his pulse. "God, oh god, oh god, no."

He can't answer her. That's the worst part. He can't say anything.

And then, just like that, he unlocks. His body sinks back into the bed, his muscles all releasing at once.

"I'm okay! Stop. I'm okay." His voice comes out muffled, his jaw still clenched.

"What *happened*?"

"I just . . . I sometimes . . . It's like a glitch." He decides not to use the word *seizure*. A seizure sounds too real, too urgent, too terrifying. He rubs at his cheeks, trying to loosen the muscles of his jaw. "It's fine. I'm fine." He sits up, slowly, and tries not to mumble. "Your map is really good. It's incredible. I thought you knew, that's all. Now it seems like I'm making everything a bigger deal than it is. It isn't a big deal." His voice is recovering, but he sounds *pleading*, he can hear it and he hates it. He hates himself. He hates the goddamn Shark Club. But he played into it, didn't he? With the whole Seven Dates thing. He was trying to be cute. He shouldn't have. He should have known it meant that much to her, that she'd . . . conflate it. With him. He should have known the second he saw the white towel.

She's staring at him, wide-eyed and confused.

"I saw a video. There was a video. It was . . . I don't remember exactly. Something about moths. And you punched Chloe Bean in the mouth."

"Oh, well, yeah. *That's* a thing that happened." He laughs. Then he laughs some more. Then he's laughing too hard, tears on his cheeks. She didn't know. It's okay. She really didn't. She obviously didn't.

She looks at him, her expression uncertain, her glasses sliding down her nose. "What aren't you telling me?"

"I just thought you knew." Presley is dazed, from the seizure, from the roller coaster of emotions, from the *map*. "Mum's not a fan, she's an author. She's *the* author. My mum wrote *The Shark Club*."

Hattie freezes, the map half-folded in her hands. "Oh my god," she says. "You *are* Topher."

And the abyss opens and Presley falls in, headfirst, pulling in lungfuls of bubbling tar, sinking fast. His voice rises up from everywhere and nowhere. "No, I'm fucking *not*."

HATTIE

Presley's anger floods the room. Hattie steps back.

She doesn't understand what's happened.

"I . . ."

Presley is looking at her with something like disgust, and suddenly her chest is tightening, and her lungs feel small, so small, too small to take in air, and her heart—her heart feels like it's not beating at all, like it's solidified, hard and unyielding as stone.

She gasps, then tries again. "Presley?"

But he's turned away from her, he's opening the door, his footsteps are in the hall, then on the stairs, then the front door slams and he's gone.

He's *gone*.

PRESLEY

Presley is running now. He's on the street, and he's running, and everywhere cars are honking, and people are shouting, and doors are opening and shutting, and the air feels wrong: hot and thick in his burning lungs. Sweat stings his eyes or he's crying or both and he doesn't care, he's stopped caring, he can't *care*.

That's some bullshit right there, my little green salad.

"Fuck off. You weren't even alive when the stupid book came out. You weren't even *here*."

He's running and he's yelling at the ghost of his dead brother, and he's lost Hattie now, he's sure of it, and he doesn't know the point of anything. His phone buzzes in his pocket, and he ignores it and keeps running, and Mac keeps talking.

Yeah, sure, I'm not an expert, but I'm pretty sure this isn't about the book.

"Of course, it's about the fucking book. Everyone who knows Mum wrote that stupid thing thinks I'm Topher. And they're all disappointed. Because I'm a mess. I'm not some shark-saving hero. I'm just not."

I know what it's about. I might be dead, but I can still read. And seriously, bro, no one is reading that book and thinking it's real life. They just aren't. Why are you really so pissed? I kind of think you should think about that, about who you're mad at, because I'm pretty sure it's not Hattie.

Presley is staggering now, and he has a stitch in his side. "What are you, my therapist?" His phone buzzes again. He feels in his pocket for it, rejects the call. "Because I've had more than enough therapy."

Therapists make you figure out your own shit, right? I don't want to do that. I'd rather cut to the chase. You're not mad at Hattie. You're mad at MUM. And it's probably time to deal with it and let me go.

Presley stops running, bends over, clutching his side, then slowly sits down on the ground. "I'd hang up on you if I could," he says. "I'd punch you in the face if you were in front of me."

That never really turned out that great, tbh. Maybe also time to rethink that punch-first-figure-it-out-later approach. Dad did that and it was pretty shit, honestly.

Presley's vision swims. He's so dizzy. Everything is blurry and smoky. His eyes sting so much. He tries to take a deep breath, but he can't. He lies back, his head clonking against the hot pavement. "Mac?"

His phone vibrates. He looks at it. It's Ellie. *We have to go. Fire's too close. You're okay to go with Hattie, yes? Text us when you're safe.*

Then from his mum: *Love you across the universe and back. We've got the goat. Be SAFE. Don't come here.*

He dials their number, not waiting for it to ring or for them to answer. He's shouting, "Wait! I'm close! I'm coming!" but the phone is going to voicemail, and his heart is in his throat, and he doesn't know what to do, and he presses his forehead into the gritty sidewalk and cries.

HATTIE

Applejack sputters and coughs as Hattie starts her up with shaking hands. She's trying to make everything make sense. Presley's mom is . . . Bianca Stark? She's having a hard time processing what happened, his *glitch*, the fire, the look on his face, the way he ran . . .

Someone honks and she jumps, hadn't noticed the light was green. She doesn't know how to fix anything, but she does know she has to find him. It's practically dark now, even though it's the middle of the day; the smoke is blotting out everything, the sun, the sky, the sea.

People are panicking now, cars slamming on brakes and squealing around corners, a vibration of urgency, the constant beeping of her phone, of every phone. She drives slowly, squinting into the smoke, her window down so she can call him.

"PRESLEY!"

At his tiny house, Hattie stops the van and gets out. She's never been here before but from what he'd described, this is the only place it could have been, the place where Meka showed her the butterflies, where the picture that's in the van was taken, which makes perfect sense because . . . everything is connected. Isn't it? The smoke is impossibly thick here now, the butterflies long gone. Her eyes are streaming. Her lungs burn. She can barely make out the skeleton of their huge new house rising up out of the ground.

Her phone buzzes with a second evacuation warning.

Thirty minutes.

Thirty minutes and then the road will be deemed unsafe and they might be trapped. Where is he?

The fire is considered extremely dangerous, her phone tells her. *Evacuate immediately.*

If the town burns, so will this tiny house.

And the half-built house.

And her house.

And the school.

And the El Amado Activity Center.

It seems impossible, even though they've known all along that it's happened before. That it could happen again. But she didn't believe it. She never quite believed it. She thinks about her mom's blue guitar, her mom's surfboard, her mom's hiking boots. She thinks about her mom's stupid toothbrush, melting against the porcelain of the sink.

She thinks about the photo she went back for, and then forgot in her rush to catch up to Presley. The photo of her mom. The only photo of her mom. Her mom staring at something out of the frame, Applejack, Hattie crying.

She lets it go. She drops her face down on the steering wheel. She feels disoriented. Dizzy. Sick. Exhausted.

Then someone knocks on the window and Hattie screams.

PRESLEY

Presley feels defeated. He'd thought . . . He'd hoped his mum and Ellie would still be here, but they aren't and Hattie is, and he has to get out of town.

There isn't any choice.

"I need a ride," he says.

"I could kidnap you?" Her voice is shaky, and he wants to forgive her and make everything okay, but he can't, not yet, not now.

He shakes his head. "I just need a ride." His voice is so angry he hardly recognizes it, all hard-edged and jaggedly dangerous. It isn't him. But it also *is* him. Isn't it? He is angry. He's angry with his mum and with the book and with his dad and with a world that would wreck his life and take his brother and let him fall in love with someone who thinks he's someone else. He kicks the dirt with his sneaker, again and again, Mac's urn cradled in his arms. *Mac.*

"Get in," says Hattie. "We're not going to die. Not today."

HATTIE

The fires, black and orange and huge and angry, are consuming a 7-Eleven on the opposite exit as they pull out onto the I-5. It looks like they're literally in hell. It looks like the end of everything. It looks like a movie about itself, all Hollywood effects and too much of everything, too dramatic to be real, yet here they are, living it and breathing it and it is real, maybe more real than anything has ever been. Black plumes billow across the I-5, hurling ash into the smoke-thick wind. In the near distance, sparks shoot into the sky like fireworks.

The smoke is permeating everything, the inside of the van, the inside of them. The heat from the fire is intense. It must be so close. Unbearably close. Fire trucks are everywhere, red lights flashing through the haze.

Hattie and Presley aren't talking. Both of them shine with sweat. Hattie imagines her tires popping. She imagines an ember, landing on the van, the way it would ignite. She pictures the gas tank exploding.

Hattie presses the gas, harder. *Love is bullshit. Love is the point. Love is bullshit. Love is the point. Love is bullshit. Love is the point.*

She doesn't know how to be forgiven.

Which fits because she doesn't know how to forgive either.

Maybe Mom will come home for my funeral, she thinks bitterly, pushing Applejack so much she starts to vibrate from the effort of getting them out of there.

PRESLEY

Presley closes his eyes because he can't look at Hattie and he can't look out the window because out there, everywhere, he sees his dad's red car, engulfed in flames, and the smell is in his throat, is in his *heart*, and Mac's body is on the ground and there's blood puddling behind his head and his skull is . . .

His whole head is . . .

I'm sure you've got better memories than that, bromigo.

Presley shakes his head, shakes it, shakes it again, trying to shake it clear, an Etch A Sketch of a memory that refuses to be gone, the faint shadow of it always there.

He opens his eyes and in front of the van, a man is pointing and waving an orange flag. "Move over, move over, other lane, other LANE!" and Hattie is swinging the wheel sharply, and they're now in the *wrong* lane, the wrong side of the highway, and he's braced for a head-on crash, and they keep driving and driving, both ducking like they're going to avoid something coming at them from above. He'd pray if he believed in God, but he doesn't, not really, so instead he wraps his hands around his knees and squeezes and squeezes like the strength of his wanting to make it out will somehow get them out of here.

HATTIE AND PRESLEY

They're out of the smoke in twenty-six minutes. Safe. Beyond the reach of the jumping sparks and the choking black smoke and the red flashing lights of the emergency vehicles and all the other drivers who were doing exactly what they were doing, putting their feet down on the gas, keeping their heads down and *surviving*.

The smoke is thinning, thinning, thinning, and blue sky exists and the sun is still shining and there's the sea and they're still alive.

They survived.

And now they have to figure out what happens next.

EVERYTHING HAS CHANGED

HATTIE

At the first opportunity, Hattie exits off the freeway, cutting over to the old 101. She needs to see the ocean, to reassure herself that it's still there, that some things haven't changed even though it feels as though everything has. She glances over at Presley, but he's looking out the window, the back of his head the only part she can see. His hair is sticking up from sweat and smoke, and she knows they both stink, can still smell the smoke, which has permeated everything. She thinks maybe when they get to the sea, she'll dive in. She'll go and keep going. She'll swim and swim and finally she'll be clean and then she'll get tired. She'll get tired and she'll start to sink.

Eighty-seven seconds.

She'll sink for eighty-seven seconds, and then she'll inhale because her body will make her inhale, and either her larynx will spasm to keep the water out and she'll suffocate, or she'll inhale water.

Either way, her oxygen supply will be cut off. The blood cells moving emptily through her veins, carrying nothing nowhere, spreading emptiness into every organ, every cell.

If she's lucky, there will be a moment, a second of euphoria.

If she's lucky, she'll hear the mermaids sing.

Just like in *The Shark Club*. It will all be just like the book.

A horn blares, and she lurches awake. Was she falling asleep at the wheel?

"Jesus, Hattie," says Presley. "You swerved!"

"I'm sorry! I was thinking about something else."

"Well, please don't. Maybe we should stop. Pull over."

Hattie is shaking. They have to stop. They *have* to pull over. She isn't okay. Nothing is okay. But she wants—needs— to see the Pacific. She's not going to swim, nothing like that. She just wants to see it. She needs to know it's still there.

PRESLEY

"We have to stop," Presley says. His throat feels raw and sore. He coughs. Hattie is driving with grim determination. "Where are we going?"

"Five more minutes," she says. "We'll stop in five minutes. Maybe ten."

All the fight has left him. He's so tired. "Okay," he says. His phone vibrates in his pocket. He takes it out. His mum. Ellie. Ellie. His mum.

Safe, he types. *Driving north.*

We went south! His mum. *Heading to the airport. Flying to Phoenix early. Use the credit card and get a hotel.*

I love you, he types. *I'll figure it out. I'll let you know.*

He sends a message to Ellie: *Don't let Mum worry. I'm fine. Xo.*

He spins the phone in his hand a couple of times, then texts a picture to Henry and Big Tee. The 7-Eleven, burning. He actually can't think of anything funny to say about it, probably because there's nothing funny to say.

> **PRESLEY:**
> Literally got out with only the shirt on my back.

> **BIG TEE:**
> Holy hellfire, Batman!

HENRY:
I think I speak for all of us when I say I hope
you also escaped with pants.

   PRESLEY:
   Board shorts, bros. Board shorts.

He takes a photo of his shorts, hits send.

BIG TEE:
Dangerously close to a dick pic, old friend.
File that under: Things I don't need to see.

HENRY:
But seriously, we've been watching online.
It looks very intense. I'm glad you're safe.

   PRESLEY: Me too. Thanks. Where
   are you guys?

There's a long pause and he thinks they must have lost the
signal. He imagines they're in Washington by now, or maybe
still Oregon if they stopped anywhere. But knowing them . . .

His phone lights up with a photo. It's Henry and Big Tee,
both wearing Mickey Mouse ears, posing in front of Space
Mountain.

   PRESLEY:
   You went to . . . Disneyland?

BIG TEE:
Hell yeah. We decided it was time to YOLO a
little. After all, college next year means being
serious and cracking down.

PRESLEY:
I'm pretty sure the college
experience includes a lot of YOLO.

HENRY:
Correction: We didn't go to Disneyland, past
tense, we are AT Disneyland, present tense.

BIG TEE:
You've just survived an inferno, young man.
No one needs to YOLO like you need to
YOLO. Get your bony, board-shorted ass up
here right now.

PRESLEY:
I make no promises, but . . .

He takes a photo of the next highway sign they pass: Los Angeles 100 miles. He presses send.

"Disneyland," he says out loud, mostly to himself.

HATTIE

By the time Hattie pulls off at the viewpoint, her heart feels exhausted. She remembers reading somewhere that your heart only has a certain number of beats before it just . . . stops, and she wonders how many hers has left. It's been racing for so long now, ever since the first alert about the fire, which feels like days ago, weeks ago, years ago, when it's only been . . . She looks at the clock.

It's been four hours.

Four hours and everything has changed.

Presley is staring at his phone. He still isn't talking to her, and she knows whatever it was they had or that she thought they had is . . . broken.

She broke it.

She unlocks the door, climbs out, her legs nearly buckling when she's finally standing. She stretches. Takes a deep breath in, lets it out slowly. She thinks about her dad. She thinks about Bug and Calliope. She thinks about Presley. She slides open the side panel door and grabs her backpack. "Stretching my legs," she says.

Presley nods. She doesn't know how to end this. She doesn't know him well enough to know the right thing to say. She wants to scream. She wants to do something, anything, everything.

She walks away from Applejack and into the shade of the scrub pines where there are some picnic benches, a few overflowing trash cans. She picks the shadiest one—it's hot and the air feels like it's burning her skin, which already feels raw from the smoke, from her sweat, which has dried but left her skin feeling sticky, from everything that's happened— and sits, facing the sea. They're at the top of a peninsula, rocky and high, and the ocean is too far away to touch. Too far away to swim. Too far. She takes another deep breath of salty air, and then because it's her happy place, and it's all she can think to do, she takes out *The Shark Club* and starts to read.

The pie date was Jada's favorite. Everyone likes pie and the restaurant they found in Oregon had seven different kinds so that's exactly what they ordered. Seven slices of pie. The skating was fun, but every time he grabbed her hands or she started to fall and he caught her, she felt like she was posing for an Instagram pic and not like she was being her real self. The problem was that when she was with Topher, she was a different version of herself, one that she liked better than her usual pricklier self, but was she being . . . honest?

It was hard to compare because she was in it now. She was sitting beside him in the front cart of the roller coaster at the Santa Monica Pier, and then the train was rattling and moving and rising and falling and twisting and turning, pushing them into each other and apart, and she felt like it was a metaphor for something she couldn't quite get hold of. At the top of the steepest drop, they both put their arms up and held their breath and forced their eyes to stay wide open, even though the wind nearly blew Topher's contacts right out of his eyes. After, he reached over and gripped her hand so tightly she thought her bones might break. Everything they were doing was such a cliché, but also it was the most fun she'd ever had, ever allowed herself to have. She knew they were almost in San Diego, which meant they were almost on day seven, which was the cage diving, which meant everything and also meant nothing.

She snuck a look at him, and he was smiling, his full authentic smile, his smile that was unhampered by secrets he wasn't telling. When the roller coaster finally came to a stop and the safety belts were released and they were walking away, still surging with a little adrenalin—it wasn't exactly the scariest roller coaster in the world, but it still had that effect—she took a deep breath and said, "I think I need to tell you the whole truth about my mom and the shark and why I have to do this."

And she told him.

She told him about the beach.

She told him about the shaved ice.

She told him about the sunburn that blistered so much she had to keep her T-shirt on, even when she was swimming.

She told him about the boogie board and how there was only one and how she was fighting her brother for it and how their fight turned into fists.

She told him how her mom went snorkeling, how she said to their dad, "This one's on you."

How she walked away. Walked into the water. Started to swim.

She told him about the screams and the lifeguard whistles and the pandemonium and how her mom was dragged out of the water and how she said to Jada and her brother, who weren't fighting now, "At least I got you to stop fighting!" and then . . . she passed out.

And then someone was tying a tourniquet around her leg.

And everyone was shouting.

And Jada and her brother got pushed back farther and farther still and her mom was bleeding and bleeding and then she was being lifted into an ambulance and then she was gone.

They never saw her again.

She told him that the road trip was about her mom. It wasn't about forgiving her mom for getting bitten by a shark, or forgiving herself for fighting with her brother, or even for forgiving her dad for forgetting the sunscreen and not spending $20 to buy more, making her irritable and sunburnt.

"It's about forgiving the shark," she said.

And he understood. She didn't have to say any more than that. He got it. Just like that. He didn't point out all the obvious things, like how it would be a different shark or about how sharks don't actually have emotions and don't care about being forgiven, or how it wouldn't bring back her mom. He just understood.

And now, as they get ready to drop into the shark cage, and all around them the ocean is rising and falling *and rising and falling and they're rocking, rocking like babies in a cradle, she looks over at him and she says it. She says, "I love you."*

And he looks at her, tips her chin up so he can look into her eyes, and very gravely he says, "Thank you."

She smacks him. "You did not just thank me for saying that! It was a big deal! You have to say it back!"

"I'm waiting to say it when we surface," he says. "I'll say it if we survive this thing."

Hattie slams the book closed. They survived a thing. She and Presley survived a terrible, awful thing. In some other part of the multiverse, right now she's looking at Presley, and he's looking at her, and even though it's way too soon for either of them to think it, much less say it, they're holding on to each other, they're saying, *I love you. We're alive. I love you. Thank you.*

Just . . . not in this world.

She puts the book back in her bag and zips it shut. Part of her wants to throw it off the cliff, watch it bounce off the rocks and into the crashing surf, but she's not ready to lose it. Not yet. Not now.

They've driven over two hours and are nearing the Santa Monica Pier, and they still aren't talking. They're safe now but still *fleeing.*

Fleeing tastes thick and chocolatey, but too sweet, like a melting Oh Henry!, sticky and too rich. Hattie doesn't want to remember, but she can't help remembering, the Oh Henry! her mom stole from 7-Eleven, casually tossed to her once they got into the van, laughing and flushed, or how the man from the counter was running after her, waving his arms and shouting, and her mom squealed out of the parking lot, laughing too hard, laughing in a way that felt wrong and wild and out of control. Hattie hadn't wanted to eat it, but she had, swallowing the hard peanutty lumps of it, gagging and pretending not to cry.

Hattie hates that memory, hates that they're fleeing, hates that no one knows or cares, hates that they're not talking. She squeezes the steering wheel hard, her knuckles whitening.

"Hattie," says Presley. He clears his throat. "The thing is, he was at least partly based on me. I get why you think . . . You know."

She's flooded with relief, not because of what he said, but because he's talking. "Sorry," she says, her voice cracking. "I'm sorry. I didn't even . . . think it. Not really. I don't know why I said it."

"Hattie," he says again, in a gentler voice than she probably deserves. "You did think it. And I helped. But I can't . . . I don't . . . I'm not a character from your favorite book." He pauses. "He's made up. My mum made him up."

"I know! I get it. I totally understand." She's talking too fast, too loud, gesturing like that will make her words land in exactly the right way.

"I don't think you really do. I want you to, but . . . you can't. You don't have all the information."

"So tell me! I want to understand. I want to know all your . . . stuff."

He smiles a little sadly. "I shouldn't have done that Seven Dates thing. It was so dumb. I totally played into it. I'm sorry."

"I liked it." She smiles a little. "I was really . . . charmed."

"Yeah, but I should have done it differently. I should have just asked you out."

"Remember the multiverse?"

"Um, yeah. Why?"

"Maybe in another reality, you did. In another reality, none of this . . . bad part happened."

He shakes his head. "That's cute, but that's not how it works."

Hattie takes a sharp breath in. "Don't do that."

"Do what?"

"Patronize me. I believe in the multiverse. You don't get to invalidate it with *cute*. That's shitty."

He groans. "I'm sorry. You're right."

Hattie signals, cuts across two lanes, gets into the right lane where she can slow down. She rolls down the window and the hot wind, deliciously unsmoky, blows in on them. "I would like you if Topher didn't exist. I would've recognized you as *you*, even if I'd never read that book."

He puts his hand over her hand, and she jumps at his touch. He traces the valley between her bones. He unclenches her fingers, one by one, from the wheel, then places her hand in his, holding it gently like you would hold a baby bird, something fragile. He looks into her eyes. "I want to believe you."

She swallows. "And I want you to."

"I don't know how."

"I know." She pulls her hand away. "Can we just . . . I don't know. Just drive. Just for a bit. Maybe we can drive and think and figure it out. Or not."

"Okay," he says. "Let's drive." He hesitates. "This might sound really weird, given this whole . . ." He gestures. "Everything. But what would you think about stopping at Disneyland?"

"Disneyland?" she repeats. "Are you joking?"

"I'm really not," he says. "You can actually just drop me off there. You don't have to . . . like, come to Disneyland. Henry and Big Tee are there. You can leave me at the gate. I think I . . . I think I need to get a ride home with them."

"Home? They're going to drive you all the way back down?"

"Not down, up. I think I need to go home. Back to Victoria. Not forever. There's something I need to do."

PRESLEY

Even as he's saying it, he's figuring it out. It's so *clear*. He doesn't know why he hasn't thought of it before.

"I want to come to Disneyland with you," says Hattie. "Please can I come to Disneyland with you?"

"Okay," says Presley, and he feels a rush of something. Affection? Forgiveness? Happiness? Relief?

He doesn't know.

She turns on her signal to exit the freeway at the sign for Disneyland. "We're going to Disneyland!" She laughs. "This has been the strangest day of my whole life."

"Same," he says.

It's a conscious decision, but it's also something that just *happens*, and it might have something to do with the fact that right before the cart goes over the edge at the top of the Matterhorn, Mac is there, just for a split second, stretching out his arm to punch Presley in the face.

But a hand that isn't there doesn't knock out your teeth, doesn't bend your nose at an impossible angle, doesn't leave you with two black eyes that take weeks to fade away.

See you later, Presleygator.

"In a while, Macadile."

He lets go of everything.

He lets go of all of it.

He lets go of his past and his no-longer future and his fears and his feelings about *The Shark Club* and Hattie's feelings about *The Shark Club* and his resentment about *The Shark Club* and his anger about *The Shark Club* and his grief.

He lets go of his anger at his dad for killing Mac and for being in jail and for being a shitbag.

He lets go of his anger at his mum for celebrating turning in her revisions on *The Shark Club* by going away with Ellie so she wasn't home on the day of the fight, which meant their dad picked them up, which meant Mac died.

He lets go of his anger at Mac for being dead.

He lets go of Mac.

The ride tips over the peak, leaving his heart at the top, separating it from his body, which drops nearly into the abyss—he can see it looming, the slick black nothingness promising eternity—and explodes out through the other side, into the light, catching up to his organs on the loop

and he's

alive.

Really alive, all pumping blood and clear eyes and wind in his hair and a girl beside him who he thinks almost for sure that he really does love.

Hattie screams. She buries her face in his shoulder.

After, they don't have an honest conversation about everything they haven't said yet. Instead, they line up with Henry and Big Tee and go on all the rides, every one, until the rides shut down, and then they sit all together in a row along Main

Street, and they watch a parade and the fireworks. Everything isn't okay yet, but it will be. Soon. It feels close, but just the slightest bit out of reach.

But he knows how he's going to do it. He knows what he's going to do.

When everyone is asleep, much later, after late-night pizza and a few rounds of Crazy 8s in the nicest hotel room he's ever seen, courtesy of Henry, he texts his mum and Ellie a list of things he needs them to send. He knows they're things they would have packed out of the tiny house, things they couldn't leave behind. His passport. His favorite flannel shirt. And Mac.

He gives them the address of the hotel in San Francisco where Hattie's dad is staying. Then he climbs into bed. On the other side of the wall, Hattie is probably asleep. He knocks softly. Waits. Knocks again. Waits.

She knocks back.

Today has easily, hands down, been the strangest day of his life, but he feels okay. He feels like he's getting somewhere. He feels like things are maybe going to work out, after all.

"You can't just *go to Canada*. You can't just decide to cross a border."

Hattie is driving and Presley is with her and not with Henry and Big Tee because he decided to just . . . stop. Stop being mad. Stop worrying.

"Everything is a decision," Ellie always says. She really believes it. He's always thought it was bullshit, but he's willing to try.

He's *decided* to be happy. He's *decided* to give this, whatever it is, another chance.

Hattie sounds amused or annoyed or both. In front of her, three cars ahead, the Mercedes smoothly moves between lanes. Until they get to San Francisco, he's going to figure out how to tell her everything about the book and his mum and how badly he needs her to see that he's just . . . Presley.

Presley Jablowski, former figure skater, current dork, lifetime capital-N Nerd.

"I *can* just decide to cross the border," he says. "I'm eighteen. And I hear it only takes twenty-four hours and six minutes to get there. And that's an overestimation because obviously, we're already partway there."

"Don't tell Applejack, but I think she counts as an inferior vehicle."

"I would not recommend taking Applejack to Canada. I'm going with Henry and Big Tee. You're . . . You didn't think I meant . . ."

"What if I want to come?"

"Hattie, that's sweet, but . . ."

"Why not?"

"I . . ."

"I was kind of kidding, but also kind of not. I want to spend time with you. You *matter* to me. Like . . . a lot. Like the *most*." Her voice cracks into a million pieces on *matter*, and he pretends not to notice the glittering shards as they fall, catching the light all around them.

"Hattie, I'm okay."

"Are you?"

"Yeah. I mean, I'm working on it."

"I'm sorry, for what it's worth."

"I know. But seriously, would this old heap even make it to Canada?"

"Old heap!" Hattie pats Applejack's dashboard. "Don't listen," she whispers. "Of course you'd make it to Canada."

"Look," says Presley, pointing at a billboard. VISIT VICTORIA, BC, CANADA it reads. HOME OF THE BEAUTIFUL BUTCHART GARDENS, OVER A HUNDRED YEARS IN BLOOM. A NATIONAL HISTORICAL SITE OF CANADA.

"It's literally a sign," says Hattie, and she turns up the music and merges into the lane behind the Mercedes.

HATTIE

They sleep that night in a campsite just off the coast highway, a glorified parking lot dotted with campers. Behind the parking area, the land gives way to a giant sand dune that ends at the highway. They run down it, sliding in the hot sand, then across the four lanes—Presley and Hattie hand in hand—to the wide expanse of sandy beach. The air is cooler here and the surf is high and loud, foaming and churning, a dull roar behind their conversation. Fires are lit up and down, dotting the darkness with sparks dancing harmlessly, twirling up into the night sky.

Henry spreads a blanket down then unfolds a camping chair and sits.

"You brought a *chair*? Did you also bring binoculars and a birding guide?"

Hattie likes seeing Presley like this, likes that he's comfortable. In El Amado, he was always the New Kid, but now he's *home*, with his people.

"I always travel with chairs in my trunk," Henry says. "Sitting on the ground invites bites from sand fleas. And of course I have binoculars, but I'm not that interested in birding as a hobby. But you never know. You have to be prepared." He runs his hands through his unruly hair. "I have my phone in my pocket if I have to identify a bird. No one would carry an actual *book* with them. Unless they're time travelers. And the book would give them away."

"People have books!" Hattie interrupts. "Some people don't like to read on screens."

Henry rolls his eyes. "Technology will win out in the end."

"I guess your Boy Scout training also explains the tent," says Presley.

"Why would I take a road trip without a tent? That would be very short-sighted. Cars break down. Even rad new Mercedes."

"Rad," Presley repeats. "What's next? Totally tubular? Awesomesauce?"

"Ha-ha."

Down near the shoreline, Big Tee whoops and then turns the most awkward cartwheel Hattie has ever seen, all legs and arms, like a praying mantis. Then he does it again and again, until he falls, half in the water. He jumps up and waves. "I'm good!"

Later, they light a beach fire, stoking it with driftwood until it reaches up above their heads, dancing toward the stars, and Hattie tries to not think about fire and El Amado and what's happening at home and if home even still exists. And there's her heart beating wrong again, *beat beatbeatbeat beat pause beat pause.*

"What are you thinking about?" Presley nudges her.

"Fire," she admits. *Fire* leaves a charcoal aftertaste in her mouth, or maybe it's from the smoke she'll never get out of her hair, her clothes, her van. It clings to everything. Someone at the next fire over starts playing a guitar, and she tries to not think of the word *guitar*.

"We're officially okay, right?" she whispers.

"We're officially okay," he whispers. "Just . . . I'd rather you didn't quote the book to me." He smiles, but it doesn't reach his eyes. "I kind of wish the book didn't exist, but seeing as it does . . ."

"Okay," she says. "I won't. I promise."

She looks up at Henry and Big Tee on their camping chairs, both tipped back and looking up at the sky, arguing about stars. She hears the words *black hole*. She hears them say *neutron star*. She hears *extinction event*.

Presley lies back, tugging her with him. She gently rests her head on his shoulder and takes a photo of them, smiling up at the camera, the plaid blanket behind them and, on the other side of the lens, an infinity of stars and possibilities and alternate universes where maybe he doesn't forgive her or they don't even meet or a tidal wave crashes in right now and sweeps them out to sea, but in this one, what's real is the even, strong beat of his heart under her ear that somehow regulates her own.

Beat beat beat beat beat, as steady and strong and sure as a machine.

"Do you really think love is bullshit?" he says, a while later.

"No, I think it's . . . implausible."

"Ah."

"Implausible," she repeats.

"Are you repeating it because it tastes good?"

"No, it really doesn't." She breathes in through her nose and out through her mouth, trying to get hold of it. "It's *banana*. But not real banana, fake banana. Like . . . medicine." She has the tiny flicker of a memory that's sparking—in it, she's in a crib, crying. She's standing and trying to climb out of the crib because she's hot. Or she's cold. No, her ears hurt. She needs her mom. She's screaming. And then her mom comes in, lifts her out from behind the bars, puts her on the counter, squirts medicine from a dropper into her mouth. "I used to get ear infections. I had to take that medicine a lot. It tasted like bananas or like it was meant to taste like bananas but really didn't. But then I grew out of it, I guess. I don't remember when they stopped."

"Maybe because it *is* bananas," he says.

"What?"

"The idea that love is . . . dumb."

"Ha-ha."

"Seriously. If you're going to take my mum's word as gospel, you should know that she's more about love than anyone I know."

Hattie stares. There are a lot of things she wants to say, but she agreed to not talk about the book so instead of answering, she buries her face into his chest.

"I love that words taste like things you remember," he says into her hair. "It's like your memories are all in your taste buds and not in photo albums."

"I never thought of it that way but . . ." She tells him about how her mom deleted all the pictures when she left. It's easier to say it when she isn't looking at him.

He turns onto his side, pulling away so he can look at her. "Do you think that's why you taste your memories?"

She shrugs. "Maybe. That's what Brady thinks."

"You hate that though?"

"I *do* hate it."

He kisses her on the temple, and she turns her head so his lips can reach her lips, and then they're kissing and kissing and everything else falls away: the ocean and the beach and the fires and the dune and the campground and Henry and Big Tee who are now playing a very complex version of I Spy with constellations. Hattie and Presley are all that exists in the world and there's no Elijah or Mac or parents or rules or wild-fires or books or anything or anyone but them.

Hattie feels grubby. Sand is stuck beneath her nails, sweat from the drive dampens her hair. She's pretty sure she stinks.

While the valet at her dad's fancy San Francisco hotel drives Applejack to the underground parking, a doorman holds the door open for them. Hattie feels underdressed in denim shorts and one of her mom's soft old shirts. Presley's Nirvana T-shirt has a tear in the hem and they both look like they badly need a shower. She texts her dad from the lobby.

> **HATTIE:**
> We're here! Coming up. Room?

> **DAD:**
> You're here already?

Hattie frowns.

> **HATTIE:**
> I told you we were on our way!

> **DAD:**
> Just getting into the shower. Grab a coffee?
> Give me ten minutes.
>
> Room 1207.

"He knows I don't drink coffee," she says when Presley returns. "Something is weird."

"Maybe he forgot?"

Hattie looks at Presley, raises her eyebrows, shrugs. "Let's just go up. Maybe it's a thinly disguised cry for help."

Presley presses the button for the elevator. The elevator pings.

The doors open.

Ms. Singh is standing there with a rolling bag.

Ms. Singh is wearing the *Fearless* T-shirt.

Ms. Singh's face goes through at least four facial expressions: shock, embarrassment, horror, guilt. She settles on a flustered smile. "Hattie! You're here."

Hattie steps onto the elevator just as Ms. Singh is stepping off it. She doesn't say anything because she can't. Her mouth feels frozen. She checks to see if she's breathing. She presses the button for the twelfth floor and the doors shut out Ms. Singh's nervous laugh.

"She's wearing our *shirt*," Hattie mutters. She knows her dad deserves a life, if by "a life" she means "a girlfriend." But she still feels *betrayed*, there in the elevator, surrounded by dim mirrors and brown wallpaper and fake sconces, while a wordless version of "Rocket Man" spills out from an invisible speaker.

Presley reaches for her hand, but she pulls away.

"This elevator reminds me of Tower of Terror," he says. "They must use the same decorator."

"Yeah, well, hopefully we don't plunge to our deaths," she says darkly, the word *death* making Elijah's ghost face appear, shimmering, in the mirror. She turns, resting her cheek on

Presley's shoulder.

"Are you wiping your nose on my shirt?" he says.

"Totally," she says.

"Nice."

They're knocking on the door of room 1207 when Ms. Singh bursts in from the stairwell. She's panting. Her face is flushed. "We should have told you. I'm so sorry."

"You have nothing to be sorry for." Hattie sounds mad because she is mad even though she has no right to be mad, no reason to be mad, and anyway she *knew*, or thought she knew, so why *does* she feel so mad?

She likes Ms. Singh. Ms. Singh is kind and pretty and obviously likes her dad. And her dad is maybe, hopefully, probably happy.

So what's wrong with her that she can't just be happy for them?

Maybe, she thinks, in a parallel world, none of them are here. Maybe the fire jumped the highway so fast they didn't have time to escape. Maybe in that world, they died, horribly, their photos featured at the next Phantom Fest put on by the people who didn't die in El Amado's second wildfire.

There were so many possibilities.

So maybe this *is* the best of all possible worlds.

Maybe it isn't.

She's overthinking. She's overthinking *overthinking*, and she doesn't know what to say to Ms. Singh, and Presley's not talking either, and the three of them stand in the hall listening to Ms. Singh breathing heavily while Presley knocks on the door and knocks again. Then the door opens and her dad wraps himself around Hattie and lifts her right off the ground, and she breathes in his weird baby cookie rain-forest smell. She can tell that he's so happy, and she tries really hard to be happy for him because she loves him, but she can't quite get there.

Her dad being with Ms. Singh comes at a cost, but she can't figure out why or what the cost is. Her dad being with Ms. Singh means that even he knows it's over, this thing that they've shaped their whole lives around, waiting for her mom to come home.

It means they had it wrong. It means they were wrong all along.

It means *something*.

And even though she thinks it shouldn't, it *hurts*.

And now she knows for sure that she's *definitely* going to go to Canada with Presley.

HATTIE AND PRESLEY

Hattie and Presley and Henry and Big Tee are YOLOing.

YOLOing is a decision they've all made. Some things you can decide: to forgive, to YOLO, to move on.

Other things you can't decide: like when to stop grieving, how to love someone, or feeling true happiness.

But they're doing the best they can.

Big Tee and Henry are willing to be off schedule to be Presley's friends again, to be on an Epic Road Trip™, like they're finally living a movie about themselves being young.

They don't leave San Francisco until the box arrives from Presley's mom, the box containing Mac's urn, Presley's passport, his things. This sets them back a whole day. And then they stop in Manzanita and fly kites on the beach and ride sand bikes and eat pizza and watch the sun set. They stop in Portland and eat five kinds of doughnuts from Voodoo Doughnut and visit the world's smallest park and go to the Peculiarium for ice cream and monsters. Hattie takes pictures and more pictures and even more pictures and she'll add them to the inside of Applejack's door, the last place that needs to be filled in, when they get home, if home is still there to get to.

They make a decision to not think about El Amado, to not look on the internet for news of home.

They stop and sleep again in Washington State in the shadows of a volcano and pose in front of a wall of chewing gum in Seattle, and Hattie and Presley kiss at the top of the Space Needle.

They make their own musical montage.

They talk about everything: the multiverse, Mac, Elijah. Hattie is surprised by how easy it is for the four of them to say these things out loud: love, ghosts, the future.

Hattie and Presley kiss,

and they kiss,

and they kiss,

and Hattie decides to stop thinking that *love is bullshit*, and she decides to stop thinking about what Jada would do and just is . . . herself.

And Presley decides to stop noticing things that Hattie says or does that look like they might be from *The Shark Club*, and he decides to stop trying to be less like Topher (and so less like himself) and to stop hiding his headaches and his seizures from his friends.

Hattie doesn't think about Elijah or swimming or her mom.

Presley doesn't think about Mac or skating or *The Shark Club*.

Instead they let themselves

fall in love,

and it feels like they're stepping across a threshold, into a future that's glowing, shimmering, shining with a mesoglea of possibilities instead of one of loss and pain.

Presley draws their trip in stick figures in one of Hattie's unused red Moleskine notebooks while they're on the ferry, the last leg of their journey. He draws kites and the world's smallest park and a volcano. He draws clear skies and shooting stars. He draws Henry and Big Tee on the ferry's outer deck, trying to lean into the wind, laughing like little kids.

"Dorks," he says, watching them through the window.

"Takes one to know one," she says, flipping a page in the book she bought at the newsstand. It's the first book she's read, other than *The Shark Club*, since *before*. It feels strange to be reading it, to be loving it, to not know what's going to happen next.

"Good book?"

"So far, so good," she says.

He taps her on the nose with his pen. "Good." He draws a heart on the last page and scribbles around it, making it look like the cover of the book she's reading—*My Heart and Other Black Holes*—and then he draws their initials in the heart.

"That's *so* cheesy," says Hattie, grabbing it out of his hands. "You're a cheeseball."

"But you love cheese," says Presley.

"I do love *cheese*," she says, tracing her finger around the heart. "But cheesiness is a whole other thing. You must have misheard me."

"LOL, for real," he says, sounding exactly like Bug, which makes Hattie miss Bug so much she has to put the book down and walk away to call her and tell her where she is and where they're going and everything that's happened, which turns out to take the whole trip.

They drive off the ferry to Victoria at Swartz Bay into cool, fall sunshine, midafternoon on a Wednesday. The air is rich with salt from the sea and *home* and green and petrichor and everything Presley has missed. He feels like all the oxygen he's been missing is rushing through his blood, and he's finally thinking clearly, everything he needs to do sharply defined. They honk and wave as the Mercedes peels off in a different direction, and Presley guides Hattie to his old house, aware of the vibration of Applejack's engine, the familiar farms lining the highway, the places that all hold memories, both good and horrific. They exit onto a sharply curving road that takes them past golf courses and a market and beachfront houses, through a forest, and then, finally, they turn left down a small lane.

Hattie stops the van and the engine sputters into silence.

The yellow house has a sign out front—application for redevelopment, it reads—and the house looks abandoned, the grass long and straggly, exploding with weeds and a scattering of wildflowers. A maple tree shades the front lawn, the tree Mac planted from a seed when they moved in. It's towering over them, the leaves starting to yellow, waving and rustling in the cool, damp breeze.

Presley leads Hattie up the familiar front walkway, every crack and ripple in the pavement something he'd once had memorized. They peer in through the small glass window by the entry. The house is most definitely empty. But in the discolored patches marking the floor, Presley sees the ghosts of their old furniture: the yellow couch, the red velvet chair, the rug his mum bought at auction that always smelled like someone else's dog. He can imagine Mac, lying on the couch, his feet hanging over the back of it, the TV blasting a recording of his latest game, doing the running commentary in his announcer's voice. He can smell his dad's specialty—Hamburger Helper—and see his mum's office door at the end of the hall, the sign on it that still reads REVISIONS IN PROGRESS: DANGER. DO NOT ENTER.

He tries the front door. It's unlocked.

"We can't go *in*!" Hattie says. "I'm almost sure that Canadian jail is nicer than American jail, but I'd rather not find out."

"Yes, we can." He pushes the door open and even the squeak of it is a memory. "I'll take the fall for you."

Inside, their footsteps echo in the empty rooms, their voices bounce around, too loud. Presley traces his hand along the cool plaster walls, leans on the kitchen counter, looking out beyond the garden and the patch of trees to the dock where his dad used to keep his boat.

"This is a nice house," says Hattie. She opens an empty cupboard, looks inside, and closes it. "It feels like . . . a perfect family house. Like a TV family house."

"Yeah, except without the TV family."

They go upstairs. There's a landing with two doors, holes in each one where he and Mac put cans on strings because they thought they'd work like walkie-talkies.

Presley opens the door to his old bedroom. There's a sun-shadowed outline on the wood where his rug used to be, a scratch on the wall from his dresser, glittering stickers still glued to the mirrored closet door. He goes in. Spins around. Then he lies down on the floor where his bed used to be. Hattie follows him, sits next to him, then lies down, too. "Is this . . . weird for you?"

"A little." He moves closer to her, then slides his arm under the back of her neck so her head isn't on the wood. In the corner by the window, there's a tiny green plastic soldier, melted and stretched and dangling upside down from the ceiling.

"This was your room?"

"Yep."

His back hurts. It's uncomfortably quiet and this house was never quiet.

He helps Hattie up and they both cross the landing to Mac's room. It's identical, only the opposite, just like Presley and Mac.

Chocolate or vanilla?

Dogs or cats?

Alive or dead?

Dust has accumulated on the floor, a few cobwebs catching it in a pattern on the skylight, and the shifting shadow art of leaves comes in from the window. The air is stale. It doesn't smell like Mac. It smells like . . . emptiness, like a held breath.

Presley leads the way down the back steps and into the yard, through the gate and down the long path to the dock. The dock was never in great shape and now it's worse, broken boards they have to step over.

Hattie shivers and he pulls her in close. They sit, dangling their feet into the water, and he points up at the sky where an eagle is gliding toward a tall, dead tree, settling on its branch, silhouetted against the sinking sun. Everywhere, seagulls are calling and on the long stretch of gray sand along the shore, a huge flock of crows jabbers and caws, feasting on something in the sand.

"It's different here than I pictured," says Hattie. She makes a gesture with her hands. "Bigger, somehow. All the trees, I guess." She kicks at some drifting seaweed, drops her head on his shoulder. Mac would've given him a push, laughed when he fell into the water. It probably happened a hundred times. More.

"Presley?"

"Yeah, sorry. It's a lot. Being here."

When they walk back up to the house, they leave wet footprints on the dock, the salty water running in rivulets down their legs, leaving white paths on their skin. Back inside, he leads her up the stairs and then up a smaller set of stairs leading to a cavernous open attic.

The white walls are covered with stick figures.

"Ancient cave drawings," he says. "Our historical record."

"Oh wow," she says, stepping closer.

"I guess it's like the inside of your van. But different."

"Yeah, I see that. It's amazing. Proof that you exist."

"Well . . . *existed*." He takes the Sharpie from his pocket, breathes deeply. "The last one," he says.

He uncaps the pen and runs his hand over the familiar, slightly rough wall. There isn't much room left, but there is enough.

He draws the fight.

He draws the counselor, calling first their mum and then, when she doesn't answer, their dad.

He draws the car, his pen moving faster and faster, the cows in the barn, the explosion.

He draws himself. He draws his dad. He draws Mac.

He draws Mac dividing into two people: one dead and one alive.

His pen is moving so fast, it's like he's not even seeing what he's doing.

He draws himself, alone. He draws a bubble over his head. He writes, *Catch you on the flip side, Big Mac.*

"Someone will paint over it," he says. "They'll start over."

"I'll take a picture." She holds up her phone.

"No!" he says. "Don't. I don't want anyone to have ever seen it. It's not for people to see . . . It was for Mac. It was always just for Mac."

He comes and sits next to her, leaning on her, and she leans on him, and they sit like that until the light through the single skylight starts to change, turning pale pink, mauve, pastel.

"I feel . . . different."

"Is that good or bad?" she says.

"It's good," he says. "It's really good."

They go back out to the van, where he collects the urn of Mac's ashes. Down on the dock, he throws handfuls into the sea, and the sea accepts them in shimmering waves of bioluminescence, rippling with light and magic. He closes his eyes remembering his dad explaining how it worked, but he doesn't say it out loud.

She knows it from *The Shark Club*, he knows she knows.

He shakes all the ashes free, then he strips off his clothes and dives in.

"Wait!" But he's already swimming out, diving down, his feet kicking and his ears popping from the pressure. He turns somersaults. He floats. The water pouring off him is a glittering mesoglea under the darkening sky, shimmering and sparkling. He lifts his arms high, lets it fall over him.

Hattie lifts her phone and takes a picture. Then another one. Then another.

Brocifer, says Mac. *It's the devil's light, remember? Did you just throw me to hell?*

"Like you believe in hell."

It's true, as it turns out, there's no such thing. But there is light. There's so much light.

"Mac?"

Presley.

"Are you . . . going?"

It's all good, Pres. It's all right, all light. I can't explain it. I wish you could see it, but I'm glad you can't. This light . . . It's everywhere. It's everything. It's the end of this.

Mac's voice is fading. "Mac? Still here?"

But he's gone.

Presley dives down, holding his breath, until he can hook his foot under a barnacle-clad rock, keeping himself anchored. He swims his arms around, swirling tiny pinpricks of light all around himself like falling stars: a whole galaxy of plankton, his own infinity. He stays down until his lungs are almost exploding and the pressure is unbearable, then he surfaces.

Good-bye, he thinks. *I love you.*

"Are you okay? I was about to dive in and save you."

"I'm . . . okay," he calls back. "I'm good."

He swims back, climbs up on the dock.

"I think I'm done," he says. "Thanks for this."

"Don't thank me."

"Too late, I just did." He sticks out his tongue, and she pushes him back into the water, and he surfaces spluttering, laughing and crying at the same time. He looks up at her. "I think I love you," he says.

"Okay," she says. Then, "Me too."

She hesitates only for a second, then she strips off her clothes and jumps in. Then they're grappling in the water, playing like kids, turning somersaults, racing to the buoy, splashing and floating and *living*, the sparkling algae pouring off their skin like art.

When they climb out, she takes another picture, this one of them kissing, the sea behind them glittering in the moonlight with all the stars that are Mac, that were Mac, that will be Mac forever.

"Look!" Hattie says, later, once they're warm and dry, and lying on broken lounge chairs in the yard. She points up at the stars, poking through the darkness. Above them, Cassiopeia makes an *M* in the sky.

That's my constellation, her mom used to say. *M for Mom. That's why I painted it on your cheek before you were born, so you'd always think of me.*

"It's your constellation," says Presley. "It's literally on your face." He traces the pattern of freckles on her cheek, pressing his fingers into each one.

"My constellation," she echoes, into his hair, and her throat tightens as she turns her head to meet his lips, and they kiss, so gently and perfectly and tenderly that she stops thinking again and her mouth tastes of nothing but his mouth and everything is really, truly, genuinely *fine*.

HATTIE

They sleep on the floor of Presley's old room, on the mattress they bring in from Applejack. Hattie dreams of Elijah. The dream feels urgent. In it, she's swimming. She's *racing*. She's breaking her record, and the water is pushing her forward, faster than would be possible.

It's the pool at Stanford and above her, the sun is shining so brightly that it blots out everything but the water, her own hands. It's blinding. She keeps her eyes squeezed shut, but even then, she's aware of it, the whiteness and impossible brightness that has erased everything except her and the water.

She *feels* it, the way her hands push the water behind her, her body slicing through it like a dolphin, sleek and shining with sweat and light and power and strength, and she realizes the water is alive with bioluminescence. She reaches out and touches the wall, her hand throwing shimmers of light in its path, and then she can see the scoreboard, her own name, the *WR* beside it for *World Record*. And there's Elijah, running toward her from the stands, yelling, "Hattie, Hattie! You did it! Just like you said you would!"

She wakes up with a start, her heart racing, sweat pooling on her skin, the sun shining through the skylight directly on her face, blinding her, leaving spots in her vision.

It was a memory that was a dream that was a memory.

But that was how it happened when she broke the world record.

Elijah was *there*.

How had she forgotten that?

Hattie was his favorite.

He had a signed photo of her on his bedside table.

Last Christmas, he'd given her a card that said *To my insparayshun.*

She gets out of bed and tiptoes down the stairs, crosses the dew-wet grass barefoot. She finds the bag she packed at home and pulls out the framed photo and there he is, standing with her, holding her medal high, smiling, just like he always is when she sees him now.

He'd probably be mad, in his little-kid way, that she quit.

What the heck, Hattie, he'd say, sounding like a stern old man, like he sometimes did. *You could have won and winning's everything.*

She can practically hear him saying it. Maybe she *can* hear him saying it.

She holds out her hand and sees it: the mesoglea. "Winning has nothing to do with it, it's how you play the game," she says. "Did I teach you nothing? That's, like, the first thing you were meant to learn."

"No way, José," he says. He definitely says it. There's his voice, filling the sky, bouncing off all the trees and plants and echoing in the mouths of birds and the hum of distant traffic and the sighing of the wind. "That's what losers say. Winning is where it's *at.*"

"You'd know," she says. "You always won."

"I always won," he says, and she can feel how proud he is.

"So . . . what the heck," she says out loud. *Heck* tastes like chlorine, like damp towels, like the smell of steam and sweat and chemicals and endorphins hanging over the hot tub where she used to soak after a race.

She looks for him, but she can't see him anywhere. "Elijah?"

Her hand looks like her hand. The birds are just birds. The traffic is just traffic.

Elijah is gone.

Hattie opens her phone and goes through her deleted emails to find the one from Nikita Chan. She moves it into her inbox and reads it and rereads it.

Then she hits reply.

I'm sorry it took me so long to get back to you, she types. *If it's not too late, I'd like to come back.*

And just like that, her future unspools in front of her again in a way that's as clear as the map was on her wall: a velvet ribbon leading to college, the podium, a degree in *something*, a life beyond the house where she grew up, beyond El Amado, which may or may not still exist, beyond anything she's imagined yet.

A whole *life*.

She goes to the van and takes out her bag. *Love is the point.* She can't believe she got it wrong, that after all the reading and rereading, she could be wrong about it, but it's true that she's never really picked it apart or questioned it. She takes the book down to the dock and sits at the end with her feet dangling in the water. She opens it to the last chapter.

> *It doesn't go how Jada pictured it, but what does? There's first the awkwardness of getting into the cage, the way it's being slapped around in the waves, hitting her leg hard against the bars as she drops into it in a way she*

knows will leave a bruise. Then, as they go down, the water doesn't even look as she imagined. Instead of being clear and blue, it's more of a murky green, thick and ominous. Her own harsh breathing fills her ears. She has the note folded in her hand. It's so stupid, the whole idea of writing a shark a letter. What's she going to do? Feed it to the first shark that swims by? Her heart hurts, maybe because she's breathing too much, but probably because now that they're here, she realizes this won't fix anything.

Her mom will still be gone.

She almost wants to laugh. This had felt so poignant and right and real in her head.

Topher grabs her arm. He turns her around so she's facing the other way. There's a shadow, circling. Her heart speeds up. They're in the cage, so they're safe. She tries to imagine if they weren't. She tries to imagine what her mom was thinking when she saw . . .

Her throat is closing. She's going to suffocate. She tries to relax, to not cry, to not die in this cage. She holds Topher's hand, and he squeezes it. He's floating up, moving to the other side, tracking the fish. He gives her hand a tug, and there it is, the nose of the shark coming so close they could touch it, and he reaches out his hand and he does touch it and she gasps, chokes a little on her respirator, catches her breath.

She takes the note and holds it out. It's so absurd. What's she offering?

She lets it go. Closes her eyes. Doesn't want to see the shark eat it or not, because of course the shark doesn't eat it and it doesn't matter.

Instead, she thinks the words: I forgive you. I forgive you. I love you. I forgive you.

*They're for the shark. For all the sharks. For herself
and her brother. For her dad. For her mom. For the
shark that took that exploratory bite.*

*She feels like she might be sick. The cage is moving
in the current, swaying, and she can't find something
to focus her eyes on and she feels dizzy. How can she be
dizzy underwater? She wouldn't have thought it was
possible, but it must be.*

*There's a bang, and she startles, swirling around.
The shark, behind the cage. Hitting it again and again
with its nose. The cage sways. And then the shark, swimming surprisingly fast, swims straight up, its tail hitting
the chain and then hitting it again and then somehow—
how?—the shark is tangled. The shark is struggling and
tangled in the chains, and its desperate attempts to get free
are banging the cage, tossing the cage, moving the cage,
and they're being flung back and forth. The shark can't
logic out how to break free, so it's going for force. The cage
tilts, and she holds on to the bars, clutching at them. She
feels light-headed, like she's running out of air. How long
have they been down, anyway? She has no idea and time is
doing something strange, and she feels strange. She catches
Topher's face in her hands and tries to make eye contact,
tries to message with her eyes,* I'm scared *or* Help *or*
What do we do? *He takes his hands and puts them on
her face, and they float there, while the cage bangs around
them, and then suddenly, he's swimming out through the
opening of the cage, swimming toward the shark.*

"NO!" she screams, and the respirator drops from her mouth and she's struggling to find it, struggling to not take a breath when there's no breath to take and her heart is beating so hard, it's going to arrest, she just knows it. Where are the people who run this tour, and why is no one saving them, and what is Topher doing?

The shark is huge, easily ten feet or more, its body as wide and thick as a concrete truck and its strength is unmistakeable and she can't fit the respirator properly in her mouth and her throat has clamped shut, she can't breathe, she can't open it, and Topher is pulling at chains and she can't see what's happening, there's blood in the water and the shark is struggling and Topher isn't in sight and she knows he's dead. He's dead. And she's furious, she wants to swim up there and punch the shark, tear out its heart, but then she sees Topher, and he's not dead, and she still can't breathe, and everything is going gray and blurry or grayer and blurrier and she can't think.

There's a light.

She sees a light.

The light is moving around, and she knows they have to go to the light, which she's vaguely aware might be the opposite of what they should do, but what if the light is the surface? What if the light is the end?

And then Topher's hand finds hers and he pulls her up and the shark is gone and she's flooded with relief. But then there's music.

There can't be music but there's definitely music and she thinks, Mermaids. She thinks, Heaven. She *thinks impossible things, but it makes as much sense as anything that mermaids and angels are the same thing and that this is it. This is the end.*

Topher is bleeding from his hands, she sees that now, clouds of Topher dissipating into the water, puffing out like red clouds of paint and she no longer knows where the surface is, but she swims, she swims for her life, as hard as she can, and somehow they break the surface and light is pouring off Topher's face and he's smiling at her and holding her and she feels safe and not alone. And she forgives everyone, everything, and she opens her heart up, and she feels overwhelmed and broken and breaking. Then they're being lifted up and up and up and they're safe and they're forever and ever, light and music and water that sparkles and glows and a huge darkening sky closing in on them, tiny stars freckling through and a warmth spreading like golden light, pouring through her like eternity, like forgiveness, like . . .

I love you, *Topher says, his voice inside every cell of her.*

Love, *she thinks, closing her eyes.*

Love.

Hattie closes the book.

She starts to laugh. They aren't dead. They survived. She'd spent so much time believing they were dead. She'd made them being dead the point. She'd missed the whole thing.

She clutches the book to her chest one more time and strokes the cover. This book saved her life, she's sure of it, even if she missed the point. She gets it now though. *The Shark*

Club: A Love Story, the cover reads, and she traces the words with her fingers. *A Love Story*. Her favorite book. Her favorite song. Her favorite everything.

She picks up the book and throws it as far as she can. It splashes and floats at first, then slowly starts to sink. She watches until it's gone. Then she takes out her phone.

> **HATTIE:**
> Checking in.

DAD:
Wonderful! Rate your trip on a scale of
1 to Taylor Swift.

> **HATTIE:**
> Impossible.

DAD:
I don't know that song. Is it new?

> **HATTIE:**
> LOL, Dad. I meant I can't summarize it
> in a song. That would be impossible.
> Maybe an album?

DAD:
Which one? I'll consider accepting your
answer if you choose wisely, grasshopper.

Hattie pictures all the Taylor Swift discs that her dad keeps in his car, tucked into a folder on the visor. She already knows the answer. She thinks of "Love Story." "Breathe." "Change." "Forever and Always." All her favorite tracks.

HATTIE:
Fearless.

DAD:
Must be some trip then. Can't wait to hear
about it when you get home.

Home. Hattie swallows.

HATTIE:
The house? Is it . . . okay?

DAD:
You didn't know? I thought you'd see it on
the socials.

HATTIE:
Never say "the socials" again.
You sound like an old man!

DAD:
😎 The fire missed us, kiddo. Didn't burn
down a single thing.

PRESLEY AND HATTIE

Presley takes Hattie to the park where he and Mac learned to play baseball. It's where they've come to say good-bye to Henry and Big Tee.

They climb up on a long concrete dragon and sit on its tail, drinking Starbucks and eating muffins, throwing the crumbs to the gulls who swoop in, squawking. It's raining gently, so they jump down and run hand in hand past the swing set where he used to sit with his friends—well, *Mac's* friends—drinking and posing for Instagram pics. They climb inside a massive concrete octopus with slides as arms, leaning back against the smooth round contours carved inside its head. Their voices echo strangely, bouncing off the surfaces and the ghosts of his past, all of them present except the only one he cares about: Mac.

Mac is dead, he thinks.

It's more true now than ever. Mac is really gone.

Presley blinks away a sudden wave of tears and exhaustion and everything that he's been feeling. He ducks his head down so Hattie doesn't see his eyes, pretends to be focused on his shoelace.

"So I'm thinking of getting back into the pool," Hattie blurts.

Presley leans back and closes his eyes. "You *should*. That's great. You totally absolutely should."

"I've been thinking . . . I mean, I don't know if I want to do all the big things that used to seem so . . . important. Like the Olympics. Or anything like that. But I need the scholarship. I think I want to go to college. I think I want to figure out what I want to do that isn't swimming. But, like, I guess ironically swimming is how I can do that?"

"You don't need a big reason, Hattie. You're a great swimmer."

"I feel weird about it."

"Why?"

"Um, I don't know. It feels unfair. It's not like . . . Well, you can't start skating again."

He reaches up and gently turns her face to his. "It's not even *close* to the same thing. I *can't* skate. My leg is pinned together in two places. My spine is fused. I have a head injury. I have seizures. It isn't the same at all. You *can* swim. You should, if you want to."

"I've seen you skate though. You're amazing."

"But I *can't*, not like I'd need to, not competitively. This isn't a movie where I can work really hard to an uplifting soundtrack and everything will be okay. My body can't ever do what it used to. It's not like it's a *choice*. Or like I can fix it if I have enough gumption."

"Gumption," she repeats. Then, because she can't help it, she says it again. "Gumption."

He smiles crookedly. "Taste good?"

She makes a face. "Tastes weird. Kind of too sweet, like icing, but not the good kind, the kind that comes on grocery store cupcakes."

"Yum, I actually secretly love grocery store cupcakes. They taste like chemicals, but good chemicals. Candy chemicals."

"You have terrible taste in cupcakes." She pauses. "I'm sorry. I just . . . No, you're right. I know. I'm sorry. I'm being totally insensitive and kind of an asshole."

"God. Hattie, no, you're not. What's going on with you is important, and I want you to swim if you want to swim, and I don't want it to connect in any way at all to *me*. I don't want you to give up! No one wants you to give up. Haven't you seen the way your friends are with you? And the whole swim team? No one understands why you quit. Everyone wants you to go back, not just because you're good and you can help them win or whatever, but because you love it and life is kind of short and sometimes stupid and unfair, but you have this thing that you *love* and you choosing to not do this thing is . . . It's kind of frustrating, Hattie. And no one knows how to say, 'Just get back in the pool.'"

"Well, it's pretty simple: Elijah can't swim again. He's dead. He loved it, too. So it's not really fair, is it? That I didn't save him, but I can just keep swimming and pretend it never happened? And anyway, I don't even know if I loved swimming in the first place. *Did* I love it? Or was it all tangled up in thinking Mom would come back? But now she's married! She's never coming back!"

He reaches for her hand, grabs it, and squeezes. "Did you ever really truly believe she would?"

They watch an older woman walk by, holding a child's hand in the rain, the wind blowing her jacket up like a red balloon. Hattie thinks about balloons and strings and ties and reasons and love. She thinks about Elijah and swimming and Presley and skating and her mom and how the name *Elijah* tastes like the first lungful of air you breathe after being underwater, like the tiles at the end of a lane, like the feeling you get when your hand touches the wall first.

"I never drew your whale," says Presley. "I want to draw your whale. I promised, remember?"

"Um, yeah, I totally remember. I just figured the ice whale was it."

"Maybe I'll draw you more whales. I'll draw you infinite whales. For the rest of time, if you want a whale, I'm here for you." He takes his Sharpie out of his pocket and kneels in front of a smooth patch of cement that's not yet covered in graffiti. He sketches a whale, like the one on the bathroom door, and then beside the whale, he draws a girl, swimming. "That's you," he says. "Proud member of the Whale Club."

"LOL, for real," she says. "I love it. I love whales. I love . . . you."

"You *do?*" Presley leans closer to her and then, again, they're kissing. They kiss and kiss. When they come up for air, it's raining really hard. A black Mercedes peels into the parking lot, skidding to a stop on the wet concrete, loud rock music pouring from the windows.

"Is that . . . eighties rock?"

"It's Guns N' Roses. Long story. They— Well, we—are . . . big fans."

"It kind of fits. I should have known you were a 'Paradise City' kind of person."

"You got me. I like paradise. And cities. And eighties rock. There's nothing wrong with that!"

"You are *such* a dork."

"I never thought it would be so adorable to be called a whale's penis," he says, kissing her on the nose.

"Okay, whatever, Penis O'Whale."

"That can't be a nickname that sticks," he says. "Can't it be something more . . . dignified? Like . . . even Whale Dick sounds tougher. Cooler. Less . . . jaunty."

She laughs.

"Ready? Let's go say good-bye. And then we can go."

"Home?" she says. "The thing is that Coach Chan says I have to be at practice Saturday morning, six sharp, if I want one last chance."

"The activity center didn't burn down?"

"It didn't burn down. That's kind of a spoiler, but it's the best kind of spoiler."

"Then let's go. We can't have you missing your last chance."

He stands up and helps her climb out the octopus's eye and they run, splashing in puddles, to the Mercedes where his friends are waiting.

HATTIE

They're crossing the border between Oregon and California when Presley finds the box of tapes under the seat of the car. He slides one into the tape deck. Roberta Flack croons from the speakers and a chill runs through Hattie, a taste flooding her mouth. Cotton candy.

Killing me softly . . . Roberta croons, and Hattie pulls onto the shoulder and turns the engine off, leaving the music playing. She knew it all along, like something that had been glimmering just outside of her peripheral vision, but suddenly she understands something, something huge. She really sees it.

"Hattie?"

She closes her eyes, lets the memory in. It was the day her mom left. They were driving to the outlet mall to buy Hattie something special to wear for the talent show. The song came on the radio and her mom was singing along, when suddenly she stopped. "Do you taste it?" she said urgently. "Do you?"

Hattie had shaken her head. She didn't taste anything. "We aren't eating, Mom," she ventured. "There's nothing in our mouths." Her top two teeth were missing, so it sounded more like *moufs*.

"The song," her mom insisted. She pulled over into a parking lot and started the song again. "*Listen*. You have to listen harder. Better. Do *better*." She sounded mad at first, and then frantic, replaying it over and over again. Hattie was scared. She was so scared. She didn't understand. Her heart felt like butterflies. *Beatbeatbeatbeatbeat*. She thought she might be sick. "LISTEN."

"I'm listening, Mom!"

"Sing it, then. Sing it and tell me what you taste."

"I don't taste anything!"

"Sing it again!"

Hattie sang. She sang because she wanted her mom to be happy and she was scared and she didn't know what she was meant to *taste* and she didn't know what else to do.

"It's cotton candy, for God's sake," her mom said. "You don't *taste* it? What's wrong with you?"

And Hattie, crying, *had* tasted it. She'd tasted it. The song had tasted exactly like cotton candy.

Brady was right. It was always about her mom. It was her mom the whole time.

When the song is over, she pops the cassette out. "Let's just listen to the radio," she says. "Let's listen to something new."

Later, at home, she prints out all the photos from her phone. The kites and beaches and ice creams and roller coasters and Disneyland. The surf and campsites and forests. The weird shops and museums and roadside attractions. The Mercedes, Presley's old house, Big Tee and Henry. The octopus, the concrete dragon, the dock. She frowns, holding up the last photo she printed.

It's Presley, swimming in the bioluminescent water near the dock, but he isn't alone. She doesn't think iPhone cameras could accidentally take double-exposures, but there, in the water, are definitely two boys.

"Mac," she whispers.

She prints out another copy and slips it into a brown envelope. She'll give it to him tomorrow, after swimming. She'll wait for him to be done on the ice. She'll let him touch her warm cheeks with his cold hands. She'll kiss him. She'll give him the last possible photo of his brother.

She gets up and opens her window, letting the wind push fresh California sea air into her room, still carrying with it a trace of smoke. It's not cold, nothing like it was in Canada, and it's different, and it's home. She sits with her knees bent and pulls the *Fearless* T-shirt over them, making a warm tent. From here, she can see Mount Southerton, smoke still lifting from the backside of it, the mountain itself as black as if someone has scribbled over it with a Sharpie.

Sounds from the TV rise up the stairs. Her dad and Ms. Singh are in the living room watching *The Bachelor*, her dad's unlikely favorite show. Hattie goes to her desk and takes out her red Moleskine notebook. She writes down the story about the song in the very last bit of white space on the very last page, and then she scans the whole thing, page by page, making a stack of copied paper an inch thick. She puts the copies in an envelope, and she writes Brady's name and a message on the front. *You were right. I'm sorry.* She goes downstairs and slips it into her dad's work bag. He'll see it tomorrow. He'll know what to do.

"You going to bed?" he calls.

"Yep. Good night," she says. "Good night, Ms. Singh."

"Please call me Ana!" she says.

"I will. Maybe not yet though. Good night."

She goes back up to her room, sits back down at her desk, and finds a pen. Her phone buzzes.

CALLIOPE:
Girl, we are literally on bated breath waiting
to hear about the Great Canadian Road Trip.
Spill it.

BUG:
Seriously there is no emoji for what my face
looks like right now while I literally hold my
breath, except it's turning blue from oxygen
depletion. Is that bad?

> **HATTIE:**
> I love you. Both of you. I promise
> I will tell you every tiny detail,
> but I need a few minutes. Please
> breathe. A person can only go
> 87 seconds without needing to
> breathe. I will be more than 87
> seconds.

BUG:
hyperventilating emoji

> **HATTIE:**
> While I'm gone, type everything
> that I missed. I'll need photos of
> all Leo's latest art pieces and an
> updated sketch of Bug's future wife
> and a complete recital of any new
> music Cal's written. Back in 5.

There's one more thing she has to write before she tells them everything.

She uncaps the pen, taps it on the desk a few times, then . . .

Dear Mom, she writes.

I forgive you. This isn't a letter telling you everything you missed. You don't get to have that.

I've been writing in a notebook. It's like an album of all you had and left behind.

I was thinking about sending a copy to you, then I realized it wasn't for you at all. It was for me the whole time.

I will always remember you, even the things that were hard. Maybe especially those things. I'm sorry it was hard for you. It was hard for me, too. And for Dad. Really, really, really impossibly, painfully hard.

So mostly, I'll remember how much we missed you, and for how long.

I thought tasting words was a curse, but I've changed my mind. It's a gift. Maybe the most important one you left me, except Applejack. And the dresses.

Dad and I aren't waiting for you anymore.

In a parallel world, this all turned out differently. Maybe it was better. Maybe it was worse. Maybe it was both. Maybe it was everything. Maybe you never had me at all. Maybe you left before I was born.

Or maybe you loved us enough to stay.

I hope you find what you're looking for. I hope you understand why this is good-bye.

Hattie

She folds the letter in half, then in half again. She folds it smaller and smaller until it fits in the palm of her hand. Then gently, she lets it go.

Acknowledgments

At the risk of sounding incredibly cheesy, one of the most important things I learned during the last few incredibly difficult years is that love is what matters. I've been saying it a lot lately, probably to the bafflement of my children and definitely to the raised eyebrows of my students, who come to me to learn how to write a novel, not to get life lessons that sound like motivational posters. But . . . at the end of the day, it's love. All of it. Love is the point. Love is the way we live our lives. It's the choices we make. The way we care for others.

Even writing a novel is an act of love, because art is love. And we are all art.

You are art. You are love.

When I wrote this novel, I wanted to play around with romantic love, wanted to write something light, to experience the fun parts—yearning and certainty and joy and hope—alongside my characters. But before I knew it, I found that I was also writing about grief, which is, of course, also an act of love, although a much harder one to write. They go together. I understood that I couldn't write one without the other.

So even though it was not what I was expecting when I first sat down at my laptop to write it, I loved writing this book. It was sad and it was happy; it was light and it was heavy; it was closure and beginnings. And it was everything to me for the two years it took to write.

No novel is ever written alone, and this one wouldn't exist without my incredible editorial team: Krestyna Lypen, who believed in Hattie and Presley even when their story fizzled in early drafts, and Ashley Mason and Adah Li, who were there every step of the way. I'm also very grateful to copy editor Jody Corbett and proofreader Chris Stamey, who patiently read every word of this book and corrected details I had gotten egregiously wrong. The cover by artist Maria Pelc could not be more perfect. I love it so much. A book is nothing until it finds its readers, and I'm absolutely blessed to have an incredible marketing team—Moira Kerrigan, Shaelyn McDaniel, Rebecca Carlisle, and Ivanka Perez—who I know will find a way to get this book into your hands. Thank you all for everything you do, for believing in this book, and for making Hattie and Presley come alive in readers' hearts.

And thank you for reading. I appreciate you so much. I hope you found love in this story; I hope you find love in your life, in whatever form it may take.